EQUIPMENT

HESSE CAPLINGER

EQUIPMENT

CARL REINHART

Publishers

CONTENTS

EDITOR'S FOREWORD

Equipment is a novel primarily about men. The characters are flawed, some more obviously so than others, with some blissfully, if mortally, unaware of these defining features. Whether or not these flaws determine or contribute to the mistakes these characters make is an open question, but the consequences are significant and often final, for themselves and others. There are no heroes here, only those—like Marek Hussar or The Familiar—who wield power. Some—like Howard Charles Foster—struggle to wield power even over themselves. The collective effect is a palpable tension between the characters, each acting in accordance with their nature, stature, and position, and few, it seems, operating with a full awareness of their own flawed psychologies. Beneath the surface is a chilling reflection of male isolation in a transactional world.

In the many years I have known Hesse Caplinger, for causes known and imagined, he grew up earlier than the rest of us and seemed unchildlike even as a child. He has always been a keen observer of psychology and culture. The intensity of the writing is a direct reflection of the intensity of the author. He can be particular in the extreme, and as a consequence, occasionally challenging for reader and editor alike. The act of creation begins with the self; the philosophies, tastes, and preferences, however particular, and the product—if indeed there is such an independent thing—exists here as an intersectional examination of quality: masculinity, dignity, morality, and self-determination. The creation of a man, like the creation of art, is deliberate and careful.

Jazz music is a prominent ingredient of *Equipment*, not just to describe the preferences and sophistication of the characters, but as a reflection of the writing style itself. Improvisational techniques are a feature of this novel with its complex sentence structures, its rhythmic use of advanced punctuation, and its evocative descriptions to create a music—singular and cohesive—meant to simultaneously please and challenge the audience. Moreover, the effect is intensity, often—and oxymoronically—understated intensity, usually divulging a character's inner life, psychology, and motivations that are revealed slowly through action; there is a delicate balance between what is vividly described and what is subtly intimated.

In consideration of what constitutes a literary novel, most readers anticipate that the work reflects an elevated artistry, manifested intellectually, spiritually, or stylistically. While no formula for exact definitions and genres need necessarily exist for art—nor indeed *should* exist for art—approaching an understanding can prove useful: Is this a literary novel, in that it is serious and makes intellectual demands of the reader? Is this a spy novel—like those of Greene, Fleming, or le Carré—in which espionage plays a central role? Is it a thriller? Certainly, although the thrills often come through revelations implied by the author and awakened within the reader, who must read closely: the vocabulary, punctuation, syntax, characterization, and nonlinear plot create a borderless puzzle that only emerges through working the pieces together and realizing—with trepidation turned delight—that some are intentionally missing. Understandably, we judge writing based on what we have previously read and then try to nestle the current work into this mold. So much depends on our expectations: as with most great art, the flickering disappointment when our expectations are unfulfilled and the rising joy when they are replaced with something new and better.

Equipment presents a looping journey into the machinations of serious people engaging in serious endeavors. As a spy thriller, the book has all the appropriate elements: espionage, seduction, gunplay, car chases, shadowy figures, and mysteries. As a work of literature, it succeeds in the execution of its prose, giving the right weight to each carefully-considered word rendered in deliberate rhythm—the effect of which is, in a word, intense.

Matthew Marx

UNIVERSITY OF NEBRASKA

DECEMBER 2018

For Eva

IN MEMORY OF

————————

GLENN SAVAN

AND

DICK COLLOTON

EQUIPMENT

2005

Augustbore a tender bruise on his cheek and a livid mar at the cleave of his right ear; it was dressed and taped and he pressed it from time to time softly with the palm of his hand. August and Kyle Lewis, and Phillip and Edmund LeFrance had shouldered the reluctant skid of a door and mounted the stair of the vacant apartment house at the verge of Nebraska and Keokuk and now waited together on the second floor. It was a 9:00 a.m. meet now waxing 9:43, and August was tired and scuffed and cross with impatience, and running an appetite. He paced about the small kitchen peppered in mouse droppings and Borax dust, and was tentatively cupping at his ear when Phillip called to him from the front room.

"Say again," he said, leaving Kyle Lewis in his place. Phillip was looking up the block through a window and LeFrance was working the fold on a hand-rolled cigarette.

"I said: 'He in a Mercedes?'" repeated Phillip, peering south out over the shuttered service station on the next lot.

"No. Why?" asked August.

"There's a black one next block up. It's running—I can see exhaust," he said.

August looked, and Phillip looked, and LeFrance lit his cigarette and looked.

"No," repeated August. "Suburban, I expect."

"Maybe he's a no-show," said Phillip, and August wondered if it were true.

They all came away from the window.

LeFrance said, "I've got a piss to mark the occasion," and shuffled off toward the short hall.

"Hey, what occasion?" August called after him.

"Pissing, August," said LeFrance from the threshold. He pinched a tobacco grain from his lip. "You took a pretty good clout on that ear."

"Don't—not in there," said August.

"You want me to put it in the sink?"

"Put it in a bottle, LeFrance—we're leaving in a minute—you put it in there you may as well leave it in a labeled tube."

"Probably four hobos a day climb up here and leave samples," said LeFrance, and turned through the second room. "Too much coffee, August," LeFrance called to him, his voice now distant and porcelain-shrill. "Just a pick-up, man. Right? Payday simple. Right?"

"Cautious man leads a long life, LeFrance," August barked, and dispelled the subject with an irritable flick of his wrist.

They heard the bathroom door shunt and rattle, nearly closed against the sloped floor. "That Socrates?" came the faint sound of LeFrance.

"What'd he say?" August asked Phillip.

Phillip chuckled lightly.

Kyle Lewis, who had been quietly watching the alley from the kitchen at the back, called out, "What'd he say?"

"Confucius!" announced Phillip.

"Confusion," August thought he heard someone say, probably LeFrance.

"Ben fucking Franklin!" roared August. "Now shut up!"

August returned to the front window, and they were still for a while. "Why'd you pick this place?" asked Phillip. He'd been walking the grain of the floorboards and paused, as though stalled on a balance beam, to deliver his question.

"I didn't," replied August. "If I'd picked—" he said, but he was interrupted by a sound that was faceted and simultaneous: of fractured glass, a loud knock which rattled the apartment with the weight of a twenty pound hammer strike, and a sound which hung in the air, like the snap of a bullwhip cut from wire band.

August and Phillip were quiet and strained with their eyes to listen.

"Where was that?" asked Phillip.

"The back," said August, "the kitchen."

They listened again.

"Kyle?" Phillip called back. "Kyle?"

"Wait," August said to Phillip as he started toward the back. But as he passed into the window light of the second room his head evaporated in heavy mist, the interior wall exploded with plaster dust, and Phillip collapsed with the improbable postures of a marionette. In the same instant, the report of the metallic bullwhip rang out, and August flickered at the knees and sat sharply on the floor. He drew the pistol from his jacket and rest it on his leg, but against his grip it felt formidable as a worry stone.

The building shook with two blows in quick succession. The first sounded of masonry and thick porcelain shards and put a shaft of light through the bathroom door onto the hall. The second resounded with the cast-iron inflection of a stricken tub and skittering debris.

The wall to his left was solid and windowless, but it opened at the far end with a hole waist high that blew wood lathe and brick meal, plaster fume and light everywhere into the space. A second passed, and one after another then, holes opened every two and a half feet toward him along the same horizon, showering brick and light and dust.

I.

Charles Foster offered no acknowledgment when Jeffrey Sachs had been seated. Instead, apparently immersed, he continued in reading and occasionally typing messages on his phone. In fact it wasn't until Sachs began craning round in search of wait staff that Foster greeted him at all.

It was early evening February when the pair met at the back of Blueberry Hill. Foster was making the unusual great length of him comfortable, his knees jutted beneath the table for fit, and splay either direction along the bench of the high booth. The two had met on several occasions, however Sachs had taken to hoping that few such meetings remained. American blues played over the din, and an amber light—imparting the outdoors an illusion of warmth it did not have—lapped at the capstones of buildings across Delmar and settled through the large window nearby. For a narrow space of time Sachs observed this light and it gave him a feeling as though the high-stain and wear-scarred angles of the booth were like the enclosure of a four-place shriving pew: economy class. It was a mood which struck briefly and passed, where it was replaced instead by an impulse for beer, if for no purpose but the chance to improve Foster's company by it.

"It's still early—they should be by in a minute," said Foster, still arrested in the small green light of his phone.

"I know," said Sachs. "But I don't feel like waiting." He craned around again and began to stand.

"They'll be by in a minute," Foster repeated.

"That's alright—want a beer?"

"I'll wait."

"Right. Anything while I'm up?"

"No," was Foster's uninflected reply.

Jeffrey Sachs was a graduate student in computer science—jeans, cowboy boots, and a formless woolen coat—who some four semesters prior had taken 'Engineering Real-Time Systems: Theory and Practice' from Foster, most commonly from his graduate assistant. It was apart from Sachs' major in programming languages, but was nevertheless an interest, and satisfied one of several School of Engineering and Applied Sciences requirements. In fact, though little of the rhetorical theater of the course now replayed for Sachs with any narrative coherence, still the image of the over-tall Foster teetering excitedly around the lecture hall like a circus performer on stilts, burping out phrases—'duality and optimization,' 'min-max equals max-min,' 'quadratic,' and 'game theory'—as though the words themselves were imbued with the power of their own meaning, and all the while gesticulating in that slow-motion manner of the very tall. He'd been impressed more with Foster's air of ill-defined ideological entrenchment and considerable self-approval than by any other particular of the man. Otherwise the class had gone off as well as might be expected, unmoving subject matter and boorish instructor not withstanding. Sachs, to his knowledge, had demonstrated no care beyond the usual, and Foster, no special interest either way— and for this and his work Sachs completed the course to the award of a lowish and slightly soggy 'A.' For a time the simplicity of this arrangement persisted: matriculation in its natural state. Weeks later however, and seemingly at random, the two met again at the threshold of Graham Chapel.

It was the preceding January following a lecture, 'Ethics and Security in The Digital Space,' that Foster, crouched upon a bench near the heavy doors had seemed spontaneously to recognize him from the crowd. Three-day-old snow lay everywhere daytime shade prevailed. Flurries danced in the changing motion of the air. It was cold. And Foster, draped in his heavy hunting coat and boots, chatted Sachs cordially—and with the casual familiarity which holds between comrades—all the cobblestone paths back through the portal of Brookings Hall; the descent of the long stair to the lots where they both were parked. Until, with no clear idea why, Jeffrey Sachs found he'd agreed to a lunch, with Foster.

2.

In Washington, H. Charles Foster, PhD, had visited with his separated wife and his infant daughter. The girl had writhed and hollered when he held her, and her mother had snatched the child away as though the reaction belonged to some premeditation on his part. The entire apartment seemed done in a singular palette of virginal white, and the living room was crowded with a fresh sofa set in overstuffed linen he understood he'd purchased with the currency of her discontent. For a moment he considered the likely volume of that currency, the reservoir of that disaffection, until he felt a sharp pain in the sinuses behind his eyes, and dabbed his nostril with a tissue from his breast pocket. Catherine, his wife, held the cloying child and spoke to him over the arm of a matching chair. He sat on the sofa in an ill-fitting suit and salmon cuffs and collar. His hands wedged numbly beside his legs. But from where his gaze fell he could make out only the sound of her voice over a soiled footprint in the form of his shoe, which lay opposite the coffee table.

She was saying she couldn't be happy with him, she had realized. That little frail Pauline deserved a more dutiful and present father. And that she needed—they needed—to be back in D.C. near her family and her friends, of course. The words at first came to him as through a bowl of water, but at last he'd risen from the hollow of a sparkling stillness and spared the shoe print to look at her. In the enormous chair Catherine looked small, like a child pacifying a doll.

And as Foster observed this, he observed also the lack of demonstrable conflict. There'd been no revelation—no grand reckoning. However ham-fisted or absent, neither had ever mattered. She'd married his family through him, and through them exhausted his usefulness. How long she'd have played along he couldn't say. He tried to guess it in her expression as she spoke. In the end, he felt convinced, it was as simple as that she hadn't required him since their wedding day, and certainly since he'd armed her with the child. And she wouldn't suffer another day in the dreary town at the bend in the river. She didn't need to. His reassignment to Saint Louis had been for her the beginning and the end. This is what Foster thought as she spoke. And when he stood on the stoop at last to leave she said, "Oh wait," and after a moment reappeared with a stainless folding knife. "Here," she said, "you said it was supposed to be good, but it's broken." He opened it and examined its badly bent tip.

"How'd you do that?"

"One day when the nurse was off, like today, the lid on one of Pauline's food jars was stuck. I couldn't find anything to open it."

"You tried to open a jar of baby food with this?"

"You always said it was a good knife."

"So you took it?"

"You said it was a good knife. But it's not, look at it."

"That's not what it's for."

"You said it was a good *utility* knife—what's it supposed to be for then?"

"That's not what it's for. You're lucky you didn't cut your hand off."

"How could it do that, it couldn't even loosen the cap on a jar of baby food?"

He moved down a step and shook his head at the knife in his hand. "That's not what it's for."

"Well it's broken, you can take it with you. Maybe you can have it fixed—and maybe then it'll be more utilitarian."

"I can't take it on the plane."

"Well, it's broken—check it—I don't care what you do with it."

But Foster did take it. For some time he turned it over in his palm in the taxi, until he traded it for the phone from his pants pocket. As a matter of habit he compared the time with his watch, and dialed a number not stored in his phone. It rang once and a male voice said, "Where are you?"

"In a cab. Where are you?"

"Closing out a visit with one of your old familiars at the D.O.E. Do you know the Freer?"

"Who's that?"

"No matter. Know the Freer?"

"I think so."

"It's across the street. Do you know the Peacock Room?"

"I don't think so."

"You know Whistler?"

"Is he a musician?"

"Painter. All that schooling and no art history?"

"I know what I like."

"You and everybody else. How long till you're there?"

"Probably twenty, twenty-five minutes with traffic."

"Alright. Go in through the Sackler, it's next door. There's a passage into the Freer. The room's on the third floor in the corner toward

Jefferson and 12th." The line went still. And changing the phone for the knife, again he occupied himself, and gazed over the seatbacks and shoulder-lump of driver, until at last he was deposited before the cylindrical façade of the Hirshhorn.

3.

His name was Steven Smith. There was no plaque on the door or the desk, but a thick wedge of business cards in a holder from which they were never taken. Howard Charles Foster had no idea what Smith's middle name might be, but he felt a conviction, just here in a chair facing him from across his busy desk, that it was every bit as vague and white as the card stock and the other two names on it: a mayonnaise between bread slices. Foster had been in the new—and it seemed to him—non-assignment several months before he had been called in. It was an office Foster had visited several times prior, but it could not be said that he had visited often. It was an airless business on the third floor; it was white too. The door was a heavy wood-laminate composite with a substantial lever. There was a large window overlooking the parking lot below and the Virginia wood which crept firmly to the edge of an enforced clearing. Behind him were file cabinets in the one beige in which they are made. There was a high worktable set with working files, fat with documents, and cinched round with file bands and clips. On its corner was a light box with transparency and loupe. There were topographical maps and pushpins, and schematics tacked to the walls.

To arrive in this chair, from which Foster watched Smith listening patiently into a telephone receiver, Foster was born to an old

French-immigrant family prospered by cotton, the labor of children, and the otherwise compelled; by a Yale undergraduate in 'something useful': Electrical Engineering and Computer Science; by a nomination for the Skull and Bones, and like so many, through it a recruitment into the Central Intelligence Agency; a Masters from M.I.T. and eventually a doctoral dissertation on the predictive relationship between Moore's Law and the scalability and speed of proliferation of enrichment technology among non-nuclear powers; by matriculation through the Langley Farm during breaks in his graduate study—while otherwise purportedly hunting in remote northern climes; eventually landing a shallow-water Asia station post as a Core Collector, under pretence of an Asia markets specialist for a Washington-based risk consultancy—mostly skimming talkative executives for rumors, and unhappy mid-level engineers and developers for substance and plot twists; he travelled perpetually, gradually cultivated a taste for whiskey and cold tea, and cocaine by the long line as pop-up Asian tycoons prefer it; attended Sunday sermon with his wife and infant when the wheels came down in D.C.; sat red-eyed on the veranda with his parents through brunch; forwarded his reports to a Langley-bound handler—Smith—who expended himself making cross-words of bills of lading, commercial invoices, spirited internal corporate communications, and Foster's reports; and for a time this arrangement held, and they saw that it was good.

Smith listened; his eyes leapt sightlessly across the objects on his desk, and he drew a curl of phone cord flat beneath his thumbs.

Tastes had changed, however. There was a new premise, and with it a determination that Foster's post was too thin and entirely too loud for the new way. He would be reassigned: an engagement which after some deliberation installed him in a quiet professorship at a university in Saint Louis—Washington University—warming a lectern

beneath the dewy, complacent gaze of a patronage intent upon pur-
chasing the terms of their future. These were the steps that brought
him across the seal in the lobby, brought him past the credential
check and through the turnstiles, and up, into the rigid, taupe-cush-
ioned armchair from which he sat patiently watching Smith on the
phone, nodding an unseen acknowledgement—nodding again. "I
understand," he said, and rest the handset quietly in the cradle. He
traded the cord for a pencil and bit on the metal crown. The thought
of the salivated eraser soured Foster's mouth. "Well, Charles, they
don't know," said Smith.

For Foster the voice was the familiar thing—its firm nasal cadence
and slurred, rural Virginian vowels had become the intimate sound
of the institution itself; but here in the flesh, the embodiment was an
abstraction: a flaccid albino bloodhound, with a sparse, reedy mustache and a truss of dusty auburn hair, seeming never combed or
cut, but of a length and state simply arrived at by some sedentary
gestation. Smith was an ageless middle place; suspended anywhere
between a hard-rode twenty-eight and a soft-worn fifty with equal
plausibility—the way an oiled cog's properties all become indeter-
minate with use. Smith's necktie lay over the hood of a large beige
computer monitor. He wore a wrinkled white Oxford going threadbare at the collar-fold over an undershirt the perfect match to his
skin tone: Foster thought them summer and winter hides worn at
once. "They don't know," he repeated, rubbed the blue bags beneath
his eyes with a pinch, and smoothed his sparse mustache with the
same finger and thumb. "Well, somebody knows, but not me—and
whoever does won't say."

Foster looked over his cluttered desk and his oil-tanned keyboard
and his coffee mug of chewed pencils.

"You've been given a new handler, Charles. That's the point," said Smith.

"But we don't know who," said Charles, " and we don't know why."

"Charles, you sat right there. You heard me. The answer was, no—I don't know—I wasn't told; and if you want my guess, it's going to stay that way."

"Am I being moved out? You would just do me a favor and tell me if they were moving me out," said Foster.

"I don't think that's it, Charles. Nothing about it looks that way."

"I don't know," said Foster, "but you can see how it might look that way. You can see how that might be the impression. Right?" He searched with his elbows for the narrow rails, and clasped his hands. "I mean, I'm yanked from circulation like I've got plague, and promoted to wilderness station. Three months in I lose my case officer . . . You can see what that might look like?"

"It could've been Lawrence, Kansas—it's a good post, Charles." Smith bit on the end of his pencil. Foster watched the stamped metal slowly deform beneath his bite, rotate and compress, rotate and compress. Foster wondered if Fabre Castle and Sanford and Trusty had different flavors: he wondered if Smith favored a brand. Smith swiveled in his chair and looked from the window with his pencil. "It's a fine posting," he said. His eyes flicked across the landscape, and Foster eventually glanced to see what they were seeing. "I don't know, Charles. The best way to prevent a rollup is to keep things on a thermostat, you know: turn things down when they get warm. And the consensus was things were a little warm. Prevents your people from getting dangled, and keeps my people viable: you. Besides, talent scout is at the ground floor of what we do. It's an honorable trade."

"Why trade handlers then?" asked Foster.

"It could be you've been tapped for an escalated project. Right skill, right zip code—something like that."

"Fine. But then why wouldn't you know—why wouldn't you be told who the handoff was?"

"It could be need-to-know. It could be firewalled, Charles. It could be somebody's pet-fucking firewalled op; and then wouldn't you feel stupid with all your glum-faced soft-shoe. Look," said Smith, "I'm sure to find out if it's some corporate style introduction. Otherwise, I'll let you know what the paroles are when they're handed down."

Now they both turned to the window.

"You're bound to hear something—forty-eight hours probably," Smith said, and turned the pencil.

It was an image of Smith which Foster held firmly in mind when they talked later that day by phone. Foster envisioned the scene from earlier—the light from the window, the dusty slats of the Venetian blinds, and the dental-molded pencil: "'Familiar,'" said Smith, the parole was 'familiar.' It was a password repeated only the next day in a call taken by taxi from Catherine's apartment.

When after some twenty minutes, he unfolded his graceless length from the taxi and onto the pavement, the air was bright and humid, and his ill-fitting suit quickly vented its cool atmosphere into the day. Foster strode down Independence remembering the knife in his trouser pocket with his fingers. In the opposite pocket, with the fingers of his other hand he also remembered his paper rose: a small, carefully-creased, 92 Bright, 20 lb, acid-free origami envelope; and if necessary, edible paper attaché for his daily measure—the travel dose of cocaine he generally kept on his person with the same habituated ease of a matchbook or spare key. He passed the Hirshhorn and mused at the paradox of displaying flat things on curved walls.

Crossing Ninth he tugged his cuffs from the cling of his coat sleeves, and inside the Haupt Garden he paused apprehensively to flick the paper rose into a concrete trash barrel, and resisted a spiteful temptation to send the folding knife with it.

Through the street-level entrance the Sackler spilled down a limestone shaft on a floating terrazzo stair of turquoise metalwork and polished brass handrails. He descended, followed a passage into the Freer, up into the main galleries, along the marble hall against the courtyard, and into a room like the interior of a Fabergé egg—composed entirely in emerald green, gilded shelving, and frail blue and white porcelain. As he entered, to Foster's left hung a painting of a woman in a pale robe and red sash; and to his right, on the far side of the room stood a man examining a depiction of two peacocks— or as Foster thought them, two turkeys—in gold on a large green leather panel.

The man stood with a broad, slightly exaggerated stance, his hands clasped at the small of his back. His figure was substantial, but compact; something like an athlete in off-season. His suit was a tidy pinstripe over a banker's blue—and Foster saw from the beam of the shoulder to the lay of cuff, it was finely shorn and fitted. But the attire, the form, and the posture, left Foster with a sense for the details of an irresolvable whole: Savile Row finery over a steeled frame—it left Foster with an impression which came formed in the single word: Navy. The man tipped his ear slightly, as though placing Foster in the room with it. "Certainly you know it's impolite to stare," he said. He turned toward Foster in a quick, uninterrupted motion. "Aren't you supposed to be pretending to appreciate something, or is that too great an exertion?"

"I hadn't gotten that far," said Foster. He scanned the room with the sense something had escaped his notice. The man was reasonably tall, though Foster's own unusual height confounded accurate guessing. He bore sharp features, a pair of silver glasses on a cord which lay professorially against his lapels, and a shock of black and gray hair which rest only reluctantly toward one side. Foster put him near sixty, and handsome if slightly sun-wizened. Foster was certain they'd never met. "You're the 'familiar,'" he said.

"I am," said the man. "And you're no fan of Whistler."

"Since I guessed he was a flautist, I suppose that counts for a 'no.' Is that his?" asked Foster with a gesture toward the painting above the mantle.

"It is. But it's his credit for the room which has it here."

"The whole room?" asked Foster.

"It's credited to him, but no—not all of it. A fellow name of Jeckyll designed it. And was nearly finished with it, too; when Whistler was fooling about with something one day—painting in the front hall or some business. In any case, Jeckyll—rather unwisely it might be said—asked Whistler's opinion on some painted shutter doors; concerned they might clash with *The Princess*, I believe," he said, indicating the painting. "Whistler said he would retouch a few details, and all would be well. Thinking this sounded fine, Leyland, the homeowner, and Jeckyll fucked-off to Liverpool or wherever—and left Whistler in London to the business of the room. Meantime, Whistler covered half of everything in gold leaf, and painted gold peacocks on the rest—he entertained guests in the room, and then wanted two thousand pounds for work that Leyland had never agreed to. Leyland paid him half, and to commemorate the occasion, Whistler painted this cockfight on Leyland's expensive leather," he said. "In the end he won a pittance and lost a patron. Artistic temperaments—so single minded. Sighted like a mole: sharp to the inch; blind to the foot. But that," he said gesturing rigidly toward the painting, "was the start of it."

Foster stood in an appreciative and deferential silence.

"I tell you this because I believe you know nothing of it," said the man.

"Is it important?" asked Foster.

"There are no facts which are important; there are only facts which are relevant—what is important is having the relevant facts. I know this because it is a fact relevant to what we do." On the final syllable there was the hollow snap of flip-flops from the hall, and both Foster and the man turned to see a couple in short pants, straw hats and print shirts at the threshold of the room. The couple looked about, and at the man whose angry gaze had stayed them from entering. Behind them in the hall, Foster noted a figure in heavy green long sleeve, with cropped hair and a roundly muscled head. He had emerged from nowhere in particular, but watched the couple as they gawked at the porcelain and shelving.

"No playing through," said the man to the tourists. But they were transfixed and did not move. "Can't you see I'm with a pupil?" he snarled at them, to which they seemed visibly discomforted, and turned away. The man in the heavy shirt followed them off, but Foster noticed that a second figure emerged and replaced him in the hall.

"Smith explained everything to you?" said the man abruptly.

"He didn't explain anything to me, other than that he wouldn't be my handler anymore—and to give me the parole for your call," said Foster.

"Good."

"Did he know?"

The man sway with a single soundless laugh—"If he did, we're keeping secrets in a sieve. No. I don't think so," said the man. "I'm from the Executive Office," he said, and provided a pause sufficient to take this up. It was a pause Foster used, and when he offered nothing but a searching gaze, the man said, "How are things with your wife, by the way?"

"We're separated," said Foster, and the sound of his own voice seemed to jar his feet free of the floor, where they restlessly shuffled him toward a velvet stanchion near the shelves.

"It's no consolation of course, but it's common: our lot, you could say. How was your visit?"

"Short," said Foster before the question had even registered. "Cold," he continued. "Hopeless. Probably."

"It's a shame to hear," said the man. "You'll be reporting to me directly from here on in. Exclusively."

Foster nodded uneasily.

"You're signed for. Entirely mine. Nothing left to do—so no concern. Was it Saint Louis? I hear it's lovely."

"She," Foster started, "she wasn't taken with it."

"Family?" asked the man.

"Yes. Possibly a shortage of admirers, too."

"In due time," said the man.

"Then it would just have come to pedigree, I think—or something else," said Foster.

"Power is context, Doctor—there is nothing else. A queen in Siam, is a beggar in Thebes. This is for you," he said, and produced a small black jump drive from the breast of his jacket. "Something which ought to be in your power."

"What is it?" asked Foster, considering the innocuous little rectangle between his fingers as if it were the ampule of a foreign serum.

"Your specialty really. Or so I'm led to believe. Software. Industrial software," said the man.

"For which machines?"

"That'll be plain enough—you'll recognize it."

"And what are we doing with it?" asked Foster.

"You," said the man, "are looking for vulnerabilities. Openings for disruptive access—remote access."

"You want me to write malicious code—for this?" asked Foster gesturing with the drive. "You want a virus."

"I think of myself as open minded. Consider it an opportunity for artistic interpretation. Trojan, virus, worm; whatever: the matter is academic so long as it operates in the deep background and allows real access—but in the end, I want a functional piece of discreet malware."

"What should it do?" asked Foster, slipping the flash drive into his coat pocket and shifting uneasily on his feet.

"Whatever is possible: that is what it should do—is what it should allow us to do. Anything. Everything. As an industrial control system, it's used in a range of applications. We should exploit every weakness and every feature. Nothing is too good for us, Dr. Foster."

"Where is it? Will we have access to it—access to the machinery?" asked Foster.

"No. It's in the wild. It's everywhere. So delivery must be taken into account."

There was a silence in which the man from the Executive Office studied Foster, studied him staring blankly at his shoes, his nervous hands dipping briefly into his pants pockets, and his bent and reluctant pose.

"We do have whole labs staffed for this sort of thing," said Foster at last. "I guess I don't understand. Why me? Why me—a man in the field in his spare time—and not a hardened resource already in place? I don't want to disappoint you, but why isn't that a better tool? Not to mention: this is hardly my field . . ."

"I thank you for the inventory of our resources, Doctor," said the man with a bitter chuckle, "but I think I have a very good vision for them. And besides, you should have faith! You won't disappoint—it's impossible for you to disappoint—I promise. We're laying new road," he continued, "pulling it up after us. We're off script, and you are a systems engineer—are you not?"

Foster tried to respond but the man continued over him.

"Yes. Yes, you are—so I think between the pair of us, you're the man for the job." The man quickly lifted his cuff to check the time, and continued. "We're entirely off the books, Doctor. This isn't a line item anywhere. For now, at least, this is drawn from my own discretionary budget, and is as dark as you like. As I said: you're all mine." He checked his watch again. "Proof of concept, Dr. Foster. Proof of concept. That's what I want: a prototype." The man inhaled deeply, drew himself up, straightened his tie. "Look it over, Doctor. Look it over, find your method, gain access, and then concern yourself with a wonderful and invisible little container."

"Have we established a point of penetration? A means—is there an angle of attack I should be looking at? A strategy, special access—anything?" Foster began to feel weightless, falling.

"Do I strike you as the hand-holding type? There is no we, Dr. Foster: no me. There is only you." He lifted his cuff one last time. "I'll be in touch," he said with a saccharin, conciliatory tone. "You're just the man for it, Doctor—I just know it. I can feel it in my bones. There's Whistler at the National Gallery as well—it's lovely—you should see it before you leave," he said, and left Foster there to the sound of his heels and the footfalls of his cohort receding along the hall.

The drive had rattled around in a pocket of his briefcase for several days unminded, not unlike the little stainless folding knife which, delivered back to Saint Louis in the belly of Foster's garment bag, hung now forgotten in the breast pocket of his suit.

It was an evening some time later—research papers strewn along the dining room table with a bachelor's care, the windows prized open to a mild breeze, the unfolded petals of the paper rose trembling gently in the air—that the jump drive had tumbled from Foster's reclining briefcase out onto the table, mirror-slick with polish. Between papers and the solvent fume of red correcting pen, he'd downloaded the contents of the drive to his laptop and found the man was right: the man from the Executive Office, The Familiar. He did recognize the software. It was Siemens Step-7: a package of industrial management software used to govern the lattice of machinery driving everything from amusement rides to manufacturing operations, power stations, refining medical isotopes, or—assuming the appropriate political and financial motivation—enriching weapons grade Uranium 235 from the garden variety vapors of Uranium 238.

But while contributing to such a system was well within Foster's ability, merely recognizing, designing, or coding were a matter quite apart from weaponizing its zero-day vulnerabilities—defeating it without breaking it, or manhandling it without leaving bruises, much less prints. It wasn't impossible, he thought, but the scope of the thing ran to—and it seemed to him—beyond, the comfortable edges of his conception—his slightly, perhaps increasingly, addled conception. For this reason he'd come to courting Jeffrey Sachs—the young graduate student and gifted programmer—and for this reason come to find himself seated in a wear-marked, tobacco-stain booth beneath the failing light of day and a menagerie of trophy heads and jukeboxes on chalk-blue walls in a dusky corner of Blueberry Hill.

4.

S achs landed the pitcher and nested pint glasses before Foster, who hadn't moved in his absence, nor had he been served.

"Expecting company, or just keeping one for each hand?" said Foster at last sliding the phone into his pocket.

"You're company. I didn't figure they'd have gotten you—we're at the witching hour."

"I'm not much of a beer man," said Foster.

"Every man's a beer man, Charles. With the exception of tipplers and 'totalers, they only come that way."

"And what are those?" asked Foster, watching Sachs negotiate the glasses and the pitcher to fill them.

"Well the one simply abstains; the other prefers champagne and hugs," he said with a broad unselfconscious smile.

"Where'd you hear that?"

"Dunno, maybe I just made it up."

"I suppose I have no choice, then."

"None at all. Savor this choiceless moment while it lasts. Cheers."

The story had been meted out in bipolarized parcels of good-natured shoulder swatting and recondite evasiveness, but as Jeffrey Sachs had come to understand it, Foster was contracting with a security consultancy tasked with providing a suite of proprietary security instruments. The client's concern was their hardware and software products falling into the hands of competitors and unlicensed users. But rather than devising a lock-out protocol alerting unauthorized users, and supplying them opportunity to purge or dispose of proprietary material, there was a concerted interest in alternatives—allowing the machinery and software at least the appearance of normal function, if also frustrating the results and products which licensed and rightful acquisition would achieve. The concept, as described to Sachs, was merely a variation on the theme of patent and proprietary defense; in this case allowing the lawyerly rank to lace and polish their briefs, and perhaps even capture offenders, hardware in tow.

How precisely to do it was the question, and it was one for which Foster proposed to pay twenty thousand dollars for an answer. With his academic and other consultative obligations for the client, he was pressed for time and overburdened. Were Sachs to provide a viable draft of a discrete executable script, it would be well worth a small piece of Foster's fee for the collaboration. To Sachs' dismay, however, that *collaboration* never transpired. Foster provided five of the twenty thousand at the start and in the ensuing months, nothing but a compensation in fits of harassing urgency broken by spells of a silent and absent indifference. It wasn't a mere business of brain chemistry, Sachs felt sure, but as though Foster's very mechanisms were bi-polar—like as all his cogs were toothed on one side—so that even flat-out he would idle for half the rotation and surge with paroxysm for the other.

Sachs, however, held out hope that this chill, ebbing February day, broadcasting the flares of its final luster from beneath the brow of window cornices across Delmar might mark the completion of their relationship. But it was a hope otherwise divorced from hopefulness; his desire was fastened by a skepticism which had grown up around Foster and the whole business, and weighed upon all the buoyancy of completion.

Foster smiled as he picked up the flash drive Sachs placed on the table. "Is Adata the only company that makes these things?"

"Thumb drives?"

"I swear to god, I've never bought a single one of these things, and I bet I've got a half-dozen that are identical."

"Everybody makes those."

"Really?"

"Everybody."

"Well I'd never know, mine are all the same—each and every one, I bet."

"If they're from the university maybe that's not surprising."

"No, no—I've gotten them other places too. It's uncanny. Anyway—so this is it?"

"That's it. Dinner is served."

Foster considered his pint glass for a moment. "In the spirit of the occasion," he said, and visited a sip.

"In the spirit of any occasion."

"Alright, what's in the soup?" said Foster, examining the jump drive as though he might divine its contents by close looking.

Sachs worked down an effervescing mouthful of drink and then guarded the glass with a two-handed grip. "Muddled mints, turtle-doves, and partridges in a pear trees," he said, and tried a fleeting smile on Foster. "Let me show you. Can I show you?" Sachs drew a heavy laptop from his satchel and cleared the pitcher and glasses for room. It bore a faint patina of original finish and a jumbled livery in band decals one full generation out of register and was white-silver with handling everywhere it might be clasped or touched or carried. The machine was hot with readiness and Sachs set it out and opened it and stabbed the jump drive in its flanks. He accessed the drive and a command console into it and spun it round for Foster to see: "It loads into and boots from memory rather than hard-disk. It's five basic modules together: a carrier file used for delivery, although the physical reality of making connection with the right hardware is a question for you and your clients—I wouldn't know where to start. There's a loader that forks it into memory on boot-up; an access panel, concealed back door that allows you to adjust functions and settings if you choose, but also to view or cull data from the hardware itself. And there's a key logger—I wasn't sure if you'd want that or not, but I thought I'd leave it in—if you guys want to defeat it you can. But I would assume that more information about the ways the systems are being used is preferable to less. I mean, that's the point, isn't it? And then there's the five golden rings."

Foster scrolled down the code lines. This time of day it was onion cutting—the squinty text gave him eye water; it was all optical Braille, digital hieroglyphs. Now he was no longer seeing; now he was no longer looking—just scrolling as a decorous succession to being shown, as the necessary antecedent to speaking.

"The access panel—where is that?"

"You're looking at it."

"It's all command-line?"

"It is."

"Are all my client staff superusers?"

"I have no idea what your client staff are."

"They're not. Can it replicate?"

"Why would you want it to do that? I mean, no—not now it doesn't—but I suppose you could make it. I'm not sure why—"

"What are the five golden rings, then?"

"Well, that's your dessert, right: chocolate truffle cake—your pièce de résistance."

"Dessert is the enduring feature?"

"I like dessert. So, I had a hell of a time trying to figure out what would let you get in, and not just observe an errant system, but affect it—but all this without rousing the guy at the keyboard with his donut fingers. It's the clock—I mean that's all I could think of, anyway."

"What'd you do with the clock?"

"Well, the more you've daisy chained together the greater the potential effect, and less likely I'd guess to ring any bells—but basically you backend the clocks, the device clocks, so that you can still feed a user the clocking specs they expect to see, but that's just a feed—like mirroring the telemetry they dial in, for example. You want to be able to alter the clock settings in order to slow things down, speed them up, turn them on when they should be off, off when they should be on—you know."

"And this does that?"

"In spades."

"In golden rings."

"Sure."

Foster followed Sachs' thread despite feeling his attentions were lolling on their stem. In the moment, here opposite the young man in his t-shirt and crumpled pea coat, this electro-mechanical achievement and its metaphor of conveyance felt insoluble, unmasticated and raw. The source of his flickering attention was in part strong boredom seizing upon him in waves, and manifest principally as a sensation of being pierced through at the nasal flange. But more generally Foster recognized it as the 'nag': that irritated hollow of the sinus, that un-chaffed scab yearning to be peeled, to be abraded.

Foreground to this ambient physiological itch, however, was another persisting distraction, in the form of Foster's astonishment at the casual acceptance of his fabulous pretence. So far as Foster could tell, Sachs had nothing for him but a student's resentment for his lack of participation, and a freelancer's tactful concern not to disturb impending monies. But whatever the static, there seemed none for premise, so that for a moment listening to Sachs' earnest tones, he wondered that he might persuade him to deliver the bug as well.

"It's an executable, I assume?" said Foster.

"Of course . . . I just said that. All plug n' play. I mean I can tool it differently, make it a remote exec for example . . . if that's what you want." Sachs worried a mole on his cheek, and his gaze veered suddenly away as he said this. He could, but had no desire to—Foster noted from the tell—evading the alternative as though their gaze might complete the unwanted circuit.

"No. That's fine. That's what I wanted. Let's just add replication— we'll need that—and a graphical user interface for the access panel. Think ease of use. Keep it neat."

"That'd be almost half again the work."

Foster closed the computer and slipped it toward Sachs. "You're a great talent, Jeffrey." He felt oddly rejuvenated by Sachs' onset of ill ease and drew a checkbook and pen from his coat. "Here's another five-thousand. You don't mind waiting till we've reviewed the work for the rest."

II.

The barn was humid with the smell of stale shit, rotting straw, the sweet tang of the M5's exhaust, and the eternal must of forgotten places. Marek Hussar rest between the headlamps with the spade handle in his left hand and gloves knotted in his right, and surveyed what lay where the light speared the turgid air. An occasional winter breeze rattled the boards, and where they gapped, set the car-light aflame with dancing chaff. At the back of the barn, Hussar had parted the heap of moldering hay to the ground, where, unlike the masonry-hard soil outside, it had been kept warm and moist beneath the decomposing straw. In that space, he'd excavated a trough some six feet long and four feet deep, leavened the cavity with a one-hundred-sixty pound zipper-bag from the trunk, stanched the gap with its own displaced earth, and paused to mark the time on his wristwatch. Beneath the rafters and the drooping loft, it had been full dark for thirty minutes. But beyond the barn wood cladding, the brisk day was still forty minutes to dusk, and its textures flared with pink and bronze as the last flush of an ember.

Again he referred to the watch, replaced his gloves, and set to dressing the straw over the earthen gash to form a heaping, shapeless drift—much as it had been before. Now with a composite interval for the process through to the end, he fetched a pair of binoculars from the car and stepped out between the barn's wide doors, and onto the rutted path parting the vast, untended grasses. The barn rest two-thirds up a rising and neglected pasture, and was closed on all sides by a wood, which in the rapidly changing light seemed to have barred even the aperture of the road with shadow. He circled, looking for trampled grasses, and scanned the wood again for any sign of structures with line-of-sight. He found nothing to see. And when Hussar had finally resolved to an imperfect satisfaction, he drew the car out through the huge doors, and fastened them closed with a keyed padlock.

He turned down the long aggregate drive, through the shaded portal of the trees, and eventually onto the county road where a sign nailed to a vague remnant of fence proclaimed 'Acreage for Sale.' The phone number listed was illegible for the height of weeds, and so far as Hussar could tell, the property had been out of use for the better part of a decade.

The two-lane switchback hove to sides and pitched blind over crests. A patchwork of amended asphalt and sudden irretrievable verges, Hussar swept along it, bending and falling, throttling up until the engine gained the breath of life; the exhaust rang in quick emphatic shouts, and the valve train spun off its lope and lethargy for snarling induction clockworks. The tires warmed through long sweepers, and the chassis danced into corners and lit on toes over the precipitous crown of rises. Occasional squat clapboard homes stumbled down toward the road, their chalky drives sailing out, as stockings from a line. Copse of wood broke between the houses, and by stages full-up against the roadside; a streaking panorama, deep invulnerable evergreen and tendril-patient deciduous brown. Only the balking punctuation of slow and unimaginative traffic disturbed his mechanical indulgence—his vestibular concentration of feet and

Equipment 37

hands—and his carefully sighting the road-line for the mount of antlers and light racks.

When at last he'd reached 44, he wound up to speed and settled into the left lane, where he moved past emerging taillights like mile markers, and for an hour and a half, slipped east toward Saint Louis and into the blue dark of early evening.

2.

The woman who left had short black hair and tattoos. The woman who returned was thick, older, wore a formless black dress, and scowled at him disapprovingly through a pair of bifocals in the guise of fashionable glasses. In the five minutes between them, Marek Hussar sat beneath the tarp-like smock, his feet on the stirrup, a bitter light swelling his unshaven pallor, his hair a swerve of damp tangle; gazed at the weary squint which peered back at him from the mirror, and decided: a competent mechanic, a good barber, and a tolerable woman are the rarest things an obsessive man will ever know.

"I'm Lauren," said the woman whose dress fell in a line from the precipitous ledge of her breasts, much as Hussar's smock from his knees. "I've excused Kim for the afternoon; I'll be finishing your haircut," she said into the mirror when she arrived.

"Then much shorter on the sides and back, if you please," he said. "For all I care, you may leave the rest as it is."

The woman, Lauren, despite her contemptuous glances, had begun to work into the scalp with her fingers and comb—the sensation as always, made Hussar drowsy—before her curiosity had the better of her. "Was there a misunderstanding, perhaps?" she hazarded. "Perhaps a . . . miscommunication?"

Hussar felt amused by her proposal, and pulled away from the scissors to look at her. "Does she speak the King's English?" he asked.

"What?" she said. "Yes. I mean . . . yes."

He turned back to the mirror. "Well then, I hardly expect there was a misunderstanding."

"What, if I may ask, did you say to her?"

"You may," said Hussar, "but frankly it's interrupted my haircut once already. As it is," he said, extracting his arm from the smock, and lifting his cuff to bare the watch face, "in thirty-two minutes, I've an appointment eight minutes away. If it's all the same to you, I'd rather keep things simple."

In fact, what he'd said had been simple. The woman with the dark bob and the tattoos, called Kim, had been dividing her energies unequally between cutting his hair and chatting him up. She was cute in that indiscernible past tense one presumes of girls defiled beneath an indiscretion of ink and piercings. And she'd prattled on interminably:

Where was he from? She didn't care for an answer. She was from Hazelwood. Did he have children? Was he in a relationship? The questions were merely preludes for her own response. She'd just moved in with her boyfriend of a year. How did he feel about apartments? They were constricting, she thought, and was happy to have rented a small house. What about pets? Did he like pets? She loved pets—dogs most of all: at which point she launched headlong into a detailed accounting of how her Labrador, Titus, had worked himself free of the house just last night. The final scene involved the boyfriend's heroics, snatching after the trailing leash, hurtling fences after the dog, circling the property, the neighbor's yards, and a near four block radius before the emboldened Titus ultimately secured his escape; and concluded with a quavering moment of sympathetic offertory into which Hussar was expected to tithe. What he thought, dryly, was: the lot of you are idiots of the first order. But what he said—and with no special intention, was, "The only thing more foolish than a man chasing a dog is a man chasing a woman."

At which, the woman, Kim, had straightened, and seized. She raised and lowered her tools, pinched her eyes, turned away, and finally, back into mirror, where, Hussar could see her eyes glistening mist. She dropped the comb into the Barbicide, clapped her shears on the counter, and after five minutes of blow dryers and the receptionist lavishing supernatural enthusiasm into the telephone, Lauren, her fabric bolt of a dress, and her disparaging eyeglasses, had emerged in her place; and from Hussar's reply forward, failed to utter another word. When she'd finished, she dusted his neck with a brush, straightened his collar, removed the cape, and pivoted the chair to the side.

"They'll ring you up at the counter," she said.

"I can see we're on a roll," said Hussar.

He collected his linen suit jacket, slipped it on at the counter and corrected the lapels as the receptionist worked the checkout.

"Would you like to schedule your next appointment, sir?" she asked.

"That won't be necessary."

"Total's thirty-five. Would you like to add anything, sir?" she asked.

"I think it would be lost in the moment."

"I'm sorry?"

"No," he said.

Outside, his breath emerged in fuming vaporous snorts, his hair had grown suddenly stiff and chill, and he navigated the sidewalk crowded everywhere with university students in their daily migration, downed and fleeced and flannelled, on their harried and self-certain way; each a point on a graph of convergences: resources versus academics, versus substances, versus time. All of them, Hussar mused, ingredients committing to a dish whose recipe they cannot fathom.

The portal of a narrow footpath between buildings opened onto a cluttered parking lot, where Hussar found the car still with the warmth of an hour ago, and bulwark against the air which had begun to sting in his nostrils and bite through the middling weight of his suit. With a few moments of running, the cabin was balmy and he'd wheeled west up Delmar, past the ornate octagon of the City Hall, beneath the gaze of the lion's gate, along the boulevard's great, leafless sycamores, and eventually left, through the wrought iron gate at Purdue, and following the leftward split at Creveling, to a stop before the second house on the right. He waited there with the V8 burbling idly for a further eight minutes and fifty-five seconds, by the hands of his watch, before the realtor drew up behind in her lipstick-red Mercedes Geländewagen.

"You're certainly of a piece," he said, stepping from the car and into the gritted street. The woman approached, prancing vehemently across the noisy pea-stones in a silk jacket printed with golden ropes, and a brimmed hat, scarf, and suede boots, each the identical saccharin red of the truck. "I nearly missed you," he said.

"Mr. Degen! Oh, what a pleasure to finally meet you! I'm Patricia, of course. Did I say that right—Degen? Is that right?" she asked, advancing toward Hussar with her arm thrust out rigidly as though to gore him with it.

"That's fine," he said, and received her hand, small, cool, and frail as an iced herring, but studded everywhere with jeweled adornments. At the touch, Hussar wondered if she could imagine the whimsy with which those improbably ornate digits might be rendered a snapped and opulent gristle. The butterfly whose grace is the spider's incredulity, he thought.

"Oh, lovely—what a lovely car you have. Very pretty," she said.

"The one woman with whom I always agree," said Hussar.

"And white after Labor Day, aren't you the daring one! Come!" she said, and led him up the front walk toward the door.

"Is it white?" he asked, briefly considering where his cuff met his glove. "And what happens on Labor Day?"

At the heavy, oaken front door, the realtor was engrossed in a procedure for opening the lockbox shackled about the handle. Stooped and muttering, Hussar suspected her of struggling to recall an incantation.

"Why Labor Day? What happens on Labor Day?" he repeated.

"Why what?" she asked, adjusting her hat brim. "Oh, well, we put up our summer whites of course . . . Oh, you're being coy," she said, spinning the key in the tumbler, and throwing the door open upon a dim tiled foyer.

"And *why do* we do that: put our whites up?"

"Well . . . I don't know, I suppose. It's just what . . . it's a . . . a convention . . . etiquette. It's just what civilized . . ." she said. But when she straightened into the full wick of his attention, she lost the fiber of her thought.

"I'm sure it is," he said. "I sometimes forget the world began in 1776. Americans have such quaint superstitions . . . and a mysterious preoccupation with color."

The home was rough-hewn brick and leaded glass, over-leaved with a deliberation of slate tiles, and trimmed the lichen green of mature copper fittings. It stood off from the street behind a lawn of crisp winter grasses, and beneath the stone archway and the shade-less overcast. The realtor rooted abruptly through her purse for her next words, and Hussar watched closely to see what she'd find.

"You've an arrow for every occasion, Mr. Degen," she said, finding at last what she sought in the red leather clutch, and closed it with a snap.

"Bravo," he said, and stepped past her into the foyer. "I try to stay well armed."

She smiled: a brief, curled smudge the precise color of her boots, and clutch, and car. "As I mentioned," she cleared her throat, "as I mentioned—I believe I mentioned when we spoke before—this is four beds, four baths," she said, laying the door gently closed. "A two-car garage as you requested; in-ground pool—though I can't attest to the condition . . ."

"What does it say in the seller's disclosure?"

"About the pool? Let me see." She produced a fold of papers from a deep coat pocket. "Oh, here, this is a copy of the listing," she said, and presented a single sheet from the bunch into the vacant foyer. But Hussar had passed into the living room and she followed. "Yes, and of course, the living room meets the dimensions you provided."

"It's larger, in fact," he said, removing his gloves and pacing off the long wall, his head bowed in concentration.

"Is that a problem?" she asked.

"No." He paused in the corner to take note of the paces, and then pivoted to mark-off the shorter adjoining wall.

"You must have large furnishings?"

"No," he said, "I have particular furnishings."

She moved to the fireplace and rest her hat on the mantle. The fireplace was simple but substantial unadorned stone, and fitted with a worked hardwood cap. An array of faceted windows stared into a brittle, gray hedge, and an anemic light shown the polished floorboards and the cherry stain woodwork of the barrel vaulted ceiling. Hussar had an impression of the light as an overpressure from the outdoors, and that the rooms were simply inflated by it.

"A little over thirty-four hundred square feet . . . Should be plenty of space if you have a lot of furniture," she offered to Hussar, who was walking off an additional series of measurements.

"I don't."

"It must be your wife," she said when she'd noticed his platinum band.

Hussar slipped his hands reflexively into his pockets and turned from his measurements to face her. "She won't be joining me," he said.

"She must have quite a bit. My husband—bless him: he claims I've never seen a Rococo I didn't—"

"She won't be joining me," he said, and rest his gaze upon her. "The garage?"

". . . is through the kitchen."

"And the beds?"

"Upstairs."

He strode from the room, across the foyer and through the kitchen portal, hands fastened behind his back. She followed. The room was white, practical, and recently clean, with fittings survived twenty years beyond their fashion.

"It could use a bit of updating," she said through the door into the garage, through which Hussar flashed occasionally turning in the unswept grit.

"It's a two-car," she said.

"It's narrower than I'd hoped. Both remotes for the automatic door?" he asked and appeared in the doorframe.

"They should be here," she said and started for the kitchen drawers, but Hussar had already begun to search them to a chorus of unladen casters. He shook his head, turned back to close the door into the garage, and checked it for play.

"Seems sturdy," she volunteered.

"Like a vault door."

She followed him upstairs where he fixed on the closets and doors and window latches. "There's just the one stair?" he called out from the master en suite.

"Yes, just the one," she said. In the bath he peered into the yard and a bitter draft through a small open window. And she fell back from the cold into the comparative warmth of the bedroom.

"Do we know the neighbors?"

"What do you do, Mr. Degen?" she called into the bath.

"Real estate," he said to the rattle of the closing window. "Real estate," he repeated as he emerged. "We're a modest firm, but we have interests in a diversified portfolio of real estate investments. Historically commercial, increasingly residential as well."

"Is it a U.S. firm?"

"By location or concern?"

"I'm not . . . I don't . . ." she attempted with a dubious shake of her head.

"Certainly," he said.

"What . . . Which is that?"

"You won't have heard of it. Wire transfer or bank draft?" he said, and turned for the door.

"Yes, yes . . . You'll forgive me, Mr. Degen—your accent, please tell me—I'm struggling to place it," she said, as he descended the stair.

"I'm a Swiss of course," he called from the foyer: "You will always know us by our impartiality."

3.

Hussar rose late into the morning, and with the grim reluctance of one acquainted with the night. The week was warm out of season and the furnace had been still for days. He bathed thirty minutes to the sound of running water, of which twenty were motionless: his thoughts suspended in the air of the stall, thick and moist as a bodily enclosure. They collected where the airborne spray beaded and released along the tile—veins of condensate born and spent in a singular pulse, slick, and humid, and sudden.

The door to the bath was fastened. The outer bedroom door as well—sealed against the limitless possibilities of an empty house. On the counter beside the sink rest a canvas duffle, which he kept near at hand bathing or sleeping. The exact contents of the bag varied based on location and circumstance, but were presently one pair of shoes; two pair of socks; two pair underwear; two undershirts; two long-sleeve shirts; one jacket; two pair of pants; one pair compact field glasses; one utility tool; gauze wrap, tape, and sterile wipes; two vials of morphine and syringe; two curved forceps, a tweezer, and nail trimmers; ½ circle surgical needle and suture thread; two virgin passports, driver's licenses, and credit cards; a ring with five safety deposit keys; twenty-thousand American dollars in two sealed plastic bags; one blacked Fällkniven F1 survival knife; two H&K USP

Tactical pistols chambered in .45 ACP; eight prepared fifteen round magazines; one hundred round box of Winchester 230 grain cartridges; one suppressor with left-hand thread; and one concealable shoulder rig.

When he'd finished, he dried, ordered his hair loosely with his fingers, and brushed his teeth. From the mattress on the carpet he dressed in jeans and shirt, rest the canvas bag in their place, removed the black knife from it, and padded in bare feet down the stair and into the kitchen, where he roused the dormant espresso machine. It was an affair in heavy stainless and commercial hafting, and was the exclusive addition to the otherwise dated kitchen appliances.

The movers arrived the week prior, threaded the storage container up the drive, and in some forty minutes of luxuriant motion, deposited the balance of Hussar's earthly effects and departed: a king mattress; an Eames sofa; a large pale rug Hussar deployed exclusively in rooms which were sonically bright; the pair of enormous piano black Bowers and Wilkins 800 speakers, the three-hundred-fifty pound Mark Levinson No. 33 amplifiers and source gear—each requiring cautious uncrating and meticulous placement; the four six-foot, double-wide, combination-locked ATA flight cases rolled on their casters and stowed beneath a vast fabric drop in the unused garage stall; and the espresso machine which just now issued the anticipated tick of status light.

These objects, barring necessity for change or the intervention of irresistible forces, represented the entire material sphere of his portable world. And sipping a stout Americano from one hand, and tossing the unsheathed knife, blade over handle in the other, Hussar ignited the components for the stereo—which like the espresso machine, required a warming—and paced the living room restlessly.

He let them warm an hour before he disturbed them again, in which time he crafted and dispatched another coffee and stalked the living room observing the dark-amber lights of electronics he'd not seen in some time, and flipped the knife round in the air, handle to handle; only the once lodging it in the floor beside his naked instep, summarily withdrawing it and continuing as before. It was common to go for extended intervals without seeing his things. The flight cases, in part or whole, were rarely far from hand; but for his nonessential gear—the equipment of human indulgence—many months may pass without it.

From a small window adjacent the fireplace a groggy wasp licked at the glass. When the stereo had warmed to his satisfaction, he played three versions of Charlie Hayden's "Silence" from digital files, and marveled at the wasp, acicular and unseasonable and precocious. It flung itself in venomous turns against the glass or the screen, a trap of inestimable boundaries it could neither penetrate nor perceive. Nowhere could Hussar make out a point for entry—the screen was whole and taught—and he wondered how it could so ingeniously enter, and with what prompt stupidity forget the ingenuity?

He retired from the window to the sofa to continue his listening, and sheathed the knife for the welfare of the cushions. From an extruded aluminum remote he advanced the volume, until the floorboards trembled with Hayden's base, and his eyes watered from the pleading horns. And as he swabbed them with his palm, he realized the wasp's trap was unsurprising: after all, determination is often comprehension's orphan.

4.

At the gym off the parkway, Hussar sat in a small office blanched by fluorescent tubes, into which a consultant entered with the brisk noise of quick-dry fabrics. He arrayed freshly-drafted papers before Hussar on a desk of wood grain plastic. The contract was a thin ream of paper vellum—a measured ploy for concealing its size while retaining a binding formality, Hussar observed—and in a script so fine he imagined it might be presented with a jewelers loupe; and when the consultant placed it reverentially upon the table which bore nothing but the loose impression of previous signatures, Hussar laughed out loud at the sight of it. "You're quite sure you haven't forgotten anything?" he asked.

The consultant, whose badge was emblazoned with the singular declarative—Roger—was a man in his middle-twenties, lightly pimpled, unskilled with a razor, slightly plump, and unaccountably earnest. At the sound of Hussar's laughter, his eyes, pink and watery, rolled to the sidelong assumption of a spooked horse, and he reared from the desk to the length of his arms and his clangorous red sleeves. "It's the standard," he said. "It's the standard," he repeated, with the cajoling note of a question. "You'd find it anywhere in the industry—you can be sure."

"Are these duplicates?" asked Hussar, thumbing wrong-handedly at the leaves with no pretence of the patience necessary to read them.

"Well—"

"No. They are not—that's astonishing," he said with an irrepressible smile and a shake of his head. "Double-sided I suppose," he said. "They are that as well! Fantastic! How many pages do we think? Don't look! Do you know?"

"Mr. Degem—"

"You do not. Twenty-three, twenty-four . . . twenty-six pages!"

"Mr. Degem . . ."

"Degen."

"Sorry. Mr. Degem . . . It's very common. Commonplace . . . a simple, very standard membership contract," insisted the consultant.

"People actually sign these?"

"Yes, Mr. Degem, of course they do."

"Now . . . Roger . . . I have a very important question."

"Of course, Mr. Degem . . ."

Hussar leaned forward, and carefully situated his palms astride the pages: "Are they shut-ins?"

"Absolutely not—"

"That's marvelous!" he roared with laughter. "Fools then! Every business must have its model. Yours is simply indentured retards."

"Mr. Degem!" the consultant protested.

"Organ donation requires less reading, and is, I suspect, less binding than what you have in mind—Roger. But perhaps there's room for additional obligation."

"Mr. Degem."

"What's one more page in the scheme of things?"

"Mr. Degem."

"Your pen...please?" requested Hussar, who was presented it by the incredulous consultant, and initialed, signed, signed, and initialed.

The consultant collected the pen, turned the pages to face him, and stared dazedly, but briefly, at the signatures. "I'll be right back with your copy," he said, but remained seated, and instead considered Hussar's features as though grappling with the glyphs of an alien language. When he finally made as though to stand, Hussar interrupted.

"Goodbye Roger."

"Let me just get your copies—"

"Mount them beside your other trophies," said Hussar, rising and with a gesture toward the bare walls.

"Enjoy your workout, Mr. Degem!" called the consultant, and scrambled out of the office after Hussar as the entry doors turned behind him.

5.

Outdoors it rained the sparse and persistent rain of cool seasons. It clicked like beads against the window glass and gurgled faintly through the progress of the gutters. A woman sat at the edge of his bed in half dress. She'd thrown on his discarded t-shirt and switched on the small desk lamp at the bedside. In this light the black shirt shown with the same Prussian Blue round the curve of her breast, as the underslope of predawn cloud through the window. Hussar knew her name was not Lilith as she'd said, but as he stood in the doorframe with the last of the Champagne ringing in two glasses, and she gazed up at him with large, beautiful, startled eyes; however absurd, he felt it oddly fitting.

The day had opened with rain: a steady mist the wipers stroked at intervals as Hussar crossed Clayton beneath the yoke of thirty-year-old mid-rise office towers. Along the corners mid-age professionals queued for lights in black hems and blue shirtsleeves and bowed beneath lunch-hour umbrellas arrayed against the levitating rain.

He'd begun at a shoe store in Brentwood, stuffed in the crook of a shopping plaza, and lighted with the vehemence of an indoor football pitch: for sixty-five minutes he'd wiled his time, committing the unique tread of men's shoes to memory, and left with black laces in an oversize bag.

He'd trundled the brief run up 170 into Clayton to the guttural per-turbations of the exhaust, and stopped by a wine merchant, where the odor of strong cheese and damp ceiling tile rest as though the opened door were a lifted lid, and checked out at a high counter, where he purchased three boxes of stemware, two foil-capped Champagnes, and a bottled whisky in a pale carton from a man heavily sweating bourbon. He'd stopped at the gym, with its scent of chlorine pool agents; fowled clothing and fresh-dried towels; the consultant, dappled in his brume of post-adolescent sebum; and its grand glass façade: a pious devotional to the commercial power of protestant ethic perseverations.

But at the blush of sunset, Hussar sat balanced between two moods, a table wrapped in lifted red laminate sheet, and a Paulaner drooling overfill from a plastic cup. He was swathed in the dark cavity of a men's club in East Saint Louis, and to Hussar's thinking it had the look of the inside of a thrift-store smoking jacket: the threadbare, synthetic interior of something which from the outside—and held to the light just so—looks the convincing counterfeit to a right idea. A soiled carpet in red paisley crawled beneath the tables and dis-appeared into the corners. A DJ loft at the back was painted galva-nized tube and diamond plate. The working bar was a convolution of Formica and corrugated sheet, and where three elevated stages marked the dusk, they shone as oases of light and polished brass. There were two near Hussar: bright and vacant. But about the third and furthest, a small residual of the daytime crowd hung helplessly from their stools, as if ensnared on the barbs of their own yearning, and spinning up thin ropes of tobacco smoke. In spite of this, Hussar found the room to be eerily scentless—still too early perhaps for the fulminate of bathroom colognes, sick, cigarettes, and spilt beer.

At the bar a heavy doorman with a headset rest his chin against his knuckles and occasionally issued drinks to the girls working tables. Hussar watched him steer his gaze about the room, over the patrons, and occasionally toward the door, with the deliberating weight of a dim searchlight. From the loft, the DJ served up expired pop singles as the rhythm of an autoerotic soundtrack, and at volume palpable as a fluid. Spangled and low-cut, the girls stopped into the narrow loft to visit him with drinks and requests, and the doorman's gaze watched this too: clients seduced occasionally down the hall toward private rooms; and from time to time it lighted downrange upon the two women on stage, their small breasts flushed and abraded, holding the stage with a nipple-bothering pantomime of wrestling and ecstasy.

Bruised peaches, thought Hussar.

A long figure in a tufted hunting jacket emerged from the threshold of the hall then, bearing an ample forelock swept back by the flat of his hand, and a nervous preoccupation with the flare of his nostrils. He crossed from the hall to an empty table in the middle of the room, where he stretched his length out over the chairback as he sat. A woman followed him shortly from the hall. She approached him with a touch to his shoulder and leant closely into his ear. He made no motion toward her except when she'd gone, when he turned to watch her at the bar. She returned with a drink, which she left with him together with a brief lingering of her fingers in his hair.

The man's silhouette jutted from the terrain of low-back chairs and tables, and from time to time, his head lolled indifferently into the upturned pitch of his collar, until at last the twosome had exhausted their vaudeville of lesbian affections; and following a short interval, the same woman who had accompanied him from the hall, appeared on stage to replace them. From the look of her, Hussar guessed her for a prime-shift talent picking up an early double: a composition almost entirely in legs, breasts, heels, and a small demure of clothing held in suspense. And when, at last, she'd thrown off these fetters, it was plain to Hussar why the man had admired her for company.

Her routine was lazy and disinterested: but if her sincerity were ever a matter for doubt, her audience seemed unaware; they were breathless with appetite. They fed her dollar bills all the while and brayed like children at a petting zoo. Even the doorman's gaze bore rare temperature. But Hussar put it to a conceit of biology: hope is an eternally suspended disbelief.

The man in the hunting jacket watched restively. Occasionally he lurched to cloy at his nose, or bat at his forelock with an unaccountable suddenness—as though it might be water in his eyes—and then rebounded to stillness. When she'd finished, and left the stage—to what passed there for reflective quiet—the tall man dispatched his drink in four prompt even measures, ratcheted himself up from the chair and onto his legs, swept by the bar for the tab, and made his path to the door. Now he was gone. But it wasn't until he'd been gone some time that the woman appeared at Hussar's shoulder.

She'd now an over-small jacket for an addition of clothes, and as she stood before him, Hussar marveled that by a similar abstract of impulse, all enterprises of men are sustained: the merest glimpse of an unlikely flesh is the fuel vapor of unrequited aspiration, he thought.

"Look at you all alone," she shouted into the space between them. It was a space she quickly narrowed.

"It's not my fault," he said.

"No?" she said, her warm breath now in his ear.

"I was born this way."

"Alone?"

"Very much. So I can hardly be blamed for looking the part," he said, but her eyes wouldn't tell whether she'd heard.

"You're clever. Where're your friends?

"I didn't invite them. I was afraid I might find something I liked," he said, and smiled broadly to the notion of playing a game which can't be lost.

"And then what?" she said and sidled onto his knee.

"And then I'd hate to share," he said.

"You're quite charming."

"I know," he said, and thought of the Paulaner on his breath, and then suddenly wished he'd had much more to drink.

"And how do those charms play on the ladies?" she asked.

"Really, it's my modesty that most impresses—"

"Most impresses . . . ?" she repeated.

"Impresses most," he said and flicked his wrist dismissively. "You're missing my best material for the noise."

"How-bout a dance, clever boy?—I give the best dances."

"Is there a ratings agency for such things?"

"Yes. And they rated me best, the very, very, best," she said, and squirmed uncomfortably on his lap.

"Was that Fitch, Moody's, or Standard and Poor's? Though, considering your features, I'm sure it was a unanimous decision."

"It was. I'm Triple A rated."

"A college girl!" he said, and suddenly had the image to mind of turning through a textbook and finding pornography. "What would I do with my hands—they generally like to be involved."

"You'd do what clever boys do, and just keep them to yourself."

"That seems an odd protocol. I crave intimacy . . . you see."

"Just what the private rooms are for—come along and I'll show you," she said, straightening as if they were poised to leave.

"What happens in there?" he asked, causing her to bring her ear close again.

"I dance . . . for you . . . in private."

"What's more private?"

"It's not on the menu."

"It sounds more work than play," he said.

"It's no work for you—I'll take care of everything."

"I have a poor imagination: feeble," he said. "Who's friendly here? Are you friendly?"

"We're all friendly, clever boy," she said, and touched his neck.

"Everyone's friendly: some are more friendly than others. I think all this business has given me an appetite," he said, with a short glance about the room. "Who offers take home?"

She looked at him carefully now and then broke off to survey the room herself, and, Hussar thought, to buy herself a moment for consideration. "Everyone's got their rhythm. What'd you have in mind?"

"Some carry out."

"To-go orders," she said, and drew his jaw toward the deep of her smile, "can be rare . . . and costly. And strictly speaking, they're not served from this kitchen."

Hussar laughed. "So much the better: keeps out the riffraff."

"You don't mind?" she asked; and Hussar thought then that despite her practiced manner, she proposed to tread rarely covered ground.

"The righteous dine alone," he said, closely into her ear, "and I happen to be a man of reasonable means."

She folded her arms round his neck, her chest to his chin.

"Comfortable means . . . ?" she said.

"Oh yes."

6.

They sat in the orange glow of instruments and cockpit switchgear. She touched the leather on the dashboard with admiration—"It's like a jet," she said. A heavy mist blew about the stands of lights which sprung from the long and vacant slope of the parking lot, and cast fine shadows from where it collected on the windshield. Her car set a few spaces away: a burgundy Dodge, miniature, round, and dirty as a schoolyard toy; fine threads of exhaust turned in the cool damp air from its expiring warmth.

"Wherever you like," she said, "the car's fine. But maybe not under the lights." She looked at him and something like a coy smile came over her features.

"It's hard on the stitching," he said, but where she waited for a change in his expression, it never came. He knocked the shifter side to side with his palm. "I had a room in mind," he said, and she noticed the way even the gear pattern shown orange from the crown of the shifter.

"What did you call it," she asked, "when you gave me the money?"

"An honorarium," he said, and set the car to motion circling round and swinging toward an exit. She was quiet until he had put the car out briskly before approaching traffic.

"It's strong," she said.

"It is strong."

"It's awfully trusting, don't you think—paying in advance? How could you be sure that I would come?"

He offered her a quick and furrowed glance: "It was the only way I could be sure that you would," he said.

She was quiet again, and watched him move swiftly and smoothly through what traffic there was. "You like to drive," she said.

"It's my religion," he said, and she laughed.

"I bet this has a nice stereo," she said, and retrieved a lip balm from the bag between her knees. "You have any music?" she asked, and drew the figure of her lips with it, practiced them against one another, then again; replaced the wand, and turned toward him.

"Of course," he said, and reached for the knobs on the dash. "What do you like?"

"Where are you from?" she asked suddenly. "I didn't notice it before—you have an accent. You have an accent, don't you?" She appeared excited at the prospect.

"Diction," he said. "Any language sounds exotic when you use all the letters."

She laughed again. "No. Come on!"

"What do you like?" he repeated.

"I don't know . . . all kinds of stuff : . . . rock . . ."

"Like that trash at the club?"

"That's not rock," she said.

"I'm aware."

". . . jazz," she said.

He looked at her now, and then again. "What's your name?"

"I told you before," she said. "I see somebody wasn't paying attention."

"You didn't."

"I did," she insisted.

"I promise. If you don't tell me, I won't have anything to call you."

"I told you."

"It never happened."

"Lilith," she said. Now her gaze was exasperated and settled keenly upon him.

"It's a pleasure," he said.

"And yours?"

"Your stage name?" he asked into a prolonged silence. He looked at her again, changed lanes, and turned off down a side street, coming to rest along the curb.

"Jazz?" he asked.

"Yeah," she said, and her features shown pale in the dash light.

"Is that a put-on?" When he looked at her now, his look was long, and his features fixed and immutable. "You're serious?"

"You want to test me?"

"No," he said. He looked through the windshield at the pool of concrete beneath the headlamps, and then returned to her. But, she thought, with a searching, distant gaze.

"Marek," he said.

"I suppose that's your stage n—"

"I have a different idea," he interrupted.

"What is it?"

"A surprise."

7.

The woman sat on the sofa at the heel of the long area rug and watched Hussar cross-legged on the floor, and before the enormous stereo. He sipped Champagne from a wide flute, and from a box of spares, carefully arranged the stemware beneath thick runs of cable which joined the amplifiers and speakers. The cables were sufficiently rigid that they ran flat and level along these supports, and crouching concentratedly as he was, installing these ad hoc piers, he looked to her like a boy fashioning a model trestle from the materials to hand.

"What is it for?" she asked as he shuffled across the floor and fitted glasses beneath the cable on the opposite side.

"It reduces the noise floor. The background haze," he offered over his shoulder, suspending the substantial cable along the lip of a final glass. "The effect is more pronounced with carpet, but it's discernable just the same." When he was satisfied with the arrangement he rose, considered his work, collected the unused glasses, and took them to the kitchen.

"Is it warming up?" she asked.

"Yes," he called out from the kitchen, "it's a bit brittle on startup."

The gear looked a complex business of cables and components, and yet from the sofa, at least, shown only a few small, humorless lights, and no obvious controls.

"So how do you know the tall gentleman?" he asked from the kitchen.

"Who?"

"The Eddie Bauer lumberjack," he said, and appeared presently with the Champagne. He replenished her glass, and with her free hand, she collected the drape of her hair, dressed it altogether over one shoulder, and with an uncomprehending lift of her brow, dismissed the question with a gentle shake of her head.

"It's very spare. Is this really all your furniture?" she asked, proposing the question to a floor lamp of cantilever joints which set beside the sofa.

"I also have a bed. I'd be happy to show to you."

"Probably that's all the place will hold."

"It's all I require."

"Your wife won't be barging in on us?" She glanced at his hand with the question. "Or do you just use the ring to bait the ladies?"

Hussar stood center of the rug, arms folded, and sipped from his glass.

"Seriously—beautiful as it is, in its own stark way, is there a woman who would live like this . . . could, could live like this?"

He said nothing.

"Beads and colored pots; plants with dangly leaves; glasses with unnecessary writing . . . scarves over the doorknobs: women are messy."

Hussar moved to top up the glasses from the bottle, and placed it beside her at the leg of the sofa.

". . . something to fill in the empty spaces," she continued.

"A man requires the space for his noise."

"... accent chairs and do-dads: not just black leather and chrome—"

"Polished aluminum—"

"And . . . wood—" she said, rapping her knuckle on the frame beneath her thigh.

"Walnut."

"Whatever . . . Does your wife live with you? I don't think there's a woman living here," she said.

"Is that your professional opinion?"

"Yes."

"I don't recall saying there was."

"The ring."

"Could it be you're straying from your mandate?"

"Then where is she?"

He said nothing.

"Where's the woman . . . !" she said pointing emphatically; and feeling suddenly inundated by the spuming tide of Champagne, she stopped, and she laughed. " . . . who belongs to that ring?"

"May it please you—she is far from here," he said, and lowered himself again, resuming a position, cross-legged center of the floor.

"You have any coke?" she asked with a rhetorical attention, and set distractedly into her purse.

"You've caught me at a bad time," he said.

"Never mind, I have some."

Hussar laughed. "Good for your grades?" he asked.

"Study aide," she said, and fished a small, intricately arranged piece of folded white paper from her bag.

"Is that origami?" he asked

She held it toward the light and shrugged. "You have a bill?"

"I seem to recall you have several."

"I 'spose I do," she said and smiled. "Hate to get them dirty."

Hussar rose and returned to the stereo.

"Some other part of the country then?" she asked, recovering her earlier thought and rolling a small bill tightly against her thigh: an alabaster plane borne beneath the brief chase of hem.

"What's that?"

"She's in some other part of the country?"

"Further," he said.

"Further? The woman who belongs to that ring?"

"The woman who belongs to the ring."

"What's further?"

He said nothing.

"Ah! That's right," she exclaimed. "We still haven't cleared up the matter about where you're from!"

"Originated? Or do you mean the location of a previous instance?" he asked. His wry smile looked to her like a gleeful suppression: an expressive indulgence clasped by its ends.

"What?"

"Do you know Eckernförde?"

"No."

"That's fine."

"Do you mind if I set this up in the kitchen?" she asked.

"By all means," he said.

"Do you have an edge?" she asked, as she walked carefully into the kitchen with the loosened paper and the tightly spun bill.

"Do you know Jarrett?" he called after her, but to no reply. He cued "Desert Sun," and followed her into the kitchen with the Champagne and the first chords from the stereo.

She unfolded the elaborate paper on the counter, and with the blade of a credit card, parted out two lines amid the creases and terrain of the flattened sheet.

"How did you say you know the tall fellow?" he said, and rest the Champagne and glasses on the counter.

She gestured toward him with the straw. "You sure?"

"Thanks, I'm full."

She took up the first line and pinched off the nostril with a snort. "I didn't say that I did," she said. "Although—he was good for this." She motioned again with the straw and set it beside the paper.

"A gift?"

"A tip," she said. "But it's very unsexy, talking about other jobs."

"I thought you said you didn't know him."

"No, I said that I didn't say that. But I don't. You're not going to ruin my buzz with this stuff, are you?"

"I merely thought he looked familiar. How is it?"

"Seems clean. I'll know in a minute, right?" She laughed. "I dunno, I've seen him maybe, like twice—danced for him twice. If he's been around more than that, I don't know about it. What, he owe you money or product or something?"

"He looked familiar."

"Whatever," she said, and retrieved her glass. "There's nobody familiar as somebody who owes you." She mouthed the Champagne and considered the stemware.

"First law of accounting? Your field of study?" he asked, and folded himself into a bend of the countertop.

"Everyone's an accountant—it's just some people are good with numbers. So where's Eckenford then? Eckford?"

"Not where I'm from."

"You're a coy boy," she said, and with great care drew another line from the low white drift set upon the paper. In a moment of unguided emptiness, Hussar's thoughts settled upon the spot, upon the miniature pile, surrounded by its vast and empty moat where he envisioned the tiny mound instead, as a great plateau rising above a boundless angular plane; and were a microbial Moses in this moment to rush up the crags of this narcotic Sinai—he wondered as she erased the line with a greedy sniff and a coordinated nod of the straw—what might he receive?

She canted her head back and cleared her nostrils with an alternating pinch and a strong, dry sniff. Her eyes closed. She blinked heavily and then looked at him as though in reappraisal. "Is it bright in here? It feels bright in here. Didn't you say you were going to show me your bed?"

8.

The room was the sound of fine sheets and stubble and the rough tread of his palm along the spline of her neck, the angle of her jaw, and every other feature where the touch was pleasing. He was patient and tender, and she was high, and cultivating an urgent delirium; and that he contradicted her practical assumptions was, by far, his greatest pleasure. Her back spasmed. And when it seized again he returned slowly to his side, and trailed his hand across her. Another followed, and then a tremor which ebbed in the wrinkle of her toes, and a slow flutter of her eyelids.

It was a deep half-light to which their eyes had accustomed, and hers bathed in it and cast up at the ceiling as though its plaster works were cloud. "That's cheating," she said, and the bulb of sound flashed starkly for its contrast against the silence. "That's not fair," she said, and moved to face him. Hussar lay with an arm outstretched, and rubbed his knuckles against the cleave of his chin with the other. On his shoulder was a dark spot, which her eyes now strained to make out—a smudge of ink, a pattern, a shark or marlin or barracuda.

"What is that?" she asked. She brought her fingers to touch the mark where it shifted against the fibers of his shoulder.

"A momentary indiscretion."

"What is it really?" she asked, tracing the features of the black, skate-like shape. He looked at her again, searched her, she thought, much as he had in the car—a look which seemed to see her, but to land beneath her surface.

"A sawfish," he said.

"What does it mean?"

"It's return postage," he said.

She looked uncertain.

"It means, when they find your carcass floating in the Baltic, they'll know who to call."

She lifted her fingers and leaned in to look for this meaning, then withdrew her hand.

"That's what it means?"

"It says . . . 'suffer without complaint," he said and smiled. It uncurled broadly between them but shone with none of the charm of the club or the boyish mischief of downstairs, and she held an urge to press her eyes closed until it had passed. "In all toil, the Bible tells us, there is profit," he said, "but in mere talk, only poverty. Let us be silent and profitable."

For a time they were.

But when his phone chimed a text, he withdrew and snatched it from the bedside where he stood deliberating in the buzzing darkness, damp, and nude, and pale; and then with a quick gesture, stole into the brief gray light of the hall, leaving her the muted knock of the latch, the door's tidal breath, cool and unseen and trembling the hairs against her brow.

Hussar moved to the laundry: padded along the hall to the stair and down, his soles across the turned lips; across the acrid chill of the foyer tile; through the glass-knobbed door, and down again. Unfinished concrete was livid beneath his feet. He thread his limbs into shirt and pants three days cold from the dryer. In the kitchen he fastened his clothes, and he examined the text, and considered the address it contained: it contained only an address. And with this done, he dropped the phone in his pocket, poured the remnant of Champagne into glasses, and tread again softly, up the stair and down the hall.

When he opened the door, she jerked with a start where she sat upon the bed in the light of the small lamp, and in the half-dress of his shirt. The closet on the far wall rest ajar where a mislaid strap from Hussar's canvas duffle resisted the door, and as he set in the doorframe with the Champagne ticking lightly in the flutes, they both paused to observe the lighted screen of her phone, nuzzled beside her thigh—which presently extinguished.

"That's a waste," said Hussar as he offered her a glass.

"What's a waste?" she asked, her beauty a lamentable and misspent inheritance.

"Warm champagne," he said as he entered the room and drew the door behind him.

III.

"**U**se this," said August. He removed the thread protector and handed the pistol to Edmund LeFrance. "You familiar?"

"I hold this end, right?" asked LeFrance when he received it.

"No."

"What is it?" LeFrance asked, peering more closely in the dim of the cab.

"Sig, Mosquito, TB. This is the clip release, this is the slide release," said August and showed LeFrance. "Your dance partner for the evening. Rack it."

"I'm a big boy, August—you wanna shake it for me?"

"Rack it. Show me," said August.

LeFrance showed him.

"The brass is clean, but don't leave any," August said, and passed the clip to LeFrance. "You've got ten, but I want nine back. You'll want this," he said, and turned over the suppressor. "Test the fit."

LeFrance tested the fit, and watched August watching.

It was quarter to six on Christmas Eve, and August and Edmund LeFrance sat in the dissipating warmth, parked at a meter on Bonhomme, in a Cummins dually LeFrance called 'the white whale,' and without the least affection. LeFrance slipped his instruments into the deep pockets of his topcoat and drummed at the wheel. August worked a pinch of chew in his lip and kept a tired paper cup between his knees for spittle. The discharge was a small watery burp, and the sound of it against the ratted slope of the cup left LeFrance thinking each time of the dyspeptic purge of flu and that final brown-sour glottal of sputum before one leaves the bowl. His mouth watered and he ground his tongue on his teeth from time to time to clear it.

Beyond the breath-dewed windows flurries leapt into the air between a heavy sky and glistening pavements they never appeared to meet. 7912 Bonhomme lay along the opposite curb. Two bare wisps of tree rose from concealed planters, two cast iron street lamps shown against the pale façade, and the self-conscious script ran three sizes in Deco stainless about the door: The Guild Building.

"Swap me," said August, who showed the expectant angles of his hand for meaning.

LeFrance soothed fingers along his bare Hippocratic verge of scalp and smiled at August. He drew a small chapbook from his coat and set himself to read.

"No, I mean it. Swap me out—trade me," he repeated.

"Why would I do that, August?"

"You can't use what you don't have," said August.

"I'm familiar," said LeFrance.

"You set that thing off in there—its gonna leave a hole a block long—and fuck this whole thing in the ear. Gimme," said August.

"You play cards, August? .22 for a .44 is a split—I should get two hands," said LeFrance, as he drew the Redhawk from his coat and August slipped it beneath the zip of his flight jacket.

They'd been parked for a quarter hour. Kyle Lewis sat in a car near the end of the block at the stop. Phillip waited in the back; in the narrow lot he thumbed the ignition key and watched the exit for LeFrance. Kyle Lewis had covered the building for several hours in turns by foot and car, and now he rang through on August's phone to report. LeFrance gazed across the street through the receding light, the yellow glare of the street lamps—their shifting halo of snow dancing like a static charge—and he listened to the attenuated notes of the voice of Kyle Lewis crackling into the porches of August's ear.

LeFrance thought then of the small AM radios of his youth—his father brought one with them to ballgames, into the high bleachers so as to hear what could only be seen—two thumb wheels, a collapsing aerial, a dial face, and a silver box the size of a Gideon's. He surveyed the wall of alternately dark and half-lit windows—those few lazily trimmed in holiday lights: sad little portals pledging unrequited hope by the foot-candle—and into the growing stillness, which LeFrance had a notion was physical as a compelling breeze or high gravity, a sociobarometric pressure rising with the failing day, pressing people toward one another, toward brighter and more splendid lights, or leaving reluctant stragglers breathless beneath its unabated force.

"Phillip tells Kyle the janitor's arrived and started work on one. Our man's in his office on four, but we're waiting out another loafer on the floor. Kyle says there's another still—corner of the first floor," said August, reaching across LeFrance to indicate an illuminated window, "but otherwise we're lookin' good. Just awhile more," he said. August had just the taper of an accent, an occasional eliding slur that scored the flanges from consonant junctures and played contiguous words through a single extrusion: LeFrance thought it had a taste of Appalachian backwood to it—something the endive slaver of tobacco chew. LeFrance returned to the chapbook held out against the wheel to read in the streetlight, but it was only a moment before August's phone interrupted him again.

"Phillip says our loafer on four just split. That leaves the janitor and the orphan on one—that should be clear enough," said August.

LeFrance slipped the book in his coat and leaned for the door handle.

August grasped him by the elbow: "Remember, behind the ear. Inside the hairline is best."

IV.

"It is just like riding the bus," had come the voice, soft and with the vague character of the vodka of which it smelled: a vinegary and granular solvent. "This is what I tell my daughter. She does not like the bumps. 'It is just the same as uneven ground,' this is what I tell her."

The voice emerged from someplace very near to Foster's ear, poured out of the gestational dim of the cabin, and from somewhere within the fibrous coherence of engine noise: the perpetual bass rumbling of thrust and drag friction and rotating mass; the whining soprano over-score of inducting turbofans, and the whistle of cabin overpressure venting with feathery reluctance into the shoulder of each window frame and through the fine breach of every hidden seam. It was the noise of common experience made bright-sharp and bowel-jostling by the ebbing chemistries of hangover.

It was a year and a month ago—last January, Beijing to Tel Aviv in coach—and he was thinking of the recent holiday: Christmas at his parents, and the nausea which marked him for the whole of the occasion; the pinion of pine logs and damp smoke, and the astringent of his wife's perfume, alive in his nostrils at the thought—like an exhaust: corrupted to its mere aroma. She'd been committed to the pageant of normalcy. A fraud accomplished for the benefit of his parents, he assumed, he hoped. And there was New Year's in D.C, too.

A gesture he'd taken to as a chaser: buttressed by old friends; a cast joined at oxidized but habituated terminations; doubling down at the stations of their first missteps, and fastened to the city and trajectory of the occasion. Nevertheless, Foster had been keened up at the prospect—and diversion—of indulging old and infamous glories.

This memory was scentless, but its remembering seemed somewhere to prize a coagulated knot loose of its fitting. And it was through this renewed wound the milky-thin, dribbling, and bilious residue—not of Christmas or his wife—but of the two prior nights in Beijing, came.

"I have to say that I do not like them very much either, but what it is to be old is adepted to dubious paths and sour provisions," came the voice once more.

Foster sat with his knees splayed either side of the seatback, one leg intruding the aisle, the other balancing a folded magazine; the voice had summoned him from a place beneath the opalescent black interior of his eyelids. His head ached, the seat poorly suited his frame, and he blinked over his right shoulder toward the voice with lethargy and discomfort. The man seated beside him craned forward, peering through the window and out upon nothing but six thousand fathoms of night. Foster observed his head was almost perfectly round; his hair was a bright gray and fleeting brown, freshly trimmed to one brief length, and standing everywhere and emphatically on end. His eyes were deep-set, cold metal-blue, bearing a watery and heavy-lidded melancholy and framed with small steel spectacles perched above the knuckle of his nose. He wore a rumpled blue suit with epaulettes of sparse dandruff, and shone an untouched cream-white pallor presently flushed with drink.

A husky, thought Foster. "And turbulence," he said.

"And bumpy and dubious paths," said the man who turned from the window toward Foster.

"Not that old I think," Foster said, adjusted the magazine on his knee and rubbed at his eyes with his palms.

"A Russian is born sad and middle-aged...and requires no calendar's contradiction."

Foster laughed.

"Do you fly often?" he asked.

"Commercially? Regularly," said Foster.

"But occasionally by carpet or fighter plane?" the man said with a red-lipped smile. "Is there another type? What is the other type?" Foster began to respond, but the man continued: "Private of course; yes, I have cousin—an oligarch—he has a private plane: a jet, like this—quite extravagant."

"Then why fly coach?" asked Foster.

"He has a vast mining and transport concern—coal principally. But when he refused a buyout from the president's friends, they jailed him for whatever came to mind. His assets were sold by the state at favorable prices. Very favorable," he repeated, nodding. "And now the minister of finance rides his plane about the oblasts—the provinces—and drinks from his Baccarat," he said, gesturing with his plastic cup.

"Were you close?" asked Foster.

"No. I don't know him. So you fly privately?"

"I'm certified."

"You're a pilot? Could you fly this . . ." he said, tapping on his tray table with the square point of his finger, "a plane like this?"

"A 767-300? No. I'm instrument rated, but not type rated for turbojet or large aircraft. They're not like cars. There's a little more to it than a steering wheel and pedals," said Foster.

"Ah, but you could?"

"I don't have a CPL," said Foster.

"If you had to."

"They wouldn't let me."

"Never mind," the man said with a loose jerk of his hand. "This is a good plane?"

"Anything that'll fly above the weather is a good plane. If you mean the airframe—as long as the engines don't fall off—yeah, it's fine."

The man swirled the contents of his plastic cup, and looked at Foster.

"Really, that was just with the Rolls-Royce RB211. When they hung them, they cracked the engine pylon. I think they've fixed that."

"The engine?"

"The pylon—they're two-thousand pounds heavier than the alternatives. Good performance though."

"It's fixed?"

"Yeah, I think so. But, it could also be the G.E. CF6," Foster said. He rubbed his eyes again and leaned his head back against the rest. "But that's not as good."

"No?"

"No. It's not as . . . robust. There've been some incidents."

"Incidents?"

"Failures. Well, if it comes apart at ten thousand r.p.m . . . four-hundred-seventy knots . . . thirty-five-thousand feet . . . ?"

"... what?"

Foster glanced at him, and thought he'd lost some of the blush from his cheek. "It's a party," he replied. "But it's probably the PW 4000. That's better."

"The PW 4000 is better?"

"Pratt and Whitney. But being it's El Al, statistically at least, the odds of a hijacking are higher than vehicle failure," Foster said.

"You are a wealth of information," said the Russian.

Foster had lain his head back against the rest when the stewardess came—ensconced comfortably as a melon on a plate—and had closed his eyes to the stutter-strobe of blinking light, common for him along the attenuated, descending arc of a healthy stimulant buzz. It was a sensation mirrored in the static shimmer in his chest and elbows and wrists, and in the clenched muscles of his jaw. He put it to the sparking of circuits pining for the surge—impatient for the certitude of maximum capacity.

The stewardess was a crafted blond with a gold chain at her wrist, and a dress with lapels, fitted navy-black with pinstripes and scarf, and was leaning across Foster to hear the Russian when he'd opened his eyes. She looked a chastened late-forties to Foster, and to have been an exquisite beauty at one time. But sleeplessness, he thought, and cigarettes, and the evasiveness of money, had worked their corrosive hand—weathered her once pristine features with a patina of concern.

"Nothing can be done about the Smirnoff? It is hateful—have you nothing better, lubov moya?" said the Russian. "You keep nothing special in your purse for such occasions—nothing you might care to share?"

"Yes, but I'm only allowed to share it with the pilot," she said. Her eyes sparkled but she did not smile.

"Well, perhaps you might make it better by making it more," he said. "And a cranberry juice perhaps."

"Cran-apple?"

"My darling, again we are moving in entirely the wrong direction," he said. "Tell the captain I'm aggrieved—deeply—sincerely—aggrieved."

"I will tell him," she said, "the very instant we set down. And you my dear?" she asked Foster.

"Orange juice, I think."

"She's a princess!" said the Russian when she'd gone. "Wouldn't you say?" "I'm Pavel Kashkin of seat A, row twenty-five," he said, offered his handshake to Foster—which was received—and returned to the dregs of his upturned cup, which he tapped for good measure.

"Howard Foster . . . of the seat beside you."

"Mr. Howard Foster. What a substantial name you have—it could be pressed from an ingot."

"Charles is fine."

"Now tell me what you fly, Mr. Foster, and feel free to spare the details."

Foster paused to look at him, to take in this abundance of retiring and bespirited energy which was called Pavel Kashkin. "I have a Beechcraft. A King Air 200; it was a gi . . . It's in D.C. Hangared at an FBO in D.C."

"Is it good? Does it fly above the weather?"

"Most of it."

"Is that where you're going from Tel Aviv?"

"No, I have a layover at J.F.K., and then on to Lambert in Saint Louis."

"What's for you in Saint Louis?"

"Home," said Foster, and wondered if there was such a thing.

"And what gainful thing do you do in Saint Louis?"

"Assistant Professor of Computer Science . . . at Washington University," added Foster, intending to preempt the question.

The stewardess returned with the trolley, asked about snacks—for which Kashkin took two foils of peanuts: Foster abstained—and poured his orange juice from a plastic bottle into a low cup, and prepared the drink for the Russian. "I found one that's extra-full," she said, breaking the cap from the small, clear vial of Smirnoff, "so you won't feel neglected."

"Lubov moya," said the Russian as he received the can of juice cocktail and exchanged cups with her—one entirely empty for one slightly full. "I will be sure to think of you in my old age, when I compose my will."

"Don't you mean just after?" she asked.

"I do," he said quickly. "Be sure I have the correct spelling of your name for the occasion."

When she'd gone the Russian added enough cocktail to his drink to impart color, and tasting it, made a sudden gesture with his hand as though he'd been struck with an idea.

"Is it better?" asked Foster.

"Entirely worse," said the Russian, who now drew a worn brown wallet from his jacket from which he carefully extracted a business card. Pinched unnaturally between his thick fingers Foster reflected that they seemed better suited to grappling ax handles and ploughshares.

"It's not precious but it's nearly my last," said the Russian when he offered it.

It was of a medium stock with a turning corner, and in embossed print read: Tower and Gradzik Attorneys at Law; Pavel Kashkin, Esq.; 7912 Bonhomme Ave. Suite 400, Clayton, MO 63105; Washington D.C., Maryland, Illinois, Missouri.

"They talk of practices in California and New York one day," said the Russian, as Foster considered the card.

"Tower or Gradzik?" asked Foster.

"Gradzik is my uncle's son—he has ambitions."

"You mean, your cousin."

"Yes, he is my cousin, too," said the Russian. "Were it not for relatives all Russians would live like Dostoyevsky."

"He didn't live well?"

"I don't know," said the Russian, "but I don't think so."

"You're a large firm," said Foster, turning the card in his fingers, and offering it back to Kashkin.

"No, you keep it," protested the Russian, with a flash of his thick palm. "We are not so much big as wide," he said. "It's really just the two offices in four markets—licenses in four markets. I'm actually licensed in six. I moved a bit in earlier times."

"What's your field of practice?"

"The firm is mostly real estate and business—I'm family law, which is why my peers sometimes refer to me as the 'harbinger.'"

"And why's that?"

"Bad tidings. In all other practices, an attorney works at least occasionally as a surgeon. The family lawyer works almost exclusively as a mortician."

"The odds of that," said Foster.

". . . but with a good bedside manner," continued the Russian with a broad grin.

Foster turned the card over once more, before slipping it into a pocket.

"If I'd merely said it, you couldn't believe it. Some days it seems the world could be folded in the hand," said the Russian.

A silent lapse arose between them, during which Kashkin tried again to mend his drink with the addition of juice, and Foster again attempted succumbing to the weight with which all his tissues seemed saturated.

"Now it is merely sweet and bad," groaned the Russian. "Were you headed out of Beijing?" he asked through the strand of a tight-lipped grimace.

"Technology conference. For developers," said Foster. "You?"

"Connecting flight from Vladivostok."

Foster withdrew the back-folded magazine from his knee, closed the cover right-way over, set it beside his drink on the tray, and with his hot, dry eyes, settled on the brim of his cup.

"Are you a reader?" asked the Russian, glancing at Foster's rumpled *Economist*. "I think I don't read enough. But I encourage my daughter—happily, I think she is a reader."

"That's the home of the Russian Pacific Fleet," interrupted Foster.

"It is," responded the Russian without pause. "My father labored the whole of his years in the shipyards. Now he's a withered oak:

more tired than retired—his back, his knees—all his life his body was his currency. He gets about his apartment, but he cannot keep it up. My brother lives in Moscow, but he is an automobile mechanic: he does not visit."

"Is he alone?" asked Foster.

"The cat, his tea kettle, and the color television I bought him a few years ago—yes. He is alone. What of you? Children?" asked the Russian.

Vladivostok had baited Foster's imagination, and he considered the Russian's soft and pallid features once more before resolving any suspicions as highly improbable.

"Any children?" repeated the Russian. "Do you have any children?"

"Hmm?" responded Foster, adrift in his thoughts, and pivoting slowly toward the question and its answer. "Oh, yes. Yes. Sorry," he said.

"Little beggars," said the Russian. "And which species have you?"

"A daughter," said Foster.

"Does she fly?"

Foster had settled himself once more onto the magazine cover, the typeface, the plastic cup with the snare on the lip, the flecks of pulp dappling the surface of the juice, the smooth gray mold of the tray. "Only to the nanny," he said, ". . . from her mother's arms," and the sepia bitterness of its saying lay on his tongue, thick and acrid as spoiled food.

2.

The water had been running some time and its slapping had grown sharp in his ears. On the breakfast table before him, lemon pips lolled in a cold-filmy water, in a tall, thin glass. Across the kitchen his father stood at the sink, his back to Foster, peeling lettuce leaves from the head and washing them individually with an extravagant and deliberating care. He wore crisp trousers and a sweater vest and his shirtsleeves rolled. And when he moved the leaves from the colander to the bowl Foster could see that his hands were wet to the leather of his watchstrap. At the end of the hall, in the living room, were Foster's wife, his mother, brother, sister, sister's husband, maternal uncle, and maternal grandfather, all seated near the fire which snapped in fits above the music; and the elaborately trimmed tree was staged with glittering lights and presents in potentia: ribboned and ornately-bound boxes entirely empty but for the spirit of Christmas. The voices of his uncle and grandfather had fallen silent and Foster imagined the company staring cautiously into their drinks until one of them would begin again.

The housemaid had spirited baby Pauline away to some distant corner of the house in order that Catherine, Foster's wife, could bask unfettered in the familial glow; the kitchen was warm with the running ovens, and the cook had gone to busy herself in the butler's pantry when the pair had encamped there. There had been nothing between them but the water slapping half-measure into the sink when Foster had tired of the sound. "Why are you doing that? You don't need to do that," he said.

His father grasped a Manhattan from the counter with his dripping hand. He took a drink, replaced the glass, and with a lazy flick of his finger, spun the holiday charm round the stem. "I've heard the Nutcracker before," he said. "Your mother wanted me to wear a tie," he offered a moment later.

"And why didn't you?" asked Foster.

His father glanced over his shoulder in response, spun the charm once more on the glass, and returned to his careful work.

The sink continued to run until Foster's brother-in-law entered, and his father had diminished the greens to a shapeless core. Foster's father had made himself respectable by way of a real estate firm—mostly commercial; Foster's grandfather was the hereditary gesture of a two-hundred year old French textile dynasty made fat on cheap labor—now mostly Asian; and his brother-in-law was named after an Irish poet, who's name he could never remember; and for all Foster knew he might have been one too. But today his hair was trimmed, wet, and neatly combed; his sparse and wiry beard was cut smooth; and he was dressed almost within pantomime of Foster's uncle: a fussy light brown hound's tooth, tan slacks—possibly they were his uncle's—and looking every bit as dated and costly. He looked a boy playing dress up in old man's clothes: only he wasn't a boy; and perhaps he was missing an ascot, thought Foster. Clearly he'd got the talking to.

"And where do you think you're going?" his father asked the beige apparition, as he drifted quietly into the kitchen clutching at his drink as though he'd stolen it from the other room. "Why aren't you in there manning your station?" he asked, shutting off the water finally, betrayed in the end by the finite measure of an initially infinite promise, "like a good lad."

They watched him for an answer, but what came was an evasive shrug, and only after an improbable interval. The answer of course, was that he'd fled the dangerous silence when it had come; escaped in the shade of the first passing diversion. And as if to underscore the hazard, Catherine's laugh came to them just then from the other room, sharp and sudden and eager, and the three of them turned briefly to face it.

"You flew in?—well of course you flew," said his brother-in-law, clearing his throat in hopes of landing the desired tone. "I mean your plane."

"It's parked," said Foster.

"Where do you keep it?"

"It's here . . . in D.C. The engines are houred up. They need to be taken down. I haven't had it done."

He lifted his glass again furtively, but his expression peered blankly into the tail of Foster's sentence. Foster looked at it too.

"It's hours not miles," said Foster. "With planes—aircraft—wear is measured in time, not distance."

Foster thought his brother-in-law had come to the kitchen perhaps to worry a keyhole in his discomfort. He wondered if he'd have been able to drink at all without it.

Manhattan was house drink of the season. There were other drinks for other occasions, but the Manhattan belonged to Christmas, and lay over it like a velvet tree skirt. The glasses were served and collected from everyone in turns—with their spent maraschino stems and lather of graduated rings—everyone but the cook and the house-maid, and Foster, who despite what was a strong urge for one, pre-ferred to cultivate the air of a non-drinker among family, and other occasions of high-pretence: the non-drinker brims after all with righteous opinion, trusted virtue, and his views and behavior pass without a reflexive imputation. His father, however, held no interest in stemware, patience for mixing, or the dishwater-sweet result, and would prefer the untrammeled bourbon they were mixed on; but was growing frisky on them just the same.

The brother-in-law replied to Foster's explanation with a lift of his chin. But he looked no more convinced than before.

"That's an expensive paperweight," said his father.

"With storage fees—yes, it certainly makes for one," said Foster.

"Well, we all have our hobbies—though not exactly the game of kings, is it?" said his father. "You golf, Cobb?" his father asked the in-law, whom he had always called by his last name, Foster suspected because he couldn't retain his first name either.

"He's been golfing with the Grandfuncle," Foster answered for him, referring to his uncle and grandfather, who kept in each other's con-stant company, and of which Cobb today looked every bit the emer-gent connubial bud.

"Twice," added the in-law.

"Sport of kings," repeated his father.

"Overrated," said Foster mostly into his water glass.

"Fucking hangar fees are overrated," said his father in a sud-den flare. "C'mon, you play all the time with your free-wheeling Orientals."

"More before, than now," said Foster watching the in-law for traces of an additional discomfort which never appeared.

"That's right, you're in Saint Louis now—how do you like it?" asked his brother-in-law.

"It's very proud of itself, but for what, I can't tell. Otherwise, it's pretty—like here. And where it's not pretty, it's ugly—like here."

His father shooed the question away with an emphatic wave of both hands, as though it had already exhausted him. "Ask him what he did before. Ask him what he did before—don't you want to know what he did before?" he directed Cobb.

"What did you do before?" he asked as instructed.

"I worked for a risk consultancy."

"Do you know what that is? Ask him what that is," he gestured sharply .

"What is that?" asked the in-law, dutiful and aloof, and looking from the one to the other.

Foster had an uncomfortable intuition for this new direction, and felt a sudden preoccupation with his forelock, which he caught himself pawing. "Corporations," he said, "or governments—agencies, all have strategies, or products; they want to expand—put factories in new markets, etc; and all of these activities present risks, vulnerabilities. They might be political or civil, or competitive—technological. But they want to know what they are, and assess them. And, as much as possible, protect against them."

There was a pause in which they drank, the in-law, as though he were nursing a medicine, and his father, as though he were thirsty— and with a look of satisfaction as though he had been. He fixed on the charm which he now spun in consecutive turns. His lips were thin and still, but the muscles of his jaw clenched and writhed.

"Did you enjoy that work?" asked the in-law, tentative, and desperate to expel the same stillness that had squeezed him from the other room.

"No! No! No!" said his father, the words cleaved between by the edge of his rigid hand. "That's not the question at all! The question is: tell me about your clients. Your clients! Who were they? Did you like it . . ." he repeated dismissively.

"Who were your clients?" asked the in-law, his eyes now fixed on Foster's father. Foster looked at him too.

"Corporations. Governments," said Foster.

"Large corporations," said his father.

"Yes. Large corporations," said Foster.

"Government agencies," said his father.

"Government agencies," affirmed Foster.

"Department of Energy," said his father.

"Yes. That was one," said Foster. "Are we going to catalogue them all?"

"You get that, Cobb?" asked his father with a rap of his knuckle against the white marble counter.

"What was your field?" asked the in-law. This time rather than veto, his father also awaited the answer.

"Technology," said Foster. "Some hardware, but mostly software. Software and security."

"Flying out to dine with Orientals three times a month," said his father.

"We had many clients in Taiwan, Singapore, and China," said Foster to the in-law. "In fact, I'll be at a conference in Beijing—"

"Now, ask him what he does now," his father instructed Cobb. The in-law turned to Foster, but was stayed by a shake of Foster's head and his lifted hand.

"Professor," answered Foster, no longer entirely certain to whom.

"What do you teach?" asked the in-law, of his own.

"Assistant Professor of Computer Science. At Washington University," Foster added summarily.

"The Yale of East Jesus," said his father. "And Catherine?"

"What about Catherine?"

"Where is she now?" asked his father.

"On the sofa, probably!"

"Where is she staying now? Howard? Is she in this Middle-West oasis with you?"

"No," said Foster, and looked at Cobb, and wished to God he had the common sense to go away. "No—you know that answer."

"Where is she then?" continued his father.

"She's here," said Foster.

"Did she ever go?"

"Yes, she went."

"For how long? How long did she stay, Howard?"

"She came for two months," said Foster. "Two," he said, and held up two fingers on his hand, and kept them there.

"Did she like it?" asked his father.

Foster laughed. "No. No, I don't think she did."

"Did she like your new position?" asked his father. He spun the charm violently once more. When it eventually stopped, he lifted the glass for a drink which no part of him seemed to enjoy.

"I have no idea," said Foster.

"Do you think she'll come back? To you. In Saint. Louis?"

Foster looked dully at Cobb, and Cobb returned his gaze, but with a voyeur's curious appetite.

Foster moved to speak.

"No!" roared his father. "Because, now you're a fucking school teacher!"

Foster had closed his eyes to the gale of sound, and when they were opened, his mother stood in the doorway to Cobb's shoulder. She wore a smart dress, and boots, a holiday wrap, and a stern countenance.

His father looked to her, and then to Cobb. "You enjoy cigars, Cobb?" he asked.

Cobb looked suddenly ashen, and shook his head imperceptibly.

"Good!" said his father. "I have just the thing. Come along," he said, dumping the half Manhattan in the sink with a thrust, "and we can have a drink."

The two had gone quickly through the servants' exit, but his mother followed them with her eyes as though they might still be seen. And just then, Catherine came striding up the hall behind her—bearing a smile residual to some other joke, some other thought, some other happiness. Whatever it may be, Foster hated the smile; he hated its timing; and it occurred to him with a rare and vivid clarity, that he hated her.

3.

The departure hall at Tel Aviv's Ben-Gurion airport was a vast inverted dome of polished stone pavements, departure boards, bistro tables, and duty-free shops. There were low, chrome and leather chairs and a fretwork of potted plants. There was the trot of baggage casters, and the cry of soft shoe rubber, and a marbling of the tones of human conversation as though it were a smoke on the air. There was a reflecting pool made rough and viscous by a fountain raining silence two-and-a-half stories the look of glass beads, and landing with a weighted punctuation. And there was a skylight through whose great round pupil a severe illumination shot down into the hall and onto the pool, and at this time of day, made it unbearable to see.

Foster had drawn his wheeled carryon with the limp resignation of a child towing a short-handled wagon, shuffling from the arrival gate through the crisp corridors of glass and stone. All airports have a character, however similar they may be—some resemble malls, others high school gymnasiums—this one, Foster thought, had the mood of a conference center; with the consequence that his tired clothes and greasy hair, and deep chemical emptiness, the way his shoes felt moist in the sole and serrated at the instep, cast him as materially apart from the chic and genial tableau. When he'd made his way to the fountain and the low chairs of the departure hall, he'd turned one away from the pool with a loud chromoly bark, and fallen heavily into it. The fierce light bit into the back of his eyes and he attempted to shield them by laying them upon everything but the blazing water.

Foster had drifted into a warm daze of rotating advertisements and crimson departure board text, and was entirely unsure whether it had been ten minutes or twenty, when the man from the Executive Office appeared with two coffees.

"An aperitif for the consciousness," said the man when he'd set them on a small table and taken the chair opposite Foster. "Perhaps you could use one."

Foster took it, carefully prized the lid and blew across the cup with an effort whose sound vanished within the roar of the fountain. Foster noticed that The Familiar, after only a moment, seemed already to have forgotten his. Foster also noticed his shoes, which were spotless and unmarred by casters or baggage. In fact, as Foster performed a quick survey of the hall, The Familiar and two dire and substantial looking men at a nearby bistro table were the only souls unencumbered by some form of luggage or another.

"Were you traveling?" asked Foster, "Or were you already here?"

The man, who'd been staring into the impossible light of the fountain, massaged the bridge of his nose, and turned to Foster: "You are improbably tall for the service. Nobody thought better of it when they signed you?"

"My recruiter thought I'd be a good situational fit—a double-guess at the edge, or worst case, mistaken for a Throwaway. But he also thought I'd probably be an analyst," said Foster.

"I suppose he did," said the man. "You had a family trade: why not that?"

"I don't know," said Foster, "a couple hundred years of textiles is enough, isn't it? Besides, isn't that the whole Skull and Bones angle?"

The man rubbed his hands together and glanced at Foster. "How are we coming?" he asked.

"It's going slowly," said Foster, "but going well."

"Going well. Oh, that's excellent—and where are we then?"

"About the middle; maybe just past," said Foster trying for a calibrated optimism.

"And what does that look like?" asked the man.

"How do you mean?"

"The middle: what does it look like?"

Foster's struggling mind went suddenly blank and damp: a yellowed leaf of paper with all the type shaken free. Foster peered at the man—lost momentarily to anything but the search of his features for the exact tenor of his question. "Like a bunch of unfinished code," he said. "Like a nest of wiring that's been made but unconnected."

"I see," said the man. "I appreciate the visual. Virtual warfare is so ephemeral, it makes for a difficult image. But thankfully, now I've got it: an irredeemable knot of diminishment and misconception."

"That's not what I said."

"I get a strong impression of it," said the man.

Foster set back into his chair as deeply as possible and breathed over the coffee clasped between his hands.

"But it's going well?" asked the man.

"Yes," said Foster, "I think so."

"And you're somewhere in the middle?"

"Yes," said Foster. "I would say so."

"This middle: is of an object, or of a novel?"

Foster looked at the man and drank from his tall paper cup.

"One is marked by coordinates, Foster, the other merely by a mood," said the man.

"The middle of a process," said Foster, after what seemed to him an intolerable interval of the fountain's heavy body falling against itself in long, shifting, unbroken consonants.

"Enjoy Beijing?" asked the man. "Keeping the old fires warm?"

"So far as I know, being moved and being blown are different things," said Foster. "The conference was a fit."

"You feeling defensive, or is that just a sound you make?" asked the man. His suit was a gray pinstripe today, whose jacket was unfastened. He adjusted the lay of his tie; he inspected the glasses on the cord round his neck closely for clouds or prints, and then gazed unflinchingly into the fountain and its cauterizing light before turning again to Foster. "I think it's a paradox," he said.

"What's a paradox?"

"Your chair. Your chair Dr. Foster—is a paradox. Do you know what it is?"

Foster glanced vaguely at the leather arms as he blew again across his coffee. "If the answer's anything but, 'a chair,' I think I've lost this one already," he said.

"You're feeling glib," said the man. "All limbered up on prawns and fortune cookies?"

"No," said Foster, the man's remark striking at his tenuous buoyancy. "Not really—just tired as all hell."

"Do you know what it is?"

Foster began a gesture which upset his cup. When it had settled, he said, "I guess not."

"Corbusier."

Foster shook his head.

"French designer."

Foster took a sip and shook his head again.

"He was an architect; he was a designer. He designed your chair, which by the way, is called Le Petit Confort," said the man. "'Comfort,' is the temptation for the Anglo tongue, but the French is 'confort.'" He added: "They have the same meaning of course," and idly adjusted his cup as though it were a large piece on a small board, but did not drink. "Fear not, Dr. Foster," he said, " you're a well-established philistine, and hardly expected to know these things."

Foster's mind felt heavy and keenly unlubricated, and he realized now that he'd lost any intuition for the path of the conversation.

"Design classics, Dr. Foster. This means nothing to you, of course, but the licensed versions are quite costly."

"Why would they be here then?" asked Foster.

The man from the Executive Office touched his bent finger to the end of his nose. "Precisely! Why *would* they be here, in the middle of a busy airport departure hall in the middle of Israel?"

Foster shook his head again. "I don't know."

"That is the essence of the paradox. Are they authentic, or are they imitations—reproductions? I struggle to make up my mind whenever I see them."

"If they're expensive, why would they be in the middle of an airport? They wouldn't be real—surely," said Foster.

"Any other airport they would be reproductions. It goes without saying." "Dubuque to Paris—they'd be fakes every time. But in Tel Aviv? In Israel? The question is more complex."

Foster drank from his coffee, briefly glanced into the fountain, and regretted it all the while blue spots dissolved from his vision and he blinked bitterly at the man.

"You doubt it—you think Jews are thrifty," said the man.

"Is that a rumor?" asked Foster.

The man from the executive office laughed a sharp, granular laugh. "Famously! They are famously thrifty! Although, if it were widely known what they spend on intelligence per capita, I promise you, that view would be properly dispelled."

"I'm feeling lost," said Foster.

"Have you ever met an illiterate Jew?"

Foster shook his head with uncertainty.

"And you never will. A Jew who cannot read, cannot be a man. He cannot be a man, and he cannot contribute to the faith. He must read the Torah to do either, and to read the Torah he must first read. It doesn't mean that every Jew is armed with a design degree; but that as a population, no other people is as intrinsically predisposed to know if that chair—your chair—in the middle of the departure hall of Ben-Gurion, is a Corbusier."

"No. I don't follow at all," said Foster, and noticed the pair of thick-necked men at the bistro table watching them intently.

"Dr. Foster . . . short a corps of Scandinavian architects, no clutch of Anglos are going to have a fucking clue as to whether these chairs were designed by Laurence Olivier, or Le Corbusier. The paradox, Dr. Foster, the paradox is—if you're right on their reputation for thrift—that these then, should be more likely than the average to be reproductions."

"This is not why we've met at Ben-Gurion," said Foster.

The man leveled a gaze at Foster, for which he immediately regretted the interruption.

"If no other people are less likely to spend for such a luxury, and no other people are more likely to recognize the object, then no other people are as likely to know of a difference to suspect. In which case, what are you most likely to put before a suspicious people—a people wise to the difference: the genuine article, or a facsimile?"

For a time there was nothing but the noise of the hall and of the fountain between them.

"That is what I think when I see them," said the man. "It closely resembles—Dr. Foster—what I think when I see you." He now shifted the whole of himself in his chair pressingly toward Foster. "What would you put before me, Doctor? Are you authentic? Are you the real thing? I needn't be a Jew to suspect—I know the difference. And whatever's left of you—I strongly encourage you to produce the genuine article anyway."

4.

McDonnell 162 seemed an outland, a far shoulder of the campus away from the warm and slender hutch of rooms which were the Department of Computer Science and Engineering. For Foster it had all the anesthetic charm of a Victorian operating theater, and today it had all the mood as well. It was a steeply-raked cavern of stepped and polished concrete, one hundred fifty molded wooden seats fixed with a scrap of carpet for grip, a towering arrangement of black boards, a projection booth, and finished from every corner in an oak paneling which soared up into a heady distance where it joined nothing less than pious scholarship. It smelled vaguely of damp metal, soiled denim, and forgotten places.

He had the air handlers for company, casting a tepid warmth the flavor of burnt toast into the grinding silence; the hard drive of his drowsing laptop whining and clicking with the aimless spasms of a dreaming puppy; and the dire likeness of a figure—which at this distance, and in this light—read as little more than an old white man in a funeral suit. It hung safely out of reach or sight above the far stair, and bore all the properties of something lifted from a boardroom tanned in Cuban tobacco. Foster had never bothered with it, or the solemn declarations of its brass plaque; but no doubt it was some benevolent corporate titan, perhaps a friend of his grandfather's; the sort who spend their first act clenching a whip in their teeth, and the second act, a cork—in that intoxicated baronial pastime:

philanthropy—the way scorched-earth warriors build churches in the flaccid amber penance of their reckoning. Nothing takes out bloodstains like a good ribbon cutting ceremony, thought Foster. And then he wondered at the thought. Today was all an off and uncharacteristic thinking: even a few sniffs of the paper rose in the men's lavatory had done little but cramp his jaw and set his mind a-fidget.

It was December ninth—last day of classes: a dusting of snow lay over the ledges, the low, brittle ivy bed, the planter mulch, and everywhere the salt gravel did not hold. The air was cold and hard and the sun presented itself as little more than an imperceptible change in temperature for the whole of the day. Foster had left the Suburban in a spot near the loading docks and the snow and grit had yet to run from the lugs of his boots when Jeffrey Sachs came visiting at his office.

Bryan Hall was one of several late-sixties architectural addendums to an otherwise strictly neo-gothic campus: a Bauhaus layer-cake of rough red quartz granite and concrete slab, with a small addition of cantilevered volumes for suspense. Foster thought its legacy would resolve as the mere proof something had been built there in nineteen-seventy. It served as one of several wings of the School of Engineering and Applied Sciences: much of the computer science faculty occupied its upper floors. Foster's own office—he was convinced it was two broom closets stitched together with drywall and paint—was a windowless box first level below grade, its rear wall intruded by a structural column as if for strength of effect. This was to be a temporary accommodation that persisted, and Foster had a notion it was some sort of tenure-track hazing.

A small plaque in close print read 'H. Charles Foster, PhD.' This was mounted to the heavy, windowless fire door. And it was in this open doorframe that Jeffrey Sachs now stood in his jaunty rumpled pea coat and his weather-slicked cowboy boots, and offered his characteristic Cheshire grin—as though a bit of mutually-appreciated humor had just preceded him.

"Professor-doctor-Foster," called Sachs, leaning into the doorframe. Foster had been composing his thoughts, and though he observed Sachs drawing up in the doorway, when he spoke he lost the fiber of his thought entirely. What arose in its place as he looked up into the white hum of the phosphorus light, and at Sachs and his heedless ebullience—heedless of wet boots and cold-bitten fingers, heedless of beguilements, of emerging and wear-slicked personal indifference, of the sum of personal failures paid in mortgage for each middling success—was: Does that tingling, ignorant urgency return? Do the fires of that stupid, warm-drooling original joy rekindle? Or does life simply outlive the sense for its own pleasure? This is what Foster thought, and offered Sachs nothing but the pallid expression of its thinking.

Sachs rapped on the opened door with a suppressed theatricality: "Bad time?"

The papers had come only a few minutes before Sachs had shown himself in the door. A mailman with a wet mustache and liner over his cap and squeaking galoshes delivered it from a parcel cart dragging a wheel on a salt grain. He took Foster's signature on a green tear-off and left him to the look of the fat envelope, and to the moist groan of the wheel retreating along the hall. What lay revealed beneath the easy-tear filament, framed in brackets and declaratory clauses, was divorce—in a brown paper wrapper. It was no filing or prelude, or other measure of procedure; but was, as far as Foster was concerned, an artifact of the state in conclusion—the thing in actual fact. It was Catherine, and purportedly frail baby Pauline as well, suing for divorce; it was a letter bomb with an utterly noiseless detonation stamped in Maryland court, blasting him with a resignation the quality of a foul odor, and spraying him with shrapnel pieces of all his loose conviction and the glass-shard of his lazy certitude. But for all its spontaneous violence, what Foster knew was that there wasn't even the least surprise in it.

This is where Sachs found him when he'd come knocking; staring down into the stagnant drift of copy: "Whereas," it said where his eye had fallen; his arms set heavily to either side: "Whereas."

"Bad time?" Sachs had asked, to which Foster had gazed up at him with a searching myopia.

"I hope'd I'd catch you. Thought I'd bring by my final," he joked, and snapped the small black drive against Foster's desk where it clicked beneath the authoritative press of his finger.

"It's finished?" Foster had asked when a dim presence of mind had reawakened.

"You'll tell me," Sachs had said. And then with an uncharacteristic glimmer of seriousness, "But, I think it had better be." His smile had dimmed just then with the brevity of a light passing behind a pole—and then returned. "But it's everything you asked for. It's everything we discussed."

"Good," Foster had said. "Good, Jeffrey." But Sachs had been silently casting his eyes about the room.

"Should we settle up then?" Foster had offered, guessing at the antidote to his sudden reserve.

"I would like that very much," Sachs had said. "It'll make next semester much more stylishly lubricated."

Foster pictured the checkbook then, snugged against a pen in the pocket flap of the briefcase lying at the corner of the desk: "My checkbook's at the house," he'd said. "Can we meet for it?" He wasn't entirely sure why he'd forestalled the payment, beyond reflex: that and an uncertainty about paying at all. Nevertheless, the moment had served up the small gratification of striking out against his own obedient resignation. Admittedly it wasn't much—a needle rather than a blow—but it pleased him just the same to let some of the air out; to bleed off some of that overabundant youth, to poultice that unchecked enthusiasm with a bit of salt, and to see the vague illness of disappointment settle over his features with the dissipating waste of aging.

"That's fine," Sachs had said, glancing at the briefcase.

"I'll treat you to some of those beers you like."

"You mean the ones that come in glasses. I should be getting on."

"I'll walk with you," said Foster, and brushed the thumb drive and legal declarations into the mouth of his briefcase.

Outside on the cold-gritted path, where it was the uniform afterglow of day at mid afternoon, they were both intent on the tread of their step and the pinwheel of their breath. "This is my stop," Sachs had said, and with a lift of his pale hand turned off along a fork in the way.

But now Foster set alone in the hall, set deep in its bowels, gazing up along the dark rows of seating: the passenger compartment. In a few minutes the doors would burst open in a frenzy of caffeine and rumpled papers, moist noses and satcheled computers still warm to the touch. The first would hunt to flip on the lights, the next would file into their single-seat pews, and eventually Foster himself would amble to the podium and begin his sermon. But right now his mind seemed a pocket lining with the stitching coming free; he was heart-sick, not for Catherine or Pauline, or himself, but for the first sense of a destiny apart from this one—small and far away, but whole; and presently setting its ember below the horizon. I'm rotting, he thought, and laughed into the silence. I'm rotting.

5.

Kashkin's was a slippery-looking leather chair that while not fine, nevertheless looked dear. Two banks of shelves sagged beneath the collective weight of legal volumes; the desk was an old piece of Steelcase three of four full incarnations beyond original use, and behind him were displayed six framed certificates without a common level or square among them. But it was the potted jade at the corner of the desk where Foster's gaze had come to fall. It was a place for his eyes unselfconsciously to rest, and so they had, his head hard-set in the crook of his palm.

"Principally, lunch," answered Pavel Kashkin. "A delicious chicken salad is among God's pleasures. Also, sometimes I buy their meats, which are quite fine."

Foster's question: 'What do you buy at Straubs?' had been launched before it had even fully formed, an utterance fired bolt-action from the thought, and now blinking dully at the wilted jade, Foster held a vague dread for the meandering, lugubrious reply. Foster had seen Kashkin, it seemed, three times in the last few weeks: first at the local grocery deliberating over box cereal, Kashkin had come gliding down the aisle to the ring of his empty cart; next, in line at the coffee house on Maryland, he'd been chatting up a tight skirt arrangement a few places back: twice it had been properly cold, and twice Kashkin had worn nothing heavier than a corded sweater. And then at Straubs, Kashkin had wandered past as Foster stood gloomily turning avocadoes, which like all his other vegetables were fated to desiccate in the eternal night of the crisper drawer.

"But otherwise," concluded the Russian, "who has need for eight dollar toothbrushes? There are humbler places to waste one's money, and grander things upon which to do it."

Kashkin was peering down onto the papers, adjusting the spectacles creeping along his nose with the back of his thumb. He swiped the tip of his thick forefinger against his tongue when he lifted pages, and did the same with his pen tip wherever he came upon the space for a signature. His top button and tie were loose. He wore beads of sweat fixed against his brow with an unmoving permanence. And he cast a scent of boiled cabbage in his wake each time he took to the copier in the hall.

"Do you always lick your pen?" asked Foster, shifting his gaze from the plant.

Kashkin peeked up at Foster, and at the pen. "Who licks their pen?" he asked.

"You've just done it five times."

"So sure?" asked Kashkin, but Foster held the same bland gaze he'd been plying on the potted jade.

"Perhaps," Kashkin relented. "A ballpoint is dimwitted cold. Where I spent my boyhood, a dab of warmth here and there lent fluency. That must be it," he said when he'd returned to the papers.

"Have you been married?" asked Foster, adjusting his briefcase between his heels.

"He who retrieves mines has no taste for laying them. No," said the Russian. "There are some dishes for which knowing the meat spoils the flavor."

"You say you have a daughter?"

"I do," said Kashkin. "You have the declarations?"

Foster probed about beneath the flap of his briefcase.

"And the electronic signature?"

"There're both here; and a hard copy of the declarations, as well," said Foster, and lay a jump drive and file folder together on his desk.

"The electronic signature? It's here?" Kashkin asked while stubbing the drive with the blunt of his finger.

"And a copy of the declarations," said Foster.

"And there is the retainer."

"Is that now?" asked Foster. A humor was intended for the question, but none came.

"It is," replied Kashkin, and flashed a brief and yellow smile at Foster.

It had been following their third encounter that Foster came upon the card snared in a fold of the paper rose, lifted from the breast pocket of a suit jacket, a bit of flotsam on a lure: Pavel Kashkin, Tower and Gradzik. It was a convenience, true; but the real allure lay in evading his parents—slipping the family attorney, his parent's reflexive alliance with Catherine, the impossibility of the conversations, and in the end, the peril of their contagious doubt, which he could neither afford, nor had the certainty to visit. Nevertheless, as Foster prepared a check and looked on the withering jade with the bored fixity of a schoolboy in a sentenced waiting, he couldn't help but wonder if it was a mistake—if Kashkin, with his yellow smile, and his dewy brow, and his straining yoke of a collar, was a mistake.

Foster leaned in toward the jade and its odd, crescent, half-eaten looking pedals. At the lightest touch one came away in the dirt. "What does that?" he asked.

"Time," said Kashkin, glancing up. "Atmosphere, neglect, and over care."

"Is it too much water or not enough?"

"Yes," replied the Russian. "But mostly it is ambition. Plants are most ambitions of all the creatures." Foster looked at him doubtfully, but he continued. "They will fill the pot until there is not a granule of earth besides, leaving nothing that sustains—just themselves and the creak of their belt. Only a touch of death will chasten them."

To Foster the plant looked modest for its pot: "Then what does this one want?" he asked.

"The forest," answered Kashkin.

6.

The Grand Basin was still. The fountains did not run, and the water was flat and smooth when the breeze lifted its fingers. The museum sat atop the steep, smooth crest of the rise to their right. The sun shone small and sharp from their left. And they faced the wind which watered their eyes, and the great, white stone balustrade which encircled the near whole of the basin, and they sat on a bench of timber and stone, and their nervous feet ground loudly in the gravel when they moved. Foster thought there would be ice in the water, but there was not.

Foster closed the newspaper on his knee once more, and noticed the perfect, round blood drop which had formed there. When he tested his nostril with his thumb there was blood there too. He cleaned his fingers against the cuff of his pant leg and tipped his head back pinching the bridge of his nose, and the light through his eyelids was a flaming orange. "I told you in the beginning I had people who could do it," said Foster. "But I didn't want to use them—I said. You said you had experience. You said it wasn't a problem."

The man beside Foster was silent. When he opened his eyes the man looked away, through the pillars of the balustrade and into the green murk of the basin. Foster dabbed at his nose again with a pinch. "You and your boys have made a long night of the last week," he said.

"If you'd had a better option, you'd better had used it," said the man. He was called August, or that's what Foster was to call him. His head was pale and smooth, skimmed to the bone and leaving little but an abrasive gray shade for hair, which joined with his beard like a hood. He wore a black flight jacket and a knitted cap he'd removed when he sat down with Foster, and now turned it over in his hands. In the still air, Foster could see faint thermals—the steam shimmer of expiration—taking up from his scalp. He looked cold, but like a man who'd worn the feeling before and knew its fit. And though Foster couldn't pin it exactly, there was a slightly mentholated Kentucky or Tennessee swerve in his speech. "How well do you know this man?" he asked.

It was a question almost without an answer, and one which cast Foster headlong into a cycle of recollection he'd been replaying near constantly the whole of the week. The imagery fell into gestures, a series of innocuous tableaus, but their memory was etched with the inalterable certainty of a photographic plate:

He was at home; the overgrown Tudor on Greenway which he'd bought for himself, and Catherine, and baby Pauline—three stories and eight bedrooms of the lifestyle to which they'd become accustomed—now an oppressively empty architectural set piece held in eternal suspense. It was a late morning quivering near the tail end of the Christmas break—a Christmas marked by the sprit of rations from the freezer drawer, a chalky punctuation of Baileys and crème, a persisting scent of paper rose, and the sigh of damp fire logs in the grand mantle. He'd stood on the third floor in the door of the nursery. There was a crib, still, tied with decorative bumpers, a stack of unfolded boxes, and an ironing board leaning against the closet as something tossed in a gale. He'd stood with his acid-black cof- fee from the kitchen, and his robe, and looked. He'd shuffled down the broad stair for breakfast: a plate of pan-grease with bacon and egg he'd slumped over at the dining table with his laptop. He'd prepared the signature documents, he'd suffered through the declarations pages, he'd sniffed vigorously from the paper rose, and by the time he lifted his wristwatch by the strap, he'd forty-five minutes between the appointment and himself. Three identical thumb drives lay at the mouth of his briefcase; he plugged one in, migrated the files to the drive, bathed, dressed, collected his things, and left for Kashkin's office when the meeting was ten minutes old. These were the motions, and they advanced in his memory with the reliability of a flipbook. A half-week had passed before he realized his mistake.

At first he rang up Kashkin's office. But he was away in D.C. on Foster's own business, and couldn't be reached there. So he rang up Kashkin on his cell: in D.C. He did not answer. He tried again later. There was no answer. He tried the following day, multiple times. There was no reply. He tried the D.C. region office: he'd been there, presumably on Foster's business, but should be back in St. Louis by now. When there was still no answer after the turn of the year, his next calls were of a different nature.

August was the recommendation of a dealer Foster had used in D.C.; he was a utility player; a finder, a fixer, a persuasive collector. But best of all for Foster, he worked in many circles but belonged to none: he was safely beyond the fold—he wasn't in the trade. And considering Foster's current bind, that was perhaps the best mark of all. "So, where is he now?" asked Foster.

"You bring any bread?" asked August. He'd noticed a quartet of Mallard ducks put down in a far corner of the basin. "I'd bet they'd feed," he said. "Good word is Mexico: cleared Juarez by car some few days back," he said.

"Who says this?"

"The people who notice comings and goings," said August.

Foster smiled a wry, frustrated smile. "And where would he be crossing to? What's he doing in Mexico—going to Acapulco? I suppose he's taking vacation? Is he running?"

"If he wasn't before, seems it now. Seems likely," said August. "There wasn't anything of use on that machine?" he asked.

"No. And now I have to break it down and dispose of it just the same."

"So, it wasn't him, then who was it?" asked August.

"According to the paper," said Foster striking the doubled newsprint in his lap with the back of his hand, "it was Stanley Burk—real estate attorney."

"Paper say what he was doing in the office?" asked August. "'Cause I'm a curious sort."

"Yes," said Foster. "Yes it does. It says his office was under renovation: says it was being painted. It says his office was being painted." Foster lay back again and worked his brow with his fingertips.

"Bad luck," said August.

"That's right. August. Bad luck."

The piece in the paper wasn't so much a story as a composite: real estate attorney Stanley Burk is working late in the offices of his Clayton law firm. His office is clad in painter's tape and plastic sheeting; thick with dust and paint fumes. He takes his computer down the hall to another office: a contemporary is away on business. His wife is entertaining at home; she hasn't missed him for dinner yet. It's a dark seven o'clock when a janitor coming in for trash and a vacuum finds a fat man collapsed over the desk. He's unresponsive: the janitor panics—she calls 911. The police arrive and find nothing special. The paramedics put it up to a heart attack and roll him off to the coolers at the county morgue. It's not until later when the coroner peeks at him and notices the .22 caliber bite mark behind his ear, and an X-ray shows the little slug rattling around in his cranium like a maraca bean, that anyone happens to think differently.

But, if it wasn't Burk's office—the paper continues—whose office was he using? Oh, some fellow name of Pavel Kashkin—an attorney for the firm away on business—maybe supposed to be back, but definitely and perhaps strangely unreachable. The rest, it seems, is mystery; one whose solution, August penetratingly resolved as— bad luck.

"There were no other drives? Portable drives; jump drives?" asked Foster again, in reconfirmation.

"No."

"You checked the drawers?"

"There were no other drives," said August. "We brought you the computer."

"And I'm still counting my luck for that," said Foster.

"That's all there was."

"Your crew wouldn't have held on to anything?"

"That's right, man; we're all getting fat on a side trade in scalped computer parts. Now, I'd say that's not polite. You know what a value proposition is?"

Foster furrowed indifferently and touched his nose again with his thumb, but he did not answer.

"Well, that's not mine," said August.

"Is laying out an alarming string of collateral damage like a handy bread-crumb trail part of your value proposition, too?"

August set again to worrying the knit cap between his hands.

"What's next for us, August? Is there something like a solution you can work out of that cap?" asked Foster.

"We make another appointment to see him—if you want my view on it."

"And what makes us think it will turn out better this time?" asked Foster.

"The presence of management," said August with a gesture toward his chin. "I plan to meet him in the living image."

"And where do you plan to do this?"

"Well, he may be running, but my mortician's intuition says he's not bound for the South Pole. You're an educated man—you probably thought of it too. Why go south by car—huh? It's not stylish and it's not pretty. You'd fly. For sure, you'd fly. If you're running, the only purpose to drive there is not to fly from here. Which leads me to thinking he means to fly from there."

"Mexico isn't just the worm—it's the bottle too. There must be countless airstrips," said Foster.

"Commercial, man: you're thinking with your top hat. If you were roading in to Mexico for a commercial flight out, where would you go?"

"Mexico City."

"See, that wasn't so hard. Mexico City. You'd have the butcher's choice for international flights. And even if somebody came calling after the fact, that's a lot of tape to sit through for a gray-headed Russian with a flash drive," said August.

"International flights," mumbled Foster to himself.

"Mexico City," said August.

Foster peered through a sparse wood opposite them beyond the basin and turned from it toward August. "International flights," he repeated. "You're going to Mexico City?"

"Yeah, man," said August.

"You're going to 'meet' him in Mexico City?"

"Yeah, man."

"When are you leaving?" asked Foster.

"Probably morning. Tomorrow morning."

Foster shook his head. "No," he said. "Now. You're leaving now."

7.

Charles Foster sat in the first booth before the wait station and opposite the bar. His keys rest on the table before him where he arranged and rearranged their blades with the idle wag of summing abacus knots on their rung. He faced the door and, by an elusive geometry, a glint of afternoon sun. Fetched out beside the keys was a bit of paper flotsam marked in pen—'Sachs 2:00 Wednesday'—as the artifactual confirmation they'd spoken. By his watch, or the light of his phone which he repeatedly checked, it was either 2:56 or 2:58, but in either case the 2:00 of record had slipped into the past; and what remained of the wheat beers he'd ordered in the high-sprinted certainty of relief, now set warm, and in the case of his own, heavily, if reluctantly, nursed.

On the phone Foster had baited him with the check—of course—and there was a problem with the drive or something: if Sachs still had a clean copy on hand—oh, he did—well then bring that along and we'll be sure to get all settled up. The peculiar satisfaction of jerking the line had drained, and however disagreeable, Foster knew now that a reprise from Sachs wasn't so much an investment as lottery winnings.

For the first half-hour Foster paid little attention to the spring-recoil groan of the door. But in this last, he watched its every motion with care. And as he tipped into the third measure of his waiting, with each disquieting whelp of the hinge, that middle-January breath that spilled the threshold and slapped his ankles stiff as frigid surf began to collect as the cool milliliters of a doubt.

For another fifteen minutes he turned his keys on their ring, expecting at any moment Sachs would emerge in a flourish of urgent conciliation, an anecdote of delay, and that sly, self-deprecating, but utterly oblivious grin. He would send the warm beer away, or drink it as tea and order another, and jam his hands into the pockets of his rumpled pea coat until there was warmth in them, and he would offer Foster the drive on the lip of a hopeful expression, and Foster would carve out the check with a languid reluctance, and at the end of it they would both be relieved—but Foster would be relieved to the center. The thought was abstract and oddly weightless: a restoration which could be so oblique, so remote—and yet so material and absolute. 'Sustained,' thought Foster wryly, was the word.

But that is not what happened. Instead, impatient and exhausted of waiting, Foster relented at last, and called Sachs. It was simple—he had to know; whatever the matter, Sachs had to come—to appear; and he had—in unconditional terms—to deliver the replacement drive. But the phone rang out, and through to voicemail, and he did not answer. And it was then, by an uncanny harmony of timing, when Foster ended the call, that he noticed the man at the bar. Foster could not make out his face from this angle, but he sat on a stool with his feet up on the bar's brass rail; his hair was short; he wore a leather coat with a heavy patina of wear; and with his elbow propped against the ledge, he held a phone out before him and considered its illuminated screen intently. Only several moments after the light was out did he delicately fold the phone and discard it within the volume of his coat pocket.

Foster tried Sachs' number several more times before he left, but neither did he answer, nor did the man at the bar retrieve the phone. And Charles Foster never laid eyes on Jeffrey Sachs again.

V.

Hoyt Gamlin landed at Aeropuerto Internacional Benito Juarez on an overcast day in the first week of January. The plane slipped sideways along the mountains and through the low feather of cloud and down into the bowl of Mexico City where it spread in every direction the color of ground crockery shard. The flight was four hours from Los Angeles on short notice—unshaven, in a field jacket he'd rolled over his t-shirt like a sock for the benefit of pockets, and all while coursing with an irritated suspense which hung in his throat as though something he were trying perpetually to swallow.

Hoyt Gamlin was thick and broad, a Briton with a uniform stain of freckles; deep creases that held his mouth in a parenthesis of inscrutability; a wispy, blond, and heavily thinning hair; swollen, muscular limbs employed to good effect in the Sheffield rugby clubs of his youth, and subsequently in the Special Air Service when he failed to make league. He'd served a full term, he was retired, he was in his early fifties, and by way of a chance encounter while providing executive security consultation in Los Angeles, he'd found himself— and his flexible world view—in the employ of the Ministry of State Security, Counterintelligence, People's Republic of China.

Pavel Kashkin on the other hand, was another matter. He was not Gamlin's own recruit, but rather an operative he'd inherited along the way. To Gamlin's thinking Kashkin was peculiar, but clever; and when Gamlin was tasked with putting someone on the curious movements of a Howard Charles Foster, PhD—whom the boys in Hubei suspected of working Chinese tradeshows for converts—Kashkin was the only situationally practical asset.

It seemed lean pickings for a time. Kashkin had settled in for the long slog of shadowing what to all appearances was a first-rate B-lister looking increasingly to have been shelved for storage—when he had a fortunate turn. Gamlin thought it was an improbable turn—Foster taking him as counsel—and warned Kashkin he may have been made, but Kashkin persisted. It helped, Gamlin mused, that Kashkin ran a near constant twenty per cent by volume: it didn't make one quick, but it made one steady, and steady was good for business.

Kashkin's message, it seemed to Gamlin, had come roaring in, cryptic, and against expectation: "Windfall! Or the lads will know. On the road. Pitchforks and torches to rear. Will follow-up." That had been the initial text from Kashkin of almost two weeks ago. A follow-up had only arrived last night. Kashkin offered his room number at the Hilton, Mexico City International Airport; and wanted a rolling handoff in the terminal, an immediate overseas launch—preferably Moscow—and someplace to foxhole for a bit. The plan was swift and simple—Gamlin would be back in Los Angeles by evening—and he was eager to grasp how anything so urgent could have come running from Foster's taps. He'd told Kashkin to stay in his room until he was on the ground. But the wheels were still crying under the brakes at touchdown and already the plan was moving sideways. Gamlin's phone had just powered up and there was a message waiting from Kashkin: "May have picked up some shit on my shoe. Would like to have a smell. Maybe pin a tail on a donkey, too. Basilica de Nuestra Señora de Guadalupe—direct. See you there."

It was a frustrating and, Gamlin presumed, pointless change that would drag him away from the lazy convenience of haunting the airport five hours; and into the corrosive noise, blaring visual stink, and flaking decrepitude of Mexico City—that set on the landscape with briny contagion. It crept along the power lines, Gamlin thought. It was Los Angeles five years left to Castro. And Gamlin hated it; every smog-farted busway and lard-tinged corner of it. Its only virtue—if in fact it had one for Gamlin—was that, in the short term at least, with the correct conversation and the correct denomination in U.S. currency, anything could be accomplished. Or, that is to say, anything could be attempted: success, as always, rest as a percentage of critical skill. In Latin America, where that ratio flagged, one simply applied the brut force of exchange value to buy in bulk. But as the plane parked up and the engines switched off and the ventilation went too, and quickly the fug of impatient quiet humid breathing filled the space in anticipation of the final stroke of the bolt in the cabin door—this small virtue was not in Gamlin's thoughts.

Gamlin strode out along the high corridor of Aeropuerto Internacional Benito Juarez, with its roof of imbricated white armadillo plate, its file of industrial gray piers; its length of cramped shop cubicles under glass—contrived as a zoological display of incidental capitalism; and its sweeping floor which rutted and rippled with the character of the heaving cobbled avenues of home, rather than the plumb of a first world concrete pour. Outside on the narrow ledge of sidewalk he stood and watched the carnival of traffic which coursed six lanes in one direction of turbulent eddies of horns, jolting taxis, and narrows of police battalions triple parked and loitering in their tall caps and decorous uniforms: beat cops dandied-up as generals and preening against their new patrol cruisers in a demonstrative ostentation against crime. A red and gold taxi was first to stop: a

Volkswagen Beetle which pealed in with a welch of tires and the sputtering rasp of a windup toy. The driver called to him: "No baggage, señior?"

"No baggage, señior," he replied and crawled in to the frantic summoning of the driver. "Basilica de Nuestra Señora de Guadalupe," said Gamlin, "direct."

"Si, si, si," replied the driver when he'd already swerved back into traffic. He wore red flannel, a wiry mustache and a tousle of uncombed hair, and a crucifix which swung round his neck, and he chatted happily at Gamlin in quick and largely incomprehensible bursts of Spanish until he'd slowed to collect another fare and Gamlin angrily thumped the windshield with the end of his finger: "Oi! Señior asshole! Where you gon'ta put him? Clip'em to the lid? Go on!" he said. From then on the driver watched Gamlin with a baleful sidelong glance and they drove in silence.

The Basilica de Nuestra Señora de Guadalupe was twenty-five minutes in a traffic which alternately sagged and surged and the driver worked daringly to chase down gaps whose advantage he invariably lacked power to take. The air sagged with sixty-degree cloud and the yellow curbs and railings glistened with a rain which never fell. The driver smoked and ashed through the vent wing, and Gamlin rode with the window down and missing the crank, and the oily scent of the flat-four and cigarillo cloud issued out under his nose, and when at last he was deposited within the makeshift cordons of a taxi lane, and the driver fixed his fee with a malicious smile, he happily quit the tiny cab for the gauntlet of peddlers working the entrance to the basilica.

The Plaza Mariana opened out as a vast granite terrace between the new and old basilica, the Capilla del Pocito, Capilla del Cerrito, and a campus of other shrines and chapels and amendments to holy suffrage. Bits of detritus still lay strewn along the damp stone, pilgrims still milled about nursing the spirit of their new year resurrections, and a small crew of workmen slowly tugged apart the joints of a nativity and tree scaffolding for which they seemed to have lost all intuition.

The old basilica was a fairly standard Roman Catholic affair—two hundred years in the making, and all with Spanish hands. The new basilica, however, Gamlin thought was unquestionably the spaceship of Christ. Built over two years in the seventies, with polished floors, an elaborate arrangement of organ plumbing, and to Gamlin's sensibilities, the interior aesthetic of a honeycomb in a wicker basket—it was a fifty-thousand seat stadium wrapped in the vestments of copper cladding and stain glass, built to watch the Trinity perform live. But there was no performance now, merely the residual adoration of shuffling pilgrims, and Gamlin strolled in through an open pair of the oversize doors which rounded half the façade and found an aisle seat near the back from which to digest the quiescent spectacle and watch for the appearance of Kashkin.

But Kashkin did not appear. There was no sign of him on the plaza, and his prickly silver head was nowhere to be seen among the camera shutters and shawls and satin black hair of the faithful. Nor did he reply to a text from Gamlin, nor a subsequent message thirty minutes later. Gamlin had sat uneasily a quarter hour when the pews began to fill and the motions of an impending service put him irritatedly back out on the plaza where there seemed no more sign of Kashkin than before. He had taken Kashkin's note on a tail for drama, a paranoid occlusion, a brief spell of the tremens—but now Gamlin slowly came to wonder if it could be the object of the delay: if it had proved real and the path of Kashkin's convolutions were holding him up. For a while longer Gamlin paced in the plaza, casting along the damp stones in hope for Kashkin, but when he'd pulled back his sleeve after a further quarter-hour by the hands of his Luminor, he left in haste.

Gamlin hailed a cab—a red and gold Nissan, furrowed with a crease at the corner—and swept back to the airport trying to puzzle out where else Kashkin was likely to be: why after all would Kashkin abort the meet at the basilica—a change of venue he requested—if the purpose was to draw out a tail in the first place? But Kashkin would know it was a quick turn, know that Gamlin couldn't wait: what Gamlin thought was certain though, was that Kashkin would have waved off the meet if he'd intended to cancel. The original plan was all that remained then: after forty minutes of stalled buses and an ass-numbing and meandering tedium, he was put down at the airport once again and worrying over the closing knot of time remaining for security, customs, the long shuffle for the gate—when he thought of the hotel, Kashkin's hotel, and his initial instruction for Kashkin to hold there: it was the last final option, and it was the very perishing moment in which to rule it out.

Signs for the hotel were few and poorly laid, and Gamlin found the Hilton as a squat and square three story arcade buried deep into the cavity of the terminal. Gamlin rang up Kashkin again as he took one of a pair of elevators to the hotel on the third floor, and with the phone to his ear and a hearty wave to a distracted clerk, he strode past the chaise in the reception hall and past the counter. He slipped past the hotel bar with a view of planes on the taxiway—looking closely for Kashkin as he passed—and down a narrow and unremarkable corridor of numbered rooms, and when he'd come round a bend to 315 he knocked lightly at the door. He knocked again to no answer. He tried Kashkin's number again. As before, there was no answer, but as he listened closely near the door Gamlin thought he could hear a phone trembling against a surface within. When he tried again, there was the same crisp palpitating drub. He'd just put his phone away and was staring along the hall after what to do when a housekeeper came slowly up the hall pushing a trolley larded with spray bottles and towels and tissue rolls. She was young and small and leaned into the handle as though she were driving a weighted sled.

"Mi teléfono: mi llave de la puerta: la tarjeta de la puerta . . ." Gamlin blurted at her suddenly. He waved to the door and the slot for the key card and patted down his pockets helplessly. "I've left my phone and my keycard in the room—I'm in a great hurry, and I have to take a call—can you help me?" he said. The housekeeper paused and looked at him with the drooped, jowly, expressionless appearance of someone roused from a slumber. "Mi teléfono: mi llave de la puerta: la tarjeta de la puerta," said Gamlin, repeating the Spanish and charades routine, patting his pockets and pointing emphatically toward the narrow slot for the keycard. The housekeeper shook her head uncertainly, explaining in Spanish, what Gamlin assumed to be a business about the front desk and the appropriate steps of a process; all the while producing a long gesture he guessed was intended to set him on his path.

"No hablo español," he interrupted. "I have an urgent call, and I've locked my phone in the room with my keycard. I can't get in. My phone and my key are inside—can you help me?" She began again with the gesture and a bit of instruction Gamlin imagined she had stored at the detent of a play button. But Gamlin foiled her prerecorded direction: he touched her hand lightly where it clutched the cart handle: "Muy importante," he said, and clasped his hands together as though in earnest prayer: "Please?"

Inside Kashkin's room the curtains were partially drawn over tinted windows. The room looked down into the arcade, beneath its translucent latticework ceiling, and on to its elevators, escalators, and into its drab white corners. The television was on with the volume down, and beyond it on a small desk lay the phone Gamlin had heard rattling from outside. Gamlin snatched it up and waved it at the housekeeper in gratitude, opened it as if to make a call, and then returned to heartily shake her hand: "Gracias! Gracias! Gracias!" he exclaimed before closing the door on her.

Gamlin quickly surveyed the room; the television remote lay on the bed. The bed sheets were disordered from use. Two shirts and two pair of pants and one jacket hung in the closet. An overnight bag lay on the floor beside the bed; its shirts and socks and underwear were in disarray. Three minibar bottles of Smirnoff and a Johnny Walker set on the nightstand along with a small, unfinished glass and the keycard in a paper sleeve. And from this perspective Gamlin noticed the uneaten club sandwich on the credenza. When he examined it, the fries and ketchup were untouched and the lettuce and mayonnaise looked passably fresh, and Kashkin's wallet lay on the floor nearby. Gamlin noticed it with the toe of his shoe, and when he saw this a great weight of resignation passed over him and he drew several tissues from a box at hand and with them turned the handle of the closed bathroom door with a reluctant care.

Beyond the door the bathroom was lined in a tawny cultured stone; a toilet, a shower, and from its abbreviated tub jut a pair of scuffed brown wingtips; and when Gamlin drew back the curtain he saw they belonged to a man in a disheveled blue suit, whom he knew at once to be Kashkin. A white pillowcase was pulled tightly over his head and pierced through behind the right ear by what looked to have been a small caliber round. The cloth perspired a thick crimson stain the scent of a meat counter. The nail on one hand had lifted from the quick and the back of both hands bore light bruising and were cool as tap water. Gamlin turned through his pockets, but found nothing.

The predominant odor was of unlaundered clothes, but Gamlin knew that would not last. He switched on the exhaust fan, closed the door, and dialed the front desk from the bedside phone. "Yes," he said when a voice came on the line, "what time is checkout? . . . One?" The Luminor shone quarter after twelve. "I've had an unexpected travel delay," he said, "and I'll be needing to extend my stay . . . Two days," he said. There was a pause. There were fingers playing at a keyboard. "Yes, 315," he said. "No, I've no interest in changing rooms . . . No, no interest . . . Mate? . . . Mate? . . . No interest . . . I will not be changing rooms . . . A sentimental attachment, what do you care? . . . I don't need the discount, just the room . . . Fine . . . Do that . . . Do that, then; I'm sure they'd prefer it. This one has a bad view in any case . . . A bad view . . . I said—never mind . . . Yes . . . Two days," he said. "What noise? The television? . . . The television? . . . When? . . . When was that? . . . Who says? . . . Who said it? . . . Well," he said, "I'll be quiet as sheep from here in."

Gamlin smashed the phone in the cradle and picked it up to do it again, but rest it gently instead. For a moment he sat and rubbed his brow, then wiped down the handset with tissue. He checked through Kashkin's bag, collected his phone and wallet, hung the 'No Molestar' sign on the door handle, and left for the terminal.

VI.

Some ten days ago I left Paris, quite ill and tired, and journeyed into a great northerly plain whose breadth and stillness and sky are to make me well again. But I came into a long spell of rain that today for the first time shows signs of clearing a little over the restlessly wind-blown land; and I am using this moment of brightness to greet you, dear sir.

His eyes cast over the words again, though this time he leaned his focus forward upon them. But there was no help in it: the words, any words it seemed, would not adhere. Absently, reflexively, he began again, as though his eyes would take up the unmediated substance of their own. But as before, his gaze merely rolled across them, tonguing at their corners.

The address was a pale brick four-family apartment house at the western curb of Nebraska. The windows of the first floor gaped stupid, toothless, and empty onto the street. The entry were a pair of green doors set beneath an arched threshold and shaded over by a sycamore clutching lifeless and noisy leaves, stabbed in the dirt between the curbstone and where the sidewalk panels lifted from the soil. An air conditioner yawned from an upstairs ledge with the limp turn of cigarette ash; there was a flagstone crown, an eroded dentil relief, and a spare, unlikely inlay of decorative white tiles which must once have promised cheer. Upstairs, the floorboards were worn and unfinished, the plaster bowed and cracked, and the air was heavy with the memory of cooking oil.

It had been ten to nine, morning of March 15th, when Edmund LeFrance made the stairhead, followed closely by August, and Phillip, and Kyle Lewis. They'd milled through the rooms. They'd taken up loose positions, and wherever they tread they disturbed decayed sediment which rose about their ankles, and which LeFrance lamented for spoiling the finish on his shoes and coat and freshly laundered pants.

After the New Year August had been away, and had returned with a fractured cheek, a separated ear, and a harrowing, which even today were still in evidence. The cheek had mended to a discolored scuff, but the ear was taped and—Lefrance guessed from the way he pressed it from time to time with his hand—still live with discomfort. LeFrance put it to tobacco—or perhaps it was the harrow that staved the completeness of healing. August had been irritable since the matter at the office in Clayton—for which his travel was thought to be a tidying of affairs—and today, as Lefrance understood it, was the final: the settlement of accounts. Despite this, though, August seemed quiet, and LeFrance thought, pensive beyond his nature; and so as the wait had drug on, it was without protest or comment that LeFrance had received the small envelope from him. A small, manila, padded mailer—sealed and folded: "I'll be calling for it when he comes—but hold it for me till then," he'd said. August drifted back toward the kitchen where Kyle Lewis carved an apple with a knife, the discarded core in the pocket of his Carhartt's; LeFrance traded the envelope into his topcoat for a sleeve of Drum and rolling papers; and Phillip peered uneasily through the front windows.

LeFrance had been setting the tobacco and wet the seam when Phillip called out. "He in a Mercedes?" Phillip had said.

August had come up: "No, why?"

"There's a black one next block up. It's running—I can see exhaust," said Phillip.

LeFrance lit his cigarette and joined them at the window.

"No," August had said. "Suburban, I expect."

"Maybe he's a no-show," Phillip had said, and they'd all turned from the window.

LeFrance had broken off for the toilet out of boredom: "I've got a piss to mark the occasion," he'd said. August had seemed uptight about the prospect and barked his disapproval down the hall after him, but it was an exchange LeFrance had already forgotten.

"Cautious man leads a long life, LeFrance!" August had shouted when LeFrance wedged the door closed. It was frustrated and disproportionate, and LeFrance had flipped up the seat, and released his zipper, and stared down through the onion burn of cigarette smoke into the dry bowl lined in a hard-pack masonry of sewage: "That Socrates?" he'd said, half to himself.

The salmon tile looked to have been spackled in places with shit. The lens of a pull chain light above the sink was a shade of silverfish. LeFrance extracted the cigarette with unused fingers, and by force of habit, derived a wet belch from the sink tap before squeezing it closed again. He'd rubbed his hands in vigorous turns against his pant legs, and then against his coat as a finishing cloth, before drawing the thin, careworn chapbook from his pocket—*Letters To A Young Poet: Rainer Maria Rilke*—and setting himself down on the ledge of the tub.

And now, fanning the pages with his thumb, he read from where the book lay open at the hinge of a relaxed and familiar crease:

> Some ten days ago I left Paris, quite ill and tired, and journeyed into a great northerly plain whose breadth and stillness and sky are to make me well again. But I came into a long spell of rain that today for the first time shows signs of clearing a little over the restlessly wind-blown land; and I am using this moment of brightness to greet you, dear sir.

LeFrance broke off and smoked. He began again. He glanced through the window. He gazed at his dusty shoes. He turned the cigarette between his fingers. He began again. But when he began, it wasn't his wandering attention, but a sharp thump from the kitchen that cut him off: the building leapt with a smart kick; there was a sparkle of separating glass; and the lash of a muffled and ferrous-snared report clung softly in his ear.

He rest the book on his knee, and he listened. He leaned into it, listened with an elbow on his thigh, cocked his head as though tuning a frequency, turned an ear toward the fractured floor tile, smoked, pricked at the smooth-perfect silence from the adjacent kitchen, heard murmurs from the front room, and then the voice of Phillip called out: "Kyle? Kyle?" LeFrance heard three or four footfalls—August said, "Wait." Immediately there was another thump: again the building shivered, calving window glazing fell, and then the sound of a great weight—two-hundred-some pounds of knees and elbows striking unchecked against the hardwood. LeFrance lurched at the impact. He slipped the book quickly into his coat, toss the nip of cigarette into the sink and began to stand, when the corner of the window frame above the toilet turned inside out with wood pulp, the porcelain sink exploded; a brick of it struck LeFrance in the chest and put him on his back in the tub. From just above the tub, then, the wall burst into brick cinders and plaster stones, and a round exited just left of the spigot and the instep of his shoe, and he was dappled with light and wood lathe and ash, and his ears rung with the cast-iron knell of the bathtub. The building leapt with another strike. Somewhere debris clattered the floor. The rent-wire snap flicked the air. There was another pause like a shallow breath, and the building shuddered again, again-again-again-again.

LeFrance lay still. The impacts rang together heel-toe as adjoining syllables, the brittle snap played for a moment and evaporated, and the clap of recoiling silence heaved closed over him. He held his breath to hear. He drew the Redhawk on the door. Thirteen inches of stainless jigged at the end of his outstretched arms. But there was nothing: nothing but his open-mouthed rasp, the flickering sights, the nap of masonry grit in his mouth and nose, and the pulse thundering in his neck and in his hands.

He spared a hand to check the speed loaders in his pockets; his book; the envelope. He climbed from the tub and cringed at the noise of his shoes and falling masonry. He listened at the door and could hear the apartment's asthmatic respiration: the ventilated wheeze of its openings—but no more. He sighted through a low exit hole. He set onto his hands and knees in the sharp gravel debris, and knelt to peer under the door. Nothing. Motionless.

LeFrance knocked the hammer back and stepped out. To his left, in the kitchen, were the Carhartt's of Kyle Lewis, limp and still, one boot inexplicably cast off. To his right, in the next room, a clot of hair adhered to the wall, an impact cratered the plaster, and the damp shoulder girdle of Phillip's heavy sweater lay before a greasy pool of gelatin onto which gypsum had settled with the look of powdered sugar. In the front room, clods of brick were tumbled everywhere, six ragged holes perforated the exterior wall, and August lay near the corner beneath the front windows. His face was a weeping bruise and his flight jacket seemed to bleed copiously from no place in particular. LeFrance felt his palm go humid on the pistol, felt the hood of his vision began to shade at the corners, and he felt the rising acid-blanch of panic; and he ran. He ran for the stair. He stumbled down on his heels and his thighs. He slammed into the door. He threw it wide, and trailing a coma of fine dust, he leapt the stoop and fled for his truck.

VII.

I t was a queer thing, thought Charles Foster. He had been pad-
dling a long-limbed backstroke when he'd stopped to think of
it—and now he lay in the thought: floated between the buoy
markers of the lane, the water lapping at his ears, and stare up into
the steel rafters where every kick and stroke and turn seemed to
catch and tangle against the welds and angles of the trusses: August
was renegotiating, Foster decided. For weeks he'd thought otherwise. He'd been desperate to get back the drive—had been steeping
in his own anxious dread from the first realization of his error. But
when he'd heard from August the work was done—Mexico was a
success—he'd suddenly cultivated a new and unexpected urge: a
paranoia. Almost despite himself, he'd told August to wait: August
would quarantine—make sure between the debacle in Clayton, and
his exploits in Mexico, he hadn't contracted anything unwanted.
Attention. Attention that might otherwise be catching. So he'd
waved off the exchange a few weeks. But, those few weeks later in
February—and this was the queer thing which had arrested Foster's
limbs with a curious doubt—rather than arrange to meet at the
Grand Basin, where they'd met before, and soon; Foster received a
text from August arranging the meet a further month out, and set it
in a vacant apartment in the leprous armpit of South Saint Louis—
Foster had driven by to see. He could also see sense in it, however
disquieting a sense it was. It was the sense of someone worried they'd

been made—rolling out a time and location isolated and unlikely. And this was the sense Foster held to it, until now. But it was also a caution beyond what of August he'd seen: a caution too far, Foster thought. This was the alternative which had freshly occurred to him: the extended date could be intended to whet his appetite for the drive, inflict him with real hunger; and the desolate location, a context for renegotiation—a safe and quiet place to sweat him for more. Foster didn't relish either as a possibility, but he knew it must be one, and just now he'd settled with a visceral certainty on the latter. And in any case it had worked, particularly since Foster had lost touch with Jeffrey Sachs—unwitting and seemingly vanished author of the work—and had suffered these last weeks in an impatient and nervously self-medicated stupor. Reconciled, he began to kick again at the pool, turned an arm back in stroke, noted the depth markers crawling past—clinging at the tissue of the waterline; and wondered what was a better insurance against this likelihood: that he should bring nothing, or that he should bring more?

The answer did not emerge from the antiseptic waters of the gym. It didn't arrive in the locker room, nor did it come down the long and narrow passage into them: a shadowed birth canal that shuttled its passengers between the worlds of light and virtuous noise, the earnest clatter of plate machines, of the multi-colored aviary; and the urine-spattered, stale man-scented silence of toilet stalls and wet bench pews, of chafed and humid steel lockers, and of the preening nude and monkish cloisters of the private interior. It was here that he snapped off his wet things, exchanged them for presentable street clothes from a sour duffle, and wheeled off in his Suburban.

Amid the funerary décor of the bank, the access form was signed and dated: March 14th—it was Monday, cool and lazy with the first calendar hours of spring break, and Foster was marked by the stroboscopic hum of morning coke, and that unshorn and wind-lashed bearing of one carried in un-denominated time—that guilt-thrill of bowing a productive and accountable resource to spend as enjoyably in its spoilage. He was led into the vault, asked for his key; the attendant spun them in unison and made crisp and officious clatter with his laden ring against the panel face. He was led to a private anteroom with an office chair, a desk of mounted countertop, a row of electrical outlets, and was left there with his opened box; sat heavily in the chair and considered the tidy rows of neat, ten-thousand dollar bundles in fresh-cut bills, each banded as though they might be fine cigars. But still he had not decided. It was a lingering thing. Nothing about the bulk of notes, their lace of guilloché, their musk of printer's ink, nor even captivity in their company had armed a resolution as Foster had hoped. He bent over them, looked down fondly, and for just an instant inflated a conceit around them—stepped in with them: for sixty quiet seconds he imagined it was unspent, not a quarter, not the whole—that their fate and his along with them, were free and undetermined—he imagined that they could be together in mysterious isolation, and he imagined that they could be unsought, would be unfound—but when he thinks this thought the quiet image coughs and collapses: he is deposited once more within his cramped confessional—a sort of ordained sinner in communion with his sinful means.

He looked at his watch—in this space he can hear it tick—and he listened as the second hand swept through the quarter-dial. Foster couldn't decide. It was as though his certainty was empty—lacked tooth—and his mind continued to slip tractionless along the subject. Lingering beside his choice began to turn his mood, began to bear down upon its delicate joints and features, and so he determined to move his determinations elsewhere. He drew out four bundles into a clasp envelope—the original forty thousand promised August for his task—and haltingly, reluctantly, he separated another three in allowance for unilateral revisions of terms—into the pocket of a separate envelope, and summoned the attendant with a push-button on the wall.

He was led out of the room, the deposit box was replaced, the keys were turned to the percussion of the attendant's chain, and Foster thought idly and unaccountably as he watched—of the lockers at the gym. He was led, again, from the vault, and he left with all his funds and decision to make.

2.

Charles Foster probed his gums against the mirror. They were pink and numb and wept blood where he flossed. His sinuses were numb as well—taught-smooth and clean from particulate erosion, and had the feel of a borehole through to open air, free from the least trace of moisture. Foster had spent last night's dinner across a table at MeKong from Kim Soong, a graduate student in a parallel program, and couldn't presently think of the first thing he'd said. The booths were low. The table was green Formica. He nursed a red curry into cold distraction. There was a low curtain along the window. A setting of soy and Sriracha sat at the shoulder of the table. Kim was Chinese—with the hooded look of a lazy dragon, a loose ponytail of hair like black wire, and other than a pair of nostrils and a small hole for soup, was devoid of the faintest discernable feature. He could picture all of this; even twice visiting the bathroom to smell the paper rose, but could not imagine a singular note of the conversation. He could remember having his curry wrapped for home, even leaving it on the table as they left—could remember it occurring to him as he'd sat there slurping his miso, that he was still carrying seventy thousand in new bills—sitting in the booth of a restaurant along South Grand. But seeing this reflection, he broke away from his leaky gums and dental tape, and hurried from the bathroom to where he'd thrown his jacket over the bedpost. And he was greatly relieved to find it there—the bulging pockets tugging heavily at the nape. He emptied the envelopes onto the bed and fell beside them, dripping naked and already half exhausted by worry. He thought of Sachs as he looked over the bundles, the undelivered check, thought of waiting evenings down the block from Sachs' apartment without the faintest sign—and for an instant Foster sensed an indiscernible moment had past, a nameless Rubicon had been overshot. But the feeling was brief and intangible: the shrug of scrotal chill, a convulsive sneeze—and it was gone. He freighted the bundles back into their envelopes. He completed his ablutions, and he dressed. He buckled his watch: 8:20 a.m. He loaded the envelopes separately into his hunting jacket, the .38 revolver from the drawer, and checked his phone: Tuesday, March 15th.

The Suburban swayed left out onto Delmar—left down Hanley, and through the lights Foster thought only of how to play the money: would he carry it on his person?—would he leave it in the car? When he came to Forsythe, however, he was taken by another thought, and he turned left again, passed down along the unfortified verge of the university, across Skinker, and into Forest Park where he stopped beside the Grand Basin. A grim wad of cloud slipped in sheet along the sky and let down strakes of light. Foster left the car to the bite of the gravel underfoot, the cool behind his ears, and the first bench along the basin. The water was still and green and where the fountain spigots blemished the surface, they were idle. Light drifted up the hill toward the museum and shown upon the sepia of the fallow grasses.

This was the sight he imagined, the location he expected, and as he'd come to the intersection at Forsythe he'd found himself answering a compulsion—coming here out of step, sitting at the waterside with the clock running out—as though the act itself might throw some illumination, might balm his inarticulable discomfort, might anneal or correct the dislocation. 9:14.

These things happen, he thought: locations are moved, times revised, dates are pushed out, motives change and strategies realign. What was puzzling then, was that he'd seized now and out of nowhere on this detail as though it were imbued with some metaphysical dysfunction. The diversion had only half-worked, however. The gravel paths were empty. The roadway was clear. Coming had placated something, but what it was Foster struggled to tell. The whole matter shifted beneath his concentration: the date and venue—the more he'd perseverated over these angles the more he'd left his own fingerprints upon the subject, and now as he sat looking into the wood beyond the basin where leaves tacked noiselessly on the air, the more he could no longer tell the subject clearly from the marks of handling. 9:15.

3.

Foster bounded cross-town with his knees nuzzling the dash-board and the seat tuned to its furthest pitch. The money itched oddly in his pockets, air buffeted smartly at his eyes through the window gap, the pistol stitched with the onset of bad digestion where it poked his rib, and the Suburban trimmed and porpoised as he rounded the cape of the Interstate 55 exchange: beneath the mulchy-scented plumes of beer wort, through the loose brocade of gas silos, and down the chute of the Gasconade exit.

He bent back up to Keokuk, waited out the metronomic tock of the indicator; glided past the hospital; the ratchet-lick progress of stops; the row houses bald and narrow; two and four family flats; tumbledown garage stalls; weed lots; half-blocks vacant as Anasazi pueblos in red brick and pressboard patches; and at every curb, workaday rust-hulks with donor limbs and delaminated rubbers. Once a coal-fire ventricle of America's victual-class heart, now feculent and forgotten.

North up Nebraska: a listing right at the service station—blue, abandoned, and rot-swole; and round the corner he leaped on the brakes with a slippery shudder and jounced to a halt off the curb. For a moment Foster sat blinking uncomprehendingly in the muted cabin; the faint lope of the engine pulsing through the seat cushion, and through the wheel. The street was an ancient blacktop, colorless and weather-beaten as the ashen sky, mottled with oil stain, and a vestige of pinstripe along its high center spine. To his left, a scrabble of pavement ran from the service station to the broadside of a four family flat, and as Foster looked on, a heat shimmer danced above the pitch roof; wisps of steam seethed through invisible fissures at the roofline; through the crowns and cracks of the second floor glazing; and through a windowless span of brick, the gaps of six tidy punctures respired with brilliant white smoke in a spluttering unison. It was his destination, it was the location for his meet with August, and it was on fire.

Foster stared on, and struggled to bring a crystalline thought to form. It was a distended instant—a filament drawn long and perilously thin. He shook his head in confusion, as though puzzling a mirage. At last, however, it was not the smoke jets or furnace light in the windows which registered, but some wordless intuition rang out to him from the penetrations through the brick. And with the shrill of sirens playing up from some invisible edge of the landscape Foster threw the Suburban into reverse, bounded unsteadily up over the curbs and off again, slung the nose round heavily into the intersection, and sped away.

VIII.

Cards were fed him, one up, one over. A pair of fives he split, and with all the deliberation of brushing crumbs from a place setting toss a weighted fifty marker to stake it. Edmund LeFrance sat among the gaming tables of a paddleboat casino along the banks of East Saint Louis. The air was heavy and granular and blue as oil smoke. The peaty dew of cigarette and whiskey evaporate was upon his skin, and he was cautious to keep it from his eyes when he smoked or braced his temples in the tactile mudras of contemplation.

Now a king joined the five and the dealer watched as LeFrance turned his glass—it was a mechanism of consideration, stretched his back, and fetched a crooked hand-rolled cigarette from his coat over the chair back. Another five was sprung at his tap, and LeFrance stayed on twenty with a limp flick of his wrist. The dealer's arm skipped to the open hand where she indicated his lone card with a taught recurve of chapped and double-jointed fingers. Her emphatic paw gave LeFrance the loose impression of a hound performing sums at a breeder's show. He knocked again: nine. Again: ace. The ace startled him and he regretted the split and he stood on sixteen with a gentle shake of his head. The dealer turned seventeen. She swept up the one hand and paid out on the other, and as she changed the shoe LeFrance attempted to unlace the elaborate embroidery of her epaulets.

It was Thursday, March 17th, Saint Patrick's Day, and since noon Edmund LeFrance had borne his place upon the anachronistic riverboat fetish, festooned with tinsel streamers and cardboard shamrocks; amidst the chain smoking retirees from collar-stain suburbs huddled over chiming Kino consoles and braced with coin buckets and low price libations. But for the special on Irish whiskey, however, LeFrance had little of the occasion in him, and while normally talkative and wry, had taken to trading cards and chips with a dire form which had spoiled the play and left a turn of dealers to ply their cards in an uneasy and avertive silence.

Through the day the tables were cool and empty. A dealer change had been tonic. A couple had played in with brightly-laminated spirits and strict ecclesiastical strategy while they could summon it. They hadn't a mote of luck between them, but they were good for LeFrance's cards, and for a time he prospered by them. But this was not to last. The cards were evasive. The dealers were toxic and confounded his attempts to mount a rhythm, and in the end he'd spent the evening working to halve back the five thousand he'd been down at the bottom. It was slow and measured work, but eventually a focus had risen up through the depths of his distracted mood and he'd gradually begun to string together hands. Hours on, round the itchings of eight o'clock, by his bracelet Timex, the dealer served from the new shoe: twenty against his comfortable-seeming eighteen. LeFrance didn't like the shoe already, and already the dealer brushed her palms and stepped out for a change. Her replacement was a man with sculpted brows and a high viscosity and fragrant hair product, and was a spoiler—a cooler, who'd dealt LeFrance such pestilential cards just hours earlier, LeFrance thought he should be emblazoned with a hazardous materials warning. Now, at the sight of his return LeFrance thought of cashing a chip against his grin.

Instead, LeFrance toss back his drink in two stern plugs, gave him the heated grimace for tip, collected his chips, and sauntered off for the cashier.

At the cage he changed for bills and a hundred in two chips he'd taken to keeping for the mysteries of habit. In the restroom he washed his face with hand soap, dried with a rasp of paper towel, and disembarked for the parking lot where his truck stood in a far and empty corner beneath the cowled yellow haze of a ticking sodium lamp.

2.

Edmund LeFrance drank warm Corona from a pottery cup—
he'd flicked the bottle from the window—and reined his
great white draft horse cross the bridge and past the towering vaginal curve of the Saint Louis Arch. LeFrance was somber
and nervous and alone with Tuesday's events at the apartment and
he spun up some of what he had: put Bowie doing "Black Country
Rock" into the dash speaker to stave off the chill of his wandering mind.

LeFrance rode the exuberant buck of the leaf springs down the
long jogging straight into the city and contemplated going home. He
was tired and what of him could not subsist on nicotine and worry
was hungry. LeFrance let a small drive-up bungalow on Zephyr at
Big Bend and he wanted to go there. He wanted to bathe and he
wanted to eat and he wanted to sleep the rest of the week. But he'd
only been to the house a few hours at a time since Tuesday. He'd
avoided private places. He'd sent his lover off to her apartment, and
had diligently preferred the company of congregations. And so it
was that LeFrance left off the notion of home, left the highway too,
and thread the truck by its bulbous hips down the narrow lines of
Skinker, to the Delmar lounge, where he left it for a station at the bar
and half the counter to himself. He cleared a pasta plate and traded
up the jewelry polish of the casino for a respectable whisky, and by
degrees he began to lend himself to the mollifying ease of food and

drink. He rolled a cigarette from his pouch of Drum and lit it on the barman's match, and opened the slim volume of Rilke's letters in a further effort to hide from his cares where they were unlikely to seek.

LeFrance read and he smoked and he knocked his ash into a clear glass tray.

> So you must not be frightened, dear Mr. Kappus, if a sadness rises up before you larger than any you have ever seen; if a restiveness, like light and cloud-shadows, passes over your hands and over all you do.

LeFrance leaned back in the stool and closed his eyes beneath his mind's working mass. And through closed eyes he saw the bar back: its amber bottles arranged on illuminated glass shelves. He saw the vivid tendrils of a smoky uncertainty in his thoughts. He saw a place in his chest that ached with a tumor of nervous discontent. He watched a heavy man in a bleak law office drop forward onto his desk with the sudden weight of four stories; and he saw himself seeing the figure of August slumped against the wall: a shadow cast without a light.

When LeFrance opened his eyes he rubbed them, rubbed at their sleeping tang and their cloying, mortal indifference. The room was brighter now, and more red, and he closed the book and held it by his fingertips—held it as he might a plate or a plaque or an antiquity—and considered it; marveled that it was not precious, or boiling off half-life, or carved from sheer granite leaves. And when he set it beside his glass, he thought of the envelope in his coat. He'd opened it Tuesday evening with a sense of expectation as though some answer were held within, some transmission from August detailing where it had all gone wrong. There was no such thing of course, only a small black thumb drive. He withdrew the envelope to examine it now. It was—he presumed—or was related to what he'd been sent into the Clayton office for, but had failed to turn up. It was nothing: a piece of industrial flotsam, a bit of buffed-up plastic. LeFrance had the vague notion August had gone to Mexico for it, but had otherwise no idea from where it had come, who had wanted it and for what purpose, or what it might contain—if it even touched the disaster at the apartment in anything but his imaginings. He rest his cigarette to turn it over in his hands. He was curious, but curious with the blunted edge of a practicing technophobe. Not a luddite—that looked too formal a position—but rather simply a disinterested party: he had a phone, of course; his lover had a laptop she trudged around—he'd used it: a talentless box, like a compact typewriter that remembered with electricity in place of indelible marks—a backlit screen with backlit windows with backlit pages with backlit type—a goddamned marvel of the age. "How did we ever make it without the electric typewriter?" he said through the hook of a sneer—to himself, and the drive in his hand, and to the barman who smiled benignly from his place.

LeFrance dropped the drive contemptuously into the envelope and slipped it beneath the book and beside the pouch of Drum on the bar. It was someone's tax filing, or illicit photos, or August's memoir preserved in eternal backlight, or whatever the hell it was LeFrance would never know, because he wasn't perfectly sure how such things were opened, and he hadn't the least intention of plugging it into a computer to find out. For LeFrance the real question was what to do with it. Dispose of it? Anywhere? Anyhow? Or to keep clinging to it as an inscrutable totem: a deadman's final and secret testament? It was a point LeFrance tried again to put down, and seeing the nub of his cigarette resting now in ash, LeFrance took up the Drum and his papers and set to fashioning another. And it was then a man took up the stool beside him.

3.

H is hair was short and autumn brown, the high ridge of his nose bore a hitch like a dog's muzzle, and a single furrow creased his brow, indelible as a scar of concentration. He bore night sky and cool pavement air in the eave of his lapels, and an old leather coat: weather-beaten and clean, and all once and uniformly black. Edmund LeFrance had sealed the paper, put the shag to the barman's match, and was working in the first clean draw when he appeared. He'd come and tugged the next stool over and slipped in, all of a motion, and was unloading Sherman's from a brown shoulder box onto a cocktail napkin when LeFrance had turned to look. He ordered a double whisky from an untapped bottle and had carefully set out five Maduro wrap cigarettes and a lighter when it came. They lay straight and even as the teeth of a comb, with a black and silver lighter beside, and LeFrance and the barman shared their bemused fascination with a glance.

The man visited his whisky and considered this arrangement, and LeFrance and the barman watched him consider it. Hours of cards and drink and lack of sleep had worked a greasy delirium over LeFrance, and when at last this new curiosity would not hold he said, "I'm guessing you've done this before."

"I have," said the man without hesitation, and removed a cigarette from the arrangement and lit it. The lighter closed with a keen dry-fire snap, and LeFrance admired the sound.

"What does it mean?" asked LeFrance. "Warding off evil spirits and bad liquor?"

"It's a special occasion," said the man, returning LeFrance's provocative grin. "I'll have to try it on bad liquor."

"What's the celebration?"

"That isn't the word I'd choose," said the man, and offered LeFrance a cigarette with a gesture.

"You wouldn't mind?" asked LeFrance. "What about your . . . symmetry?"

"Fearful symmetry? A ceremony of measure, I suppose. It's difficult to put a sense of dimension to one's doings. Also, I don't like the taste of bar top. You'd ease my burden," said the man. LeFrance bobbed with a breezy but grateful affirmation, collected a Maduro cigarette from the small napkin and moved to light it against the burning end of his handroll when the man interrupted.

"Please. Please. Allow me," said the man, and lit LeFrance with the lighter and a two-handed concentration. "It's an odd thing, a cigarette that isn't squarely lit: it never gets right." LeFrance carefully pressed out the handroll for later. He felt struck by an accent, an occasional chord played on black keys, fluid and elusive—but he couldn't train the sound to a certainty.

"What's the wine for this fish?" asked LeFrance.

"Oban," said the man, "do you know it?"

"Not personally."

"No? That's a matter to remedy," said the man, and summoned the barman with a snap of his fingers.

"Like Macallan?" asked LeFrance.

"Macallan's for cleaning brushes. Oban for my neighbor, please," said the man to the barman. "You must know it in your time."

"It's not necessary."

"I disagree," said the man.

"Really."

The man turned at LeFrance now with a spontaneous gravity: "I think . . . it's the *least* I can do," he said.

LeFrance resigned with a snigger and watched the man until the fresh glass was set up beside the old. When it came, he put back his dregs with a jolt and took up the Oban, but again the man intervened with a hand poised above LeFrance's wrist: "Don't cut that with diesel—let that set!" said the man, with an irritated urgency that brought to mind August's protestations over his tools.

When he was satisfied the man lowered the hand and raised his glass and LeFrance repeated the gesture. "Partus sequitur ventrem," said the man. "Prosit."

"Which means . . . what?" asked LeFrance.

"May it benefit your health."

"The other, I think," said LeFrance.

"It means: that which is brought forth follows the womb."

"Latin?" asked LeFrance.

"The words."

"You know it?"

"As the drone of liturgies and mausoleum script," said the man.

LeFrance smiled and drank. "You seem a literate sort," he said.

"No," said the man, who grew a smile so broad then it chapped his cheeks with creases and his eyes glittered wildly and LeFrance felt himself leaning imperceptibly away. "Oh no, I'm utterly reformed," he said. "No," he repeated, staving a feral mirth LeFrance thought would surely overtake him, "literature is merely romance reading for men, overfilled with emptiness, and punctuated by masturbations of hardship." The man snuffed his cigarette in the flanks of his ashtray and drank and took up another which he lit with the jarring snap of the lighter. "I've no idea how anyone survives it," he said.

There was the chatter of cutlery on plates, the door rapping closed with the spasms of early crowd, the feminine score of conversation, automobiles in the street, and the man's gaze, which LeFrance broke to chalk his own cigarette. "They're nice," said LeFrance.

"Be my guest," said the man.

LeFrance took another cigarette and the lighter. It was more substantial than he'd imagined: lacquer panels, knurled thumb-wheel, hinged lid with a chirping valve and deliberate action. He put the cigarette on the slender blue flame and played the lighter over in his hands. There was a mar in the bottom finish that snared against his thumb and engraving near the lid: S.T. Dupont, Paris.

"Though, I think you may be," said the man.

"Maybe what?" asked LeFrance.

"A literate sort."

"I don't think so," murmured LeFrance, and shook his head. But the mouth feel of speaking had oddly and unexpectedly gone, and he lost the certainty of having spoken at all and studied the man then for proof.

"The Rilke says otherwise. Or that was just laying about?" said the man, and he indicated the chapbook atop the envelope at LeFrance's elbow.

IX.

Marek Hussar labored some time in the stultifying full wet of the barn before firing up the car and laying headlamps on his work. He closely inspected the second trench of turned and overfilled earth, noted the burdened heel marks to be cleaned, and checked the time. In the light he rest and appraised his cultivations. Two rectilinear troughs of harrowed earth, new beside old—both tilled and fertile and sown. Strange ripe bulbs to put up dark flowers, thought Hussar. He imagined a music which played over his deep and quiet spaces as he worked—Joe Zawinul, pressed out strains of "In a Silent Way," pressed out flat block organ-chords with two ten-fingered hands. It played in crisp, full color from the stores of memory; but the idle of the sedan, which he'd run for a few minutes of true light, had thrown up a drape of noise which perturbed it, and made him deaf to the low clatter of rain on the shingles and in the field of bent grasses, and he clipped the lights and stilled the car and returned to the gap in the high doors to survey all this again.

The rain had persisted some thirty hours by his counting, rung directly from the air and shiftless slate of sky. And this too preyed on his attention. It played on the roof and the field and granule-fine on the leaves of the far trees as camouflage, an acoustic veil that hung everywhere in palpitating shelter that prolonged his earthworks with vigilance. But within the resumptive low patter, his tune took up again, bounded into the open, filled the barn and the clearing and the inky brushwork of wild spaces, just as it had coursed over his exertions in the trunk, the chuff of spade-bites, and the scuttle of soil on ninety inches of bag; on heels; on spangled clutch.

The ill-fated phone had become a litter of pieces about the city, the battery and SIM card and bits of handset had been drawn and quartered and cast off. The fateful call, as it turned out, had gone unanswered, too brief for voicemail, and the irritation of waste had lingered with him—like big-game trophies, or great sharks in mackerel drags; like defiled sculpture.

Hussar stood in the door with his music, and when he finished surveying the out of doors, he studied his gloves; studied their leather palm and spine. And he reflected on three layers of medical booties over his shoes—regarded their stupidity; their practical ugliness; imagined a catalogue for such things; an great human inventory; a genealogy—all I need's a rubber nose; a Chaplin cane, he thought— and shook his head at the indignity; resolved himself to the murk of the interior and turned himself back upon the earthen furrows and the re-dressing of hay and other cares. And when he'd finished he admired the great mound of straw, straked with mold and fragrant with common decay, and he smiled upon his work. "Whomsoever may object to this union," he said softly, "speak now!"

2.

In the days which followed, February endured in its wet, cool, and humid color—a mirthless oil-spill plumage that would neither lift nor break, and Hussar marveled at its dark and adamant featurelessness. He busied himself with the mundane gestures of his work. He restocked perishables, took coffee in fine porcelain cups, and sat in silence and music before the altarpiece façade of the stereo. And he received the key.

It arrived by post, as they generally did—stamped and postmarked and unremarkable: a modest envelope containing a fresh-cut key, sharp and bright and urgent with the capital of new-minted coinage. It was the third such key he'd received in St. Louis, in fact—the second at Creveling—and it belonged, as they always did, to the address which preceded them by text. The first key had fitted a box at the Deco brick of a post office in University City; the second a box in Clayton; and this, the third, fitted a box on Market street—across veneered marble thresholds, and through portals of brass and glazing, and low beneath grand New Deal murals of riverboat authors and lions of newsprint, traders, and trappers, and threadbare provincial generals illustrious in their abolitionist blues. There were his footfalls sparkling into vacancy, a column of postage tables fixed in optimistic permanence and lighted in smoky eye-shadow noir—an emerald jewel in an urban-pothole setting, thought Hussar, a powder magazine for convictions all spent in its care.

There was the toothy rough-saw of the key. Whine of the tumbler screw. Clatter of the aluminum paddle of door on dry hinges. And there was the vessel for the key—the envelope itself. It was a system comprised of three ingredients: the address of the post office box, which arrived via text message in thin lines of green-pixilated script; the post office box key, which arrived typically by mail; and the key-envelope's return address—a business in a tidy secretarial hand—which in its house number, contained the very number for the PO Box—a box number he'd quietly scanned from the Market street block of them, the folded slip of envelope in hand. And there was the package—or packages: three sealed one in the next like nested dolls. Three fragile paper vaults, all in the service, not so much of perfect confidence, but transmissional certitude: not a secret kept, but delivered; an agency of will conveyed; made manifest. These levers of agency came in many forms: travel itineraries, conference addenda, notices of delegatory appointment, psychological profiles, articles and glossy photos with earnest grease pencil loops. In this particular case that manifestation came as an uncharacteristic revision—a modification to the matter and manner of the first and original key, the key that had brought Hussar to St. Louis seeking its mated box to begin with. And the form of that modification came as a place, a date and time; a geo-chronological overlap of coordinates representing an end to watchful waiting. It was an escalation request.

3.

Hussar visited and reviewed the location, at different times and for different intervals, and set about his preparations. He bought buckets and paint rollers and nitrile gloves and fetched and arranged items from the flight cases cached in the garage.

He visited the gym; weights and pool, and fed down the narrow-dark and crooked passage to the untended locker room within: a long, moist gauntlet opening upon a quarter lighted in heat lamp and cared after like bus stop latrine. Littered a blight of blue-veined tumescence, unflushed turds, and Asian centenarians come to bathe their balls in the warmth of hand dryers.

He observed treadmills, and untold squads of fettered cyclists in laborious captivity: thought of calories—lamentable kilojoules; bristling watts of power exhausted in malodorous brine and fevered loathing. He thought of ancient Egyptians; masons; traded copper implements for diet pills and row-machines, and left off pyramids for sacrificial offerings in righteous vanity: self-improvement. Wheat fields turned ornamental gardens. Pharaonic deification swapped for coital fingerings of personal immortality: and with it, two splendid new follies bought for the labor of one. This is what he thought where he slipped into the pool, and carried it with him the fourteen feet to the abrasive floor. He dropped beneath a bandolier of diving weight and watched in meditative calm as the thought left him in tear-away sheets and the sweeping second hand of his wristwatch clicked off formidable sixty-second ingots, all in accumulated fine-shaven intervals.

Like the extra-physical martial art of car-craft, or sunning in the sonic arc-light of the stereo, this of the drowning—the immersion, too, had become a pleasure. But unlike the others, this ecstasy—two minutes, eleven seconds at the hypoxic edge of carbon dioxide saturation, of chlorine salts and dim green bathwater for breath—was a stillness advanced from terror. Not a perceptual or psychological fear, but a horror, pure and primal. Physical. Reflex. A panic of the body: that intravenous death-shudder; a sort of writhing certainty of crocodile teeth on skull plate. Overcoming this was no matter of measured pacifying gasps, of mollifying the senses one placid touch upon the next; but the stern rode and precipitating anchor of self-abnegation: of smiling death; of thrilling to foretake the fit limb that it may not later be taken. A full depth of watercolor pigments in blue-green silence; a chest taught with spoiling and unbreathable vapors; the heart feeding them in slowly tiring hammer fells; atria of the mind dilated in wheezing, asthmatic starvation; the second hand of the watch, knocking as though it might be pressed against his ear, marking out the edges of his diminution, sounding the curtain-draw in the brief calendrical lozenges of mechanical perfection: and all the while, however tenuous and ephemeral—a vesicular home. An absolution.

4.

The morning of March 14th opened in low and heavy turbid cloud, and trained in swift procession across the splintered window frame. Wind lapped at the soiled curtain-tails, drew them out through the fractured glass, and for a time the room hummed and buffeted with something like air. Marek Hussar was installed in the front room of an apartment house on Keokuk at Nebraska; third from the corner; second floor. He was suspended in waiting, but at pensive distance from its pleasures, and far from the forms of home. The half block leaned shoulder-to-shoulder in huddled vacancy, brown-toothed and abandoned: a weather-softened rain catch to the open roof of sky, and occasional hotel suite for those in search of private accommodation for their needled dusk. Battered saplings put up in window hems and the daylight gaps of floorboards. Feral droppings were everywhere near at hand, and Hussar had the sense that every surface had been somehow graced by a sputum of tubercular hackle.

Hussar had watched the hooded morning rise—night turned blustery scrim of day; had watched the belt-fed day unfurl; and a shoal of rain, not so much heavy as large—cold, full rain-stones cast down in spite. He had watched this pass a sort of snowflake mist that tumbled in doorways and spun up window frames. He had sat deep in the room on a milk crate, back against the wall seeping dew and cream-white base. He sat in the curried stink of mildew, the crawl-ing nasal sting of desiccating lime dander, the ammonia-scented fold of carpet. He'd held this vigil through all the hours of the cool, still night which followed, and in the early hours of the fifteenth, he'd set the bipod legs of the Barrett G82 on the flank of an overturned bookshelf; queued up three five-round magazines—AP and two Raufoss—and trained the scope through the narrow portal of win-dow and onto the broadside of the building above and beyond the remnant of service station, and some eighty meters from his sights.

At 8:00 Hussar checked the green-fluorescing markers of the Sea-Dweller, locked the suppressor over the muzzle break and rose from his many hours of listless hibernation. Some four hundred sixty feet above sea level—high-center of the Midwest, second floor; still, his undiluted mood remained a depth-pressure fully half the watch's four thousand foot dive rating. At 8:30 Hussar glanced at the shims he'd fixed to bar the door. He strung a set of muffs round his neck, thread the suppressor to the USP, advanced a round, and rest the pistol within easy reach in the case of an attempted entry. He tested the reach; practiced it twice for feel, and then he briefly rest his eyes. After long hours silent in wind and rain and the passing of rain, it was in this short crush of velvet dark that a small piece of Brubeck flickered into the low corners of his thought.

A large white Dodge truck crept to a stop near the building on Nebraska. A hulking extended cab dually; even opposite the service station, some two hundred sixty feet from Hussar and through the window frame across the room, he could hear the tappet-clatter of diesel at rest. For some fifteen minutes it rest.

Generally Hussar would be cycling his breathing by now, minding his heart rate, slowing it—feeling for the downstroke of its intersti-tial track. But at eighty meters little beyond the force of habit was required; perhaps not even that. On a still day, as it had become, eighty meters was reaching out and placing a thumbtack; pressing it home. Yesterday had been blustery—ten to twenty east-northeast turning east; today, a steady one and a half to three, northeast; over this distance it was a motion six hundred ninety-six grain .50 BMG would fail to notice. 8:45 the faint noise of tappets stopped and four men quit the truck for the apartment. They were: one middle-height in heavy corded sweater; a stocky figure with hands jammed in his coveralls; one tall and sloped at the shoulder—bald with a short wreath of hair and black topcoat; and one middle-built with a full head and face of close-shorn stubble and flight jacket; and Hussar watched them move with directed ease up and into the building.

8:55 Joe Morello was on drums, bouncy and tribal. The men moved through the apartment; beyond its windows. A black Mercedes slowed along Nebraska. S-class sedan. Crept past the apartment building; past the parked up dually; past the service station; out of view. Well, well. New player?—thought Hussar—and nestled into the buttstock; cozied into the reticle with a smile—looking perhaps to raise the stakes? 3800 block of Nebraska, a late model S-class was a chess pawn on a checkerboard: a piece out of context. A dealer pissing his territories; a drug tourist out of his depth—were certainly possible—county parishioner lost to both a sense of magnitude and direction, was possible too. The fullness of time will tell.

9:00. Purported call time. He expected five as a party of two parts, but so far had received four and a random variable. Second floor, south, on Nebraska, the men still shuffled about. Hussar tracked them through the rooms, followed them through the windows, beyond the walls, marked their motions, their distribution; emplacements. He had been to the unit, had been through it in his preparations, and he overlaid its features on the men as they milled loosely about it—its rooms and volumes, wall partitions, cover, and the blind fortification of the front room: a presentation in sashless full brick; an unfenestrated blind spot for which Hussar had only the Raufoss and an animal intuition. 9:01 the party of four took up stations front and rear of the apartment house, fell to marks like a cast awaiting stage lights. Hussar donned the muffs, adjusted them for fit, and in them found a new volume for his interior music—filled in the heavy shade. And he deliberated over the best round to begin.

Snap, dap, duba, duba, doh. Dum-dap, snap, daba, duba doh.

AP, he decided. Might get off two clean deliveries before they scatter. Magazine of black-snouted cartridges; fit it, drove it home with a pat; drew the bolt back like a sling, chambered the cartridge; bore down on the stock with his shoulder to prevent slap, and carefully squared his feet. And he waited. And he watched the men wait.

Hussar had opted against subsonic loads to maximize kinetic transfer. The suppressor wouldn't cure flight-snap, that would remain, but over so short a distance; instantaneous; they'd be there before their own noise. The suppressor would defeat muzzle flash—set deep in the unlighted room. And as for the hard enclosure, it should reduce the overpressure—reduce the dazzle—fend off the awe-strike of the untempered Barrett.

9:15 was still. What is that tune?—he wondered. "Far More Blues"?

9:30 Flight jacket figure moving in the kitchen. Pacing past the small window. Out of view. Into view. Head cast down. Out of view. Into view. No, this is 5/4. "Far More Blues" is 4/4, right? Yes, 4/4.

Whap-snap, duba, daba, doh.

9:40 Party of the second part? Sniffed some bad air, did he? Flight jacket figure, out of view, into view, cupping his ear, out of view.

Snap-dap, whap-snap.

9:45 Drum version. It's the drum version of "Far More Blues." "Far More Drums"! It's "Far More Drums"! Yes. Yes.

Motion. Motion. Coveralls to the back. In the kitchen. Flight jacket, past the center room window. Heavy sweater? Heavy sweater, front. Too long. Baldy, past the center window. This is too long. In the toilet? Yes. The toilet.

Dum-dap, snap, duba, duba, doh.

Missing pieces? Just too long. This is too long. Stood up, gentlemen. 9:45 and

31 . . . 32 . . . No. We're gonna wrap this up. I'm calling it. Time. I'm calling time.

Dum-dap-snap, dap-snap, duba, duba, doh.

"Catch," muttered Hussar into the buttstock. A deep *thoom* seemed to emanate from between the muffs. The rifle punched his shoulder. Dust leaped from the floor. A hole opened in the kitchen window glass. And where the figure in coveralls had stood there was now only haze on the air.

Hussar inched left and swept the sight picture twenty feet east along the wall. Center room window: the baited trap. This is where he'd see if he'd called correctly. Still. Still. Figure entered the frame. Rifle punch. Leap of the bipod. Lift of dust. Hole in the window glass and a pillow of atomized and over-penetrated plaster.

Toilet. Two quick shots into the toilet, over the bowl; into the tub: *thoom, thoom.* Castoff brass now ringing like chimes.

Front room. Low left corner—he'll be low by now—herd him back. Punch. Thrown casing. Perforation in the brick. Mag change—drop the can, drive the can, draw the bolt.

Dum-dap . . . dum-snap . . . dum . . . dum . . . doh.

5.

Hussar swiftly drew up the corners of a thin drop he'd laid out to collect brass. He dismantled the rifle and rolled it into a cloth wrap on a sling. He stowed his gear, shoved the bookcase into the corner, and hurled the milk crate into another room. He left by the back stair, and as he swung around the side of the building the bald man in the topcoat stumbled out of the apartment house on Nebraska. He emerged from the door in a gypsum plume and a sort of running fall, skimmed the front stair and stormed away in the white truck as quickly as it could be roused and forced into gear.

Hussar blinked irritably at the sight and moved quickly. He had only a few minutes now. He moved up the bricked alley to the apartment, and through a back gate. Above a brief sag of wooden step, Hussar collected two five gallon buckets he'd placed previously. They were lidded and heavy and he hurried with them up the back stair, which bowed and wrenched at the weight. At the highest landing he put out a small window, reached through to release the deadbolt, and entered the southern flat through the narrow door.

Hussar left the buckets in the center room, looked in on the bath with its shattered sink and punctured tub, shook his head, and searched the figures that remained. He searched the torso in coveralls and turned out an apple core and folding knife—the heavy corded sweater in the center room and the figure in the flight jacket slumped low on the wall in the front room, and drew nothing but small arms and spare rounds. He noted the six perforations through the brick of the southern front wall, and the exit wounds of the five tungsten penetrators in the plaster opposite. Hussar opened the buckets of nitromethane. He removed a thermite grenade from his kit, removed the pin; installed it in the mouth of the flight jacket figure—lever into the cheek. He collected bits of teeth and jaw bone from near the other two—"Imagine your look of surprise," he said—cast them into one bucket with their affects, and with the other, doused the three figures liberally. He inventoried his things, wet a piece of lathe in the bucket, put a lighter to it, toss it on a runoff puddle, and when he saw it aggressively light, he left immediately down the back stair.

6.

The cargo van was up the block in the alley, nosed into a garage stall with daylight holes and a twist of overhead door that could be drawn like a shade but not closed. Beside it a Monte Carlo lay flat on its oil pan, the carcass gleaned open by predations. Marek Hussar had entered at the rear, stowed his things, and climbed through to the cab. He'd made his way along backs streets, migrated with slow diligence stop sign to stop sign, light to light. He'd pulled in at a contractor supply warehouse. Rounded to the docks, changed his clothes in the van and left them and his other painter's tools and trappings in the dumpsters.

He'd looped out 55 to Highway 270, and back in along 40. In the rental lot, he'd transferred the Barrett and his gear back to the trunk of the M5. He'd turned in the van, and stood waiting in a corporate incarnation of two-room hut. A high-station carpeted shed, were it not for the spoilage of computers by rain, he wagered, would instead have been standard issue rain hats and recommendations for a comfortable shoe. He'd stood at the counter in the pretence of patience. A duo in dark suits—a blond in his cuticles; and a brunette on a call, a silk round her neck like a sailor's sash, and the deep, close eyes of a disadvantageous breeding—were staff. He'd out-waited the call and reluctant keystrokes for the formalizing measure of slip—and when he had it, cast it in a refuse bin past the door.

In the car "Yama" had come over with the ignition, played in the speakers with cool piano and soft bourbon horns, and he took it in clean restorative draughts. He was tired and filled with three days of evening, and it had given the day a queer inverted turn— made it flat-lit and false: the night in photonegative. He picked up 170 from Ladue, eased into the bend of ramp, merged, fished for his sunglasses, and when he'd checked his mirror a black sedan had crowned the ramp from Ladue; a Mercedes he thought, and Hussar dove immediately cross a lane and down the Forest Park Parkway off ramp to hand; a long eastbound sweeper that folded back beneath the highway, and presently, would cast a stamp of clarification. He passed an opening of Clayton parkland. To his left office towers rose. And in the mirror he searched for the sedan. The ramp was empty when it dropped from view. Then it appeared. On the final beat of the final plausible measure, it emerged beneath the retreating brow of overpass. It hung back, slipped along a staggered distance behind, and Hussar thought, had made a revealing effort to delay its drop down the ramp. It was a Mercedes to be sure, the features of its pointy, smug, insinuating glower were clear. The sills, hunch of roof, cut of nose, and scale, said it was an S-class. But at this standoff, the question of type remained.

The Parkway rose into Clayton, ran like a fortification in concrete pour and lane markers; bent left around the business district, and passed beneath flyovers, footpaths, and high paved embankments; a sleek gray canyon, which eventually opened out into Jersey barrier and guardrail. And all the while the Mercedes closed on him by discrete, imperceptible degrees. Hussar moved slightly above the posted limit, and he let him come; watched and wanted him to come; wanted him near; wanted a closer look. They made the light at Pershing and Hussar coasted up to the crossing at Big Bend. Traffic shot down either side through the intersection. The lane beside queued for the light, and the Mercedes drew in slowly and stopped a full car length back. Scripted security move, thought Hussar; someone a bit handy then—not just an analyst with a checked piece and a field pass.

The chin bore the aggressive AMG valence. It meant little in itself, but suggested problematic flavors. S55 or S600, thought Hussar; but judging from this view was like guessing conviction from a grimace. Windows were blacked and he could make out little beside eight Caucasoid knuckles wrapping the wheel. Hussar tuned off the stereo, defeated the traction control and cued the performance throttle mapping with a pair of switches. He cycled the gear pattern for tolerances and rhythm. And now he searched for the yellow against cross-traffic, and watched the Mercedes edge in.

At the light the exhaust bellowed: quickly rapt to a wail at the top of the gear. The rear stepped out on power: launched with a squat through the intersection. Change up: two: Hussar rolled on throttle until the clutch hooked up: flat now. Change up: three: a column of cars drifted ahead: left lane—he bounced out to pass before they spread. The university rushed by to the right: a small truck flashed an indicator to the left, and began to cut out. Hussar lifted slightly; squared right for room. In the mirror the Mercedes' nose was invisible—up the trunk. If he let up they'd touch. Turbo dump-valves chirped and whistled from the Mercedes. Gnashing teeth. Rounded the truck: flat now. Fourth: roll on power: flat now. Flat: flat: he was pulling a gap—getting some air in. Ahead, light for a side street was changing: yellow: a pair of cars lined for their turn: red: he tucked left: flat past a nose: fifth. Mercedes checked-up: went wide offline: missed the car: cleared the curbing. A space now: five car lengths. Skinker rushed up brushing three figures on the gauges. Rev-match the shifts: down four: brake: down three: brake, brake: too hot.

Mercedes was on top of him again. Five cars slowed for the light: closed the lanes. Dove for the turn lane; ripped left around the cars and straight: rolled on power through the crossing. Turning traffic honked and jolted. When the rear settled, flat down the long divided straight: change up: four. Narrow. Five. He was gapping the Mercedes again: the weight and softer springs upset it over junctions. Traffic on the right: again. Rise at the light: lift: touch of brake: change down: four. He'd given the gap back now: Mercedes mouthing at the pipes. Full compression over the rise: went light off the back. Mercedes squirreled and hopped half a lane: dropped back off the pedals. Settle: settle: back on power: five. Fast now: very fast. Pavement getting choppy: Mercedes struggling to close over the rougher ground. Traffic on the right: on the right: left: left: right. Union ahead. Lift: touch of brake: four: touch of brake: high manhole cover: center up: lift: manhole cover, two: manhole cover, three. Maintenance throttle, bending right, touch of brake, straighten left: touch: touch. Light at Union: brand new yellow. Mercedes coming up: on the right, nosing alongside. Big compression now—clapped off the bump stops. Deeper on the right: Mercedes folded full-down over the wheels— and up: lept off the rise—over it. Chassis light: wait for the front to load: the rear: settle the corners. Mercedes landed hard in the mirrors: bounded right: scrubbed the curb. Six, eight, ten car lengths now. Long open straight. Flat: change up: five. Flat: flat: flat: needles sweeping right: hurdling along tar joints: clopclopclopclop. Pair of cars shouldering up at the horizon: slow: into a right-hand bend: slow. Closing. Closing. Boxed up both lanes: flash the lights. Jersey wall on the paint line, inside—half-lane shoulder and Armco, out. Closing fast. Flash the lights. Lift to coast.

Brake

Change down: four: change down: three: brake: brake: change down: two. Pedal going soft: tires getting hot, greasy. Mercedes closing fast: still flat out: dives under braking: drops the chin: locks all four corners: slip angle drift. Car on the right merging out for Lindell exit: opening a gap: opening: dive in: power on: flat top of second: back stepping out: through: change up: three. Exhaust wash bathes the car left: rears in fright: clips the wall: cuts hard away: back over-center. Mercedes commits, behind: takes the gap: plays right: parts the mirror with a hip-check. Gap out to six lengths. Mercedes coming hard now: running center-dash like a guide wire. Change up: four: line left for traffic: one, two: square for the underpass: firm brake: water on the floor: off brakes: maintenance throttle: full shade: out into left sweeper: steep, descending off-camber left: squeeze on throttle: gentle: more: more: load the corner: more: opening into a straight: roll on power. Flat. Staggered traffic: lift: throttle, right: lift: throttle, left: countersteer jab. Flat: change up: five. Descending. Mercedes rounding traffic. Closing. Flat. Underpass into off-camber right: change down: four: set the nose: brake: feather in—firm—feather off: more water: light throttle: flash of shade. Falling steeply now: down and away: closing radius right: add throttle: gently: add throttle: more: more. Easing out from the heavy Mercedes. More: steady: balance: skirting the wall: haunches squat into the corner: ass pinned down under power. Opening out: flat now: change up: five. Mercedes surging down the short leveling straight. Uphill now: right-hand slip to a tight left crest. Inside line. Mercedes to the outside: set to square the apex. Rising. Keep the foot in it. Rising. Big speed. Stay in it. Starting left. Stay in it. Tightening. Set the nose: touch of brake. Tightening. Ease off. Tightening. Lifting. Sharp throttle now; cut into the apex. Mercedes cut across: inside. Pressing in. Gap to two. Light over the crest, and steeply down. Straightening. Change down: four: power on. Buildings rising over Kingshighway. Mercedes has momentum: filling the mirror. Shoot beneath Kingshighway: dim bunker of underpass. Back uphill. Traffic inside: out and back. Mercedes close. Gap to one. Closing. Dump valves whistling, snorting in his ear. Traffic filling in: slowing for Euclid. Rising: hurdling up: heavy embankment thinning to grade. Two lanes opening into four. Med center buildings crowding the light. Cars stacking up in the left turn lane. Signal going full orange. Cars filling out three outer lanes. One through lane inside. Wingover thought Hussar. Scrub some speed. Lift. Gap to zero. Touch of brake. Full mirror of black hood. Into the shoot. Onto the light.

Lift

Flick right: touch of power: opposite lock: e-brake: ass out: around: across the intersection: change down: two: into the oncoming lanes: power on: slipping backward: sideways: clear the corner: rear hooking up: noise turning to grip. Horns and diverging shapes. Mercedes fired through the intersection: fury of brake lights. And back downhill. Launching west: full-throated, off, and back along the parkway.

X.

Kim Soong unfastened her hair, brushed it with a fearsome tool from her bag, and tightly refit the cable as it had been. When she'd finished she resumed her position in the armchair: knees together, palms upon them, her narrow lap filled with carryall. Soong had arrived just after room service. She'd come up with a pair of suits draped in dry-clean plastics and a frisson of noise—to all appearances a delivery girl; lay them on the bed and folded herself neatly into the chair, where she remained.

Hoyt Gamlin last shaved two days ago, in D.C. He'd been interrupted from the task by room service, and again by Soong, and now finished with a blade the act of civilizing pretence he'd begun before. He followed Soong in the mirror, her gaze trailing surreptitiously in toward his bare torso and then swerving off to hold on other visual anchors. He rinsed and dried on fresh towel and felt fully and finally clean. He rolled a shirt on, retrieved a vodka from the honor bar, and settled on the sofa with his coffee and orange juice—his back to the French doors which looked out from the Ritz-Carlton, Clayton, and onto the county and the feather of winter canopy. This was Soong's anchor now, and whenever Gamlin saw that she was not contemplating her knees, or the bowels of her giant bag, this was her view.

"Those fit me?" he asked, of the suits on the bed. She appraised him openly this time, and shook her head—full no. He offered the vodka—again, no. "Suit yourself." He in-filled the juice till it troubled the brim. "If all God's children knew full and virtuous splendor by sight, there'd be bugger-all left to me. To fallen comrades," he said with a gesture, and drained off the top. He chased it with coffee and she watched him motionlessly. Gamlin drew a pair of enlargements from an envelope on the coffee table and toss them down before her. "Know him?" he asked. He smoothed his sparse, damp blond hair and reclined into the sofa with his juice and his ethanol warmth.

Soong separated the images with index fingers. "What is this?" she asked.

"Two weeks fruit-meat," answered Gamlin. "Frame captures. Closed circuit."

"Who is it?"

"You ever seen him?"

"Skinhead in a bomber? He deliver pizza?"

"You know it lovey—I can never tell when you're joking: something 'bout your demeanor."

"Next time I'll tap my foot."

"Light a flare," said Gamlin.

"I don't know him," she said, and pushed the pictures back toward Gamlin. "Who is it?"

"Some fixer. Name of August Reams."

She shook her head again.

"I wouldn't think it," said Gamlin. "Our moon-face mandarin friends were all out of ideas, too. I'd to ring up old mates to work it out."

"Is that a risk?"

"When we're all scribing Hanzi with a fucking brush, you and your people can have it all your own way. Until such time, I'll draw my own plays."

Soong lay a long, heavy look at him he took for doubt. But he couldn't be sure. She drew a rumpled pack of Marlborough Lights from her bag, and he nodded toward the balcony. She stepped out through a French door, lit one on a grape convenience store lighter, and exhaled gamely back into the room. Gamlin skimmed from his glass and settled further into the sofa. "Any other shocking habits to confess?" Gamlin called over the sofa back and smiled.

"The stills are from where?" she asked.

"Kashkin's hotel in Mexico City, and the departure lounge."

"Kashkin was yours?"

"Pavel Kashkin. I ran him, yes. He was mine."

"How'd you get them?"

"Do you know what?" Gamlin laughed, "they were all snugged away till the police took them. Rounded the closed circuit footage, and from there it was light reading. Cost me a return trip, four packs of draught Guinness—they've a Sergeant who likes it: says the widget's always wrong—and a clean 1911. He should have that by now. But, maybe that's bloody expensive for Mexico!" said Gamlin, who rose to share his expression over the sofa.

"For frame captures?"

"No. The tapes."

"Copies?"

"Nah, original tapes. Hard to say how, but I imagine their files must have got damaged. Corrupted…somehow. Call it intuition. It's a pitiable loss."

"Are you the only one who knows who you're looking for, then?"

"We are," said Gamlin.

"Is that what you want?"

"We do. No good him getting rolled up somewhere we can't reach him. Competition's for chumps and republics, right Kim Soong."

"What is a 'widget'?" she asked, as a bee struck against one of the door mullions with an audible tap, and clung to it in lethargy. Soong observed it with a shiver.

"He's bloody out of season."

"It's been unusually warm most of the week," she said.

She exhaled vaguely, pressed out the butt with the tow of her sneaker, fastened the door behind her, and knitted herself quietly back beneath the bag in the chair. Soong was young and featureless and porcelain-fine, and resumed her unstructured collapse of slouch as before. Gamlin wondered if she'd evaporate in self-dispraise. And if she did, what would become of her enormous, scrotinous droop of tote?

"Widget's a nitrogen capsule in a draught Guinness can. Ever had a Guinness?"

She shook her head.

"I wouldn't think it. You live a fevered, unbridled life, Kim Soong: low tar fags and dry-clean laundry. At this pace you're liable to blow."

"I don't think you know me so well as to dislike me," she said, and blinked, and blinked. Gamlin thought she was straining against touching her face, thought if she didn't master the urge soon she'd leave rope burns.

"You'd be right to think it; but you'd be wrong to imagine it's true. But listen: your English is perfection. So, good on ya."

"I've got it you're some speckled Anglo from danglesey: mineral rights to empire and all. But I guess I don't understand why you called in for me. I'm fed: I'm not hungry for *your* shit."

Gamlin laughed. "Ah, fuck it Kimberly! Let's be friends. I've lost the urge, and you've stole my wee heart away."

"That's the screwdriver, Hoyt. Have another and we can do lab trials: see if your kingdom expands or contracts."

"It is love!"

"What...do...you...want, Gamlin? Before I call Hubei—tell them you're wasting my time, and to have you mounted on your own shaft. I've got my own work," she said, and brushed her cheek with her hand, just once, and then smothered it beneath the bag.

"Mouth on a lamp string," Gamlin said with mock astonishment. "Fags and blowjobs made you tough after all. Well, Kimberly . . . you know Howard Foster?"

"Dr. Foster? I had his class three years ago: senior year. Yes, I know him."

"Kashkin was working him when he set off for Mexico. Followed him back from a conference in Beijing. He was working him here in St. Louis. Left for Washington. Something got hotted up and he split for Mexico City—thought he had something, and called me down for a rolling handoff. When he doesn't turn up I find him stuffed in his hotel bath."

"Dr. Foster?"

"That's who he was covering. I told him it was fallow, but he persisted. Hubei thought Foster was recruiting from Chinese trade shows—tech and security conferences. They wanted somebody on him. Kashkin was in Bejing at the time. I put him on. I thought it was a loser. Then Foster hired Kashkin—for his divorce, I presume. I thought it might be a ruse. Kashkin thought it might be gold—no clue as why. And then he said he had something: something good. Then our August Reams turns up for a very brief tour in Mexico. And now Kashkin doesn't drink anymore." Gamlin sat up to dribble what vodka was left into the glass, and stirred it with his finger.

"You liked him."

"Kashkin? If it matters. I like a man, you know what he's about."

"Is this Reams serious?"

"People in D.C. think he's capable, but say snuffing's not his main thing. Does drug logistics, mainly. Some enforcement. High-power problem solving. Runs some players through Kansas City, St. Louis, Atlanta; and loose teams in Chicago, D.C., New York, and Boston. Guess he got boxed out of Philadelphia. Mainly Atlantic corridor sort of thing."

"So, what's the connection?"

"Well that's to work out, isn't it. But Foster's here and so is Reams. Or he was. Left from here for Mexico—so I'm told. And returned here after."

"That's a close loop for a busy man."

"So said I."

Soong rose and left the bag in her place. She fetched a cup from the credenza at the door and returned to have coffee from Gamlin's carafe. She took cream and sweetener from fiddly packets, and Gamlin's unused spoon.

"Add more and they charge for dessert," said Gamlin.

"What about do-it-yourself cocktails?"

Soong wore jeans, a quilt coat she'd put over the chair, and what to Gamlin was an odd brocade blouse. It was close at the shoulder and wide at the hem and swung unsteadily as she moved, and Gamlin thought she looked the tongue of a ringing bell.

She took the time from a slender watch that might've been inert costume jewelry: "Half-past eleven, Hoyt. You could be drunk by one."

"With a little effort, sooner," said Gamlin. "And see there, I'd just thought we were getting on.

"You say you know Foster. How well?" he asked.

"Not well. When I had his class I was on light watch. But Hubei's got their internship now—so I've been concentrating on that. I know for a while he was palling with this student—we were in Dr. Foster's class together: Jeffrey Sachs."

"He is?"

"Grad student at the university. Supposed to be a slick programmer: big talent. Some mutual friends—pretty reliable parties—said he might be working on a side project with Dr. Foster, or maybe for him. But nobody's seen him since New Year's—and what is it?" She looked again at her costume jewelry watch. "The twenty-seventh? He's got family in the east, I understand—so people think maybe he ditched out and went back home for a semester. Family illness or something, I don't know."

"What might he be doing with Foster?"

"Recruiting him, maybe?"

"Where's he from?"

"Here. The U.S."

"Not likely then."

"Well, if it was side work, and you'd brought Sachs on to code, you'd have brought the right guy."

Gamlin tugged deeply from the glass and cleared its dewy sides with his thumb. "You know Foster by sight?"

"He'll be the one ducking power lines."

"Tall, is he?"

"Hard to miss."

"He look alright to you?"

"He's tall for me—anyone but Greek heroes really."

"He look alright otherwise?"

"He's fine, I suppose."

"Maybe you should know him better."

2.

Hoyt Gamlin had been on the road some two weeks—his trips to and from Mexico, his phone calls and favors and promises: his beer and a gun. He'd wheeled out by car from his L.A. condo to Pavel Kashkin's attorneys' offices in Washington, D.C. He'd pecked around Kashkin's offices as a client forlorn with questions, and elsewhere, working to untangle Kashkin's steps through D.C. to the point he'd slipped off for Mexico City. Gamlin had forwarded the digital bank of files to Hubei from Los Angeles: between the hotel and the airport, forty-eight hours across thirty-two cameras to be run through recognition software, and played for what Gamlin imagined to be a roomful of fifty Chinese all the bespectacled look of Mr. Moto, and raising a tobacco smoke like Beijing industrial fog. He floated this image receiving Soong's armchair quiz on sources—an ageless prepubescent mid-twenties waif tuning static on his methods.

His footwork in D.C. had remained largely fruitless until he'd heard back from Hubei on the footage. Whether by rock-crushing mainframe or legion of nicotine inspired Chins—the turn was 'stonishing fast. As he'd suggested, they crossed traffic near Kashkin's room with the footage from the international terminals, and swiftly provided a match. But as with Soong, this sort of thing was a categorical weakness—a blind spot the size of all Caucasia. The Chinese had become

expert at smuggling corporate data systems and siphoning off anything not bolted to the floor. Pinching files, decades of tax declarations, accounting and staff ledgers—public, private, privileged or
otherwise: they were scanned and collated and cross-referenced—
rooted and foraged with a truffle pig's flair. Mailing list or security permission: if you were on an inventory, you could be found.
Otherwise, you were in the boundless reaches beyond data. In near
Asia, their HUMINT—their human intelligence—was quite good: a
body could be dug out of hiding in Taiwan; Hong Kong—plucked
up and spirited off. In the bucolic swathes of alabaster pallor: the
chasm yawned off into imagination. Operating in North America,
if you weren't coded into a lift-able database of assets, you were as
well as unknowable to the hand-wringers back east. And it was in
large part to this point that Gamlin had been attractive to the Chin.
Castoff parts and pension back in the U.K.; security consultant like a
corporate Pilates coach to baby tech titans in California; a bit of trigger muscle off in the camel-sands; but the whole of a full-functioning
machine to Hubei—or so he was paid. But just as he with Soong
there at the balcony door; her playground lighter and diet cigarettes:
they did not trust him. But they did not trust him for the same reason that he did not like them: the isolation of tribes—mountainous
impasses; deserts gravid with emptiness; and language which grows
to cleave beyond common meaning. They wanted him, they needed
him, but they would not trust to use him as they might; and it had
become a recurring and perceptible omission.

The cross-referenced stills had come back to Gamlin in D.C. with
shrugs and blank expressions, and he'd been left to work out what his
minders, in the zenith of their inabilities, could not. He was unfamiliar with the figure in the stills as well, but it took little imagination
to appreciate he possessed physical power to manhandle Kashkin,

technique, and some measure of skill. He was no pizza boy. He'd traipsed the images round Washington a few days to a collective bemusement, until finally he'd traded them to an old friend in the U.K. for a future reciprocation: a friend who'd long ago swapped his SAS face paints for an MI6 redacting pen. It was he who first put face to name. He recognized him as a fairly competent doer and finder and mover of things. They'd used him on occasions when they'd required vendors in the U.S. eastern corridor but weren't coordinating with the CIA—or moreover, sharing.

Now, with this, a caption for his photos; when Gamlin tried around again, memories began to clear; recollections began to jog. And once he'd put this August Reams into and out of St. Louis—a line circling back toward Foster—the third figure in the geometry, he reached out to Hubei about Soong.

Hoyt Gamlin had crossed paths with Soong a few years prior on business through St. Louis: he'd taken reflexive disliking to her then, and he took viscerally to that reflex now. Kim Soong was a graduate student at Washington University; she was a native to the mainland: she was skin and kin and well liked. Moreover, she'd gained an internship at Boeing and in one stroke greatly elevated her station. For Hubei, she'd become the gilded swan or the jade duck, or the whatever- the-fuck, in her section: word was she was feeding back a steady stream of tasty morsels, and the Directorate had sincerest hopes for more and better. So, when Gamlin put in for some of her bandwidth, suddenly there was slack in the line. There was shuffling—a pandering reluctance—but in the end if someone was putting down footmen, he'd get a download from her, and some time. Nevertheless, Gamlin found her disagreeable as a taped chair leg: flawed, not by intent, but natural condition. If Kashkin were a concert in reassuring faults, Soong was a fugue in atonal virtues: for

Gamlin, a disconcerting strength of composition in all the wrong good. It was a condition of her nature that lay against him with the bristling mortification of haircloth, but with none of the mollifying pleasure of contrition. He felt it when she crossed his running toast of Kashkin quoting time from her costume watch; and days later, parked opposite the Cheshire Inn, he would feel it whenever she rummaged through her split sow of purse, its clatter of lipstick tubes and mysterious daubs and balms, its breath of old gum, and the grim silence, which Gamlin took as the welcome sound of retributive intention, levied against him by Soong as they sat watch on the hotel.

The Cheshire Inn was a brown and tan Tudor with a heavy porte cochère shading the door: a seventeenth century half-timber coaching inn, plucked from history and screwed to the curb of a frantic intersection beneath a waxing shout of Amoco ellipse. It was a location they'd covered through the thronging traffic from the opposite curb, and it was the location, with some doing, that Gamlin had put August Reams to. Soong was annoyed at the fieldwork, and restless, and oddly noisy for all her labors of silence. They'd been there four hours with coffee and a telephoto camera, and the interminable contents of Soong's bag when a large white dually drew up to fill the porte cochère, and a figure the convincing likeness of August Reams stepped from the hotel to the truck, and Gamlin started the car.

3.

Kim Soong sat on a brick step puzzling over something on the sole of her shoe when Hoyt Gamlin pulled in to fetch her. He pictured her hiking up Forsyth along the school and the quarter block off campus along Maryland: a rangy stoop of girl with a freight of backpack and a click of stone in her tread. The day was mid February dishwater and salivary mist of rain as he'd swept down Maryland to collect her; a quiet length of roof gable and pin oak which stared dead into the university's gluteal terminus—an athletic complex which rose along Big Bend as a blush battlement of mercantile apparatus. She'd sat glistening between two beds of rattling ivy—Gamlin could hear their parchment tremor when he'd put down the window—and with her slim jacket perishing warmth, Gamlin took her demeanor for a thing like relief. She was glad for the car, if not also for him.

Kim Soong hoist her pack into the back seat and joined him up front with a sigh and scent of damp fur. It had been several weeks since they'd camped the Cheshire and tailed August Reams and his ride—a local associate whose truck registration said he was Edmund LeFrance of Zephyr Lane. And what the work of between days said, was that Reams liked drive-through coffee and Mexican carryout, and LeFrance liked diesel fuel and green produce and cards; and between the two they'd recently taken unaccountable interest

in abandoned Dutchtown real estate. But as to matters of whyfor—
nothing more had emerged.

Gamlin had phoned her in recent days, but hadn't seen her in
weeks, and doing so seemed an abridgement both parties might
happily forego. And so it was in this spirit of occasion that Gamlin
thought to compliment her attire.

"You look a pussy in a windsock," he said.

"Pussy?"

"Cat. On a day in equatorial January you're running about in a bed
quilt, and now it's shitting cold, and you think a piece of nylon kite
looks just the trick."

Soong blotted her face in her jacket lining. "I was inside all day.
And don't work your bellows on my account: you'll just fog the
windows."

Gamlin smiled and set off.

"Did you talk to him?"

"Not today. Yesterday. And I saw him in passing a few days before
that."

"And? How was it?"

"I was nice and impressed."

"And he was?"

"Like he was getting spotty reception: preoccupied and aloof with
short windows of nervous attention. Also . . . he's just so fucking tall:
feel like I should be waving semaphore. It's kinda too much."

"Not your thing, is it?"

She shook her head.

"And what is?"

"What's opposite a sunburn-swollen albino?"

"A squint of black-hair drain rat, thinks it's a zoo panther," said Gamlin. "But that's just a guess. I give up, tell me."

But Soong made a pool of breath in the door glass, and touched it with the back of her hand.

"Where's he now?" he asked.

"He's got office hours for another thirty minutes or so. He likes to park behind the building off Throop."

"Then let us go see him there."

4.

Kim Soong averted her gaze. When that seemed inadequate she fixed her brow in the visor of her hand. "He'll see me, Gamlin, this is stupid."

Gamlin laughed. "Are you hiding or guarding your eyes?"

She lifted her visor to see him, and replaced it. And Gamlin laughed again.

"No. He won't," said Gamlin. "That's a promise. You could shake his hand, and he'd be none the wiser."

"What?"

"I said: He'd never see you here."

"You're wrong."

"You're shepherd's pie at a cookery fair. You're deluded. He'll never, ever, see you.

"Hey! Oi! Don't be a fool, get that hand out your face!—I said, he'll never see you—but you look a cunt with your hand up," said Gamlin.

Soong removed the hand and lay the matching pair in her lap.

They'd tucked into the deck-shade of a parking garage with favorable view and watched Charles Foster emerge forty minutes later to his black Suburban from the service doors of Bryan Hall. Twice Gamlin had her confirm it: clothes and car and man. From there they'd followed to a private gym on Forsyth near the parkway. Parking lot of slippery Europeans and second-life economy tuners in wings and flares, together in aspirational contrivance. It was sloped and broad and they sat within clear sight of the entrance. They'd watched him dismount and teeter off with his bow-stepped cowboy hitch, head tipped to the rain; and marked collecting water on the windscreen until his return. An hour and a half Gamlin wondered why he wouldn't use the campus facility; wondered it out loud to Soong, who floated indifferent shrugs at it: contract or privacy or habit. Maybe he just likes it here, she'd said, and he'd thought on it over a sideways glance.

They'd trailed him up the pea gravel streets where he lived. He'd pulled up to his house, wrong-way against the curb, and run in. He'd stopped for drive-through and then he'd streamed east out the dive and jog articulation of Highway 40, across the river and down the plunge of Route 3; the gas candles and flood-green haze of refinery light, drop-stitch pavements and crush-stone lots, and the metastasizing cairn of architectural leavings.

They'd arrived after dark and watched him park up and go inside: struggle to brush the last bit of damp from his hair, and throw the door wide, as he might an old familiar shed. She'd turned to him as they rolled off to the side and out of lamplight: You've gotta be kidding, she'd said. He'd held out his fingers in illustration: You've got five minutes to find it, and then you'd best believe: and she'd shook her head violently all the walk in.

Now they sat against a Formica table in the inaudible dip of vinyl booth-seats, and Gamlin watched Soong not watch the bare-breasted duo on stage as though the avoidance bore some needs for overt demonstration. The room smelt to him of Rosco Fog and markdown cologne. He said: You'd better have a drink 'fore you irritate piss out of me. She said: What?—and he waved to the cocktail waitress though the viscid air: tacky he imagined, with the same agents kept it aqueous clear.

"Where is he now?" she asked when the drinks came.

"You know, I was certain I'd see the hind 'aneath all your furs at some point, but I wouldn't have guessed it'd be this that bared it."

"Where is he now?"

"He's there," said Gamlin. "With the girl, near the stage. See? There. Standing—they're the ones going off to the hall."

"What's down there?"

"You are joking?" Gamlin turned and leveled a stern look, but she tapped him on the sleeve.

"Look," she said. "He's not watching the girls either." And they both looked. And there was a man seated away from a stage and to himself. Drinking from a plastic beer cup. And he was not watching the girls, but followed Foster intently, until he'd passed entirely from view.

5.

Hoyt Gamlin sat past the corner of Keokuk and Nebraska. By his Luminor's counting he'd been idling there forty-three minutes. He'd slept fitfully. He'd risen early and gracelessly. He'd bathed in slow, unconscious gestures. He'd prepared bitter coffee in the urn. And he'd left alone, with bottled waters and cereal bars dangling in thin grocery plastic. Mercifully, Soong had internship duties. She'd spend the day lifting Boeing memoranda like office supplies. He'd been free of her several weeks and was perfectly glad: free of her and her special frisson of dark silence.

He'd set up that morning again cross Clayton from the Cheshire. But he hadn't been long before the white dually had rolled in once more to fill the porte cochère—filled it like a mastiff in a travel crate. August Reams had joined the truck. There were two already packed into the extended cab, and his company made four. The quartet gave Gamlin the impression of a purposeful socializing. Today they were up to business, and with the addition of eyes Gamlin let out the cord and followed from altitude.

They stopped for drive-through coffee, deftly edged the truck through the slip, and cackled off to Dutchtown trailing soot from the stovepipe exhaust. They'd parked and waited, and eventually stacked into a four family beside a vacant service station, and when they'd been awhile he'd moved up and past and settled across the corner at Keokuk for better view. And now he'd sat forty-four minutes with the engine turning a bass note played somewhere from the audible cusp and vents whispering warmth into the cabin, and a side mirror focused back at the building, and he tried to settle on his next move when he heard something like a nail gun.

And again.

Like a nail gun, but higher and sharper: more lash in the tail. Gamlin peered from the side glass, and back at the building.

And again. And again.

Two whiffs of red masonry lifted near the corners of a window.

Again.

Gamlin craned over and between the seats to see. A puncture in the broadside of the second story wall.

And again, and again, and again, and again, and again.

A tidy row of them opened up with a small incendiary knock. "Jesus Christ!" he said and sat crouched in the car. The last report melted from the air, and it was still. Then the tall one, the bald one with the topcoat burst from the door. The driver—LeFrance; Edmund LeFrance—burst through the door and stumbled down the stairs. His black coat was pale with plaster dust and it seemed to hang in the air where he'd been. He tripped out alone and rushed to the truck and unlocked the truck and bent over the column with the key and turned the key and the diesel groaned to recalcitrant life and he slapped down the shifter and the truck lurched from the curb and past in a clamorous belch of coal dust.

Gamlin noticed a figure. A man. He emerged from somewhere on Keokuk and moved behind the service station. He bore a sling over his shoulder with paint rollers and extension handles. He was clad in painter's white. Booties and blue disposable gloves. And he moved swiftly behind the service station and beyond Gamlin's sightline. He'd let the truck leave without giving chase and now he'd run onto a flat spot for choice. He rubbed his head vigorously with both hands. "Bloody hell." He sipped water from a bottle. He checked his watch—and wondered what it could possibly hope to tell him. He leveled a sightless gaze at the dash. I'll have to work this out on the heel, he thought. And he heard a tire chirp from behind.

A heavy Suburban had just rounded the corner from Keokuk onto Nebraska. It turned the opposite direction—north, back toward the apartment—and almost immediately it checked brakes and lurched to an artless stop against the curb. It sat stationary for a moment before whelping backward and up half onto the curb. Is that Foster? "Is that Foster?" It dropped off the curb, spun round in the street, and sailed off in the direction it had come.

"Foster!"

There were sirens in a distance. Gamlin peeled round after the Suburban. But then Gamlin saw what Foster had seen. The apartment was on fire. White smoke pressed from window frames and ruptured glass and vented riotously from serial penetrations in the solid brick. And it was in this awe-ceded instant that Gamlin noticed the crisp white panel van. It crossed Nebraska down an alley at the far end of the block. Almost at the edge of view—along a trough in the landscape before the street lifted to join the horizon. It bounded down off the worried brick pavers and across and up the other side: a tidy white panel van.

The painter . . . The painter. "The fucking painter."

Gamlin cut right; east down Keokuk and along Foster's path. But wherever he may be, it was out of sight and far from Gamlin's thought. Just now, it was the van; running quick and parallel—just the van. At Oregon he looked left up the block, and once again the white tail of the van bounded across and up the alley. He sped to the next street: it was just visible, cross California and into the alley: across Iowa, and up the alley. Gamlin leapt through the intersection, but at the next half-block a large truck and trailer had swung out from an alleyway and failed to clear a parked car. Gamlin launched the brakes and swore and honked and swore. He watched painfully as the truck threaded back, lining for a better approach. Each instant brief and incandescent. The truck rocked back in guileless spasms and Gamlin reached for the shifter to abort, when; end of the block—far side of the truck and trailer—there it was. There it was, at the next intersection—the crisp white van: paused at the stop...and then crossed. Gamlin waved furiously at his impediment through the windshield: "Move! Move! Move! Move! Move! Move! Move!" When there was a gap one centimeter to the good, Gamlin rumbled through and onto the full stop of the intersection. But he did not hurl himself out. He inched up; craned up over the wheel; an inch; an inch; a foot—until he could see the tail of the white van slipping south down Ohio. Another foot. And another—until the van was several blocks out and there was an infill of traffic and it was safe.

He followed at a terrific distance. Down Ohio, till it had dumped into South Broadway. Under 55, down South Broadway till it had given up shotgun lodgings for warehouses in corrugation gray and penitentiary glass block. Scrap yards and cyclone fence. And it was in this spread of industrial bottoms that the van pulled off. It pulled into a gap Gamlin could not see from distance, behind a storehouse he could not read. Gamlin turned off to wait, but moments later they were underway again. They traced a looping circuit down 55, north on 270, and east again on 40. At 170, they split north to Ladue, and there the van turned in at a car rental and Gamlin watched closely from the grocery parking across the way.

The driver loaded out some kit to a silver sedan and thirty minutes later snapped decisively into traffic and through the light and Gamlin wrestled out after him. On the highway again, he'd immediately dipped off and down the parkway and Gamlin knew he'd tipped his hand in haste to keep up. He'd paced the sedan, paced in behind to the light at Big Bend—an M5 with a fitted exhaust murmuring vaporous dew. He sat back at a cautionary standoff and lamented his mistake. And he waited for the light.

XI.

Charles Foster had camped three days in the nursery. The nursery with its bare white walls and empty crib—an historical castoff—bumpers laced carefully to the bars and tied in bows of rabid maternal perfection. Symbols of a boundless measure in custodial care. Love knots of geomagnetism. He had slept there and sat there and lain there unsleeping—throbbing empty wakefulness—with cut-down boxes, the tipped prow of ironing board deck to the wall, the lost meter of electrical cord unjacked by head and tail, toothless and dead against the baseboard; the carpet-pile registry of footsteps and laden boxes and changing tables and mover cleats and the course of dolly casters and his own hand prints like monkey tracks in a post-industrial Pleistocene—a paleogeography in sedimentary wool-tuft and underlayment—the place-marks of his water glass, his phone, his shoes tumbled in the corner, his coat with banknotes over the crib-rail; the paper rose and straw, weightless and ephemeral; and the .38 and box of shells, just there.

Here the nightlight fizzed its residual glow. But elsewhere he'd kept the lights out. Elsewhere he'd stalked the house in dress socks and robe tugging with gun. He'd ventured from the room at random—in hunger, in thirst, in vain invisible defiance. He'd lurked in the curtains wherever the house bore portals—and cast watchful suspicions against light-fall in the street, the company of branches in wind, furtive leaves through coughing winter grasses; dog walkers; and against the field-song of high, unbounded children. Charles Foster was fear-sick and hiding.

The house was stale and close as summer bedding. Foster had cancelled the furnace. It played his nerves when it started and threw haunting silence when it stopped and its duct-rush and tapping louvers taunted him when it ran. Tree vermin clattered in the gutter eves; plaster snapped in distant corners with every shallow sigh of earth mantle; and coils of the slim elevator plucked groaning pentatonic chords each time the search lamps of his imagination were turned upon them. Worry rose like caustic belch in his throat, and Foster confided in himself a headshaking, deep uncertainty. He had seized vividly on the image of the burning apartments. The wheezing penetrations in the brick had reached out and clasped enervating hands at his shoulders. They pressed his intuition indelibly, but illegibly: they were images he could not resolve; emergent conditions he could not achieve with a calculus of known ingredients.

Charles Foster lay on his belly and his elbows and pushed back his oily forelock and prized open the paper rose—the remaining tenderness still employed to him—and combed out two long arrow shafts of potential chemistry and deployed them with a captive nostril, and they lifted against his parietal arch in vortices of dry lavender fog, and he took up his phone. And he stare at August's number. Again he stared—as he'd done many times in the past few days—cued on the screen and waiting. As though the act were a summoning, a resolving. Foster felt somewhere he must have parted lockstep with sense. He could not, for all his great labors of imagination, understand what he'd seen—what it meant. He could only feel intimations of tectonics in slip—this he could taste in his pores, feel in the irritable quaver of follicular root. This was a certainty, but a meaningless, inarticulable certainty—and it was with a strong urge to dispel it that he longed to hear from August; longed to receive the call; receive the explanation of it all; explaining the random accident; or his gang's misbegotten betrayal; or the call with threats and accusations; even a vague and belated text messaging insinuations of a last minute change of heart—a new expensive and unfavorable deal. Few were desirable scripts in their right, but Foster pined desperately for any or every one of them. Even the worst of these was the wound to heal him; the worst of these were injuries he could survive—injuries he could comprehend.

But the phone did not ring.

Foster held the fine black text—the chroma-green pulse of a solution in his hands—the afterglow of living possibility. But it refused to speak—day after day—choked in stubborn silence. And so Foster decided he would call.

He would call. He would call. Him. He would call August. He would call. He would call him now—stupid and careless and irresistible—he would call—him! Foster shook with resistance to the impulsive stupidity—but he would do it—he was doing it—pressed the call button in a paroxysm of flagging restraint—and it was ringing.

Now it was ringing . . . Ringing . . . Still ringing . . . And it rang . . . and it rang

. . . never went to voicemail, but . . . just rang . . . and rang.

Until he snapped the phone closed in a gesture that felt weightless and empty—an aping mockery to the freighted casters and thunderous shuttering passages; a barring of ways which he felt at his navel.

"Fuck . . . you . . . Fuck . . . you, August!" The invocation had only just loosened his bindings, but before he could retighten them he was standing; had snapped the phone through the doorway with the

full range of his arm, and it exploded against the hallway. "Fuck . .
. you! Fuck you, August!—and your moron crew! You sad, dumb,
hopeless, son of a bitch!" Foster shouted. He shouted and thrust his
long finger at the end of his long arm; thrust his finger at the place of
detonation, the place where August was, or had been, had exploded,
had vanished.

"God dammit!" God damn it.

Foster clutched his head in his hands, and he collapsed to the floor.
He lay there holding his head, fetal and contorted. He lay there in his
robe and socks; lay there with the pistol butt and ammunition box
piercing his rib. And he thought of Christmas. Not of last Christmas,
with microwave cuisine before the wet-smoldering fire, but the
Christmas before—in D.C. He pictured his father—the water running in the sink—the wet strap of his new tourbillion: a Cartier from
his mother, opened just that morning in private. Pointlessly washing lettuce—to escape in-laws, to feign honest toil—donning it like
Halloween makeup, while the cook and housemaid stepped from
view that he might pose alone with work. His enmity rising with
the addition of each new bath ring of bitters and vermouth—a table
chart in gathering force with a festive stemware charm. There was his
sister's husband: a middle-age boy in old man clothes. There was his
wife—his ex-wife—and there was his mother standing in the doorframe. His mother standing threateningly in the doorframe; piqued
with canine violence—storming the threshold with that matriarchal
proxy for bringing down the door. Raging for order and sense and
decorum. Foster wanted to talk to her now, he wanted to call her,
wanted to hear that tone of pitiable condescension telegraphed from
some childhood violation, some early disillusionment in him. He
wanted to call Catherine, wanted to hear little Pauline, wanted to
hear her smack her lips on the air, he wanted to hear her breathe.

Now he lamented the phone—now it stung, and he groaned into closed eyelids. Stupid. So stupid. He wanted to squeeze his skull in—press it flat beneath his fingers, between his palms—beneath the sheer hydraulic tonnage of his disgust—press the electric charge from his last tingling neuron.

It struck him as humorous then—a mechanical irony: the same load he'd apply to his cranial yolk—till it ran through his own fingers, was the same compression required to hold him in—keep him together; stop him seeping out between his teeth; the corners of his eyes. They were the same. The strength required to reduce him to vacancy and sustain him in cohesion, were the same.

He opened his eyes. He squinted sidelong at the nightlight stabbed into the wall: a small, dim lighthouse to mark the hazards of imagination. He thought of the man from the executive office—The Familiar. He thought of calling him. He wanted to call him and ask about the burning apartments; wanted to ask him what the hell was going on. But this was the one question he could not ask—perhaps the only question he could never ask. The question was a confession—that there was something deeply amiss; that he'd been a fraud; that he'd made a mistake, which like a single pebble's avalanche—had grown terrible by its own echo; that he'd launched a conspiracy of sloth— had lanced himself on the spear of his own torpor. Nevertheless, he needed to call him. He resolved that he would. The Familiar. Surely it would be horrible. He was waiting for the script—a virus—that Foster no longer possessed. Had been expecting it. Demanded it. Foster resolved to call him—to reset the whole affair.

He'd tell him the computer had failed—been lost or damaged. Destroyed. An awful, regrettable, and unforeseeable accident, had ruined it, erased it; the perfect and delicate thing was gone—evaporated as completely as August or Sachs. But with nothing more than a loan of time and patience, Foster would repeat the work—he would build it all over again—and it would be fine and beautiful. The very thing he'd asked for: a functional and potent proof of concept. And Foster would do it, too. He resolved that he would do it, just as he resolved that he would call—the man from the executive office. It was the only thing to do. He would call him, would confess to the loss, apologize for the delay—for the action of powers beyond his control. And then he would set to it. He would settle down, in honest labor, and do it. This is what he would do. This is what he would do. Would do.

Then Charles Foster closed his eyes.

2.

Foster woke in the late morning. The nightlight glow softly from the baseboard. His cheek was slick with saliva. His face burned from the bristled imprint of carpet. His hands were numb and senseless for the odd angles of his arms, and his side felt as it were spilling vivid, colorful pain from where he'd lay on the gun and box corners. In the hall a warm breakfast light fell orange and dappled over the shards of phone, and when he could move, he moved toward this with hands and knees. He rooted through debris for the SIM card, and when he'd found it in a chassis fragment, he rest on his elbow with it for some time.

At the mall he was washed and pressed. He upgraded his phone for a fee—generally reconstituted its hard alpha-numeric memories for a fee—watched an affable father of two perform the gestures for which he provided the fee; and sat in an armchair at the foot of the escalator abrading his knuckles on his chin and considering the store's Rorschach banner—a punctuation in strenuous exercise—and roused the new phone on its splash of factory charge. He was thinking about his father again: as a boy, walking in the yard, following as he trod along mole tunnels with the index of his heel and muttered curses. Cuffed trousers draped the laces. Wingtips like polished obsidian, knife-edged and uncreased. They bore into the bread-soft caverns like spade teeth; arrow points launched into the earth with ambivalent prosecutorial malice. Something in the vision turned him back to thoughts of The Familiar—the call; the reset; the work. He should do it before his courage drained—before all his temperature left. The dangling spectacles on their jaunty cord: he should do it now, while they were in view: feed the furnace while the shovel's up. But he also wanted to test his voice, run flight checks on his tongue; prime the mechanisms of his corrective deceit. He also wanted to wait: also wanted not to call. Ever.

He rang his mother's line instead, listened as it rang through five times to voicemail. He imagined her severe gaze. He imagined her mock surprise in answering, as though he might be calling out unexpected from the other room. He imagined her sitting through a boutique horticultural seminar while groundskeepers tended the lawn. He imagined her at ribbon cuttings; ship christenings; library dedications; all manner of consecration in presidential denomination. He thought again of Pauline: a furniture decoration; a human simulacra with damp eyes and feral whispers. He rang Catherine's line as he thought this. It rang five times through to voicemail. He imagined the flare of her nostril; he imagined the delicately turned undercarriage of the lower lip he had once enjoyed. He imagined her watching the phone ring through.

The rustle of warm fabrics and the shuffle and snag of shoe rubbers filled the space with a basketball court solemnity. Decorative carpet lay at his feet and the patter of footfalls across it vanished with the pause of shopping casters over entry mats. He imagined The Familiar, feet beneath his shoulders in naval brace—as though the ground under his feet might swell with whitecaps; pitch like ship-deck. He should call him. He saw him peering over coffees at him in Tel Aviv; he saw him gazing unblinking into the sky-lit fountain—the water aflame in bitter starlight. He should call him. He should call

him from the car in the parking garage. He thought of himself calling August; calling Sachs. He thought of himself calling his mother;
Catherine—calling to reach through and raise tickles of paternity.
He should call him from the car, he thought. And then, like August,
he was calling him. The phone was ringing—from impatience and
fear: dread. ring— A dread he no longer had the courage to wait to
face. Ring— He couldn't wait for the car. It was a piss that won't hold.
Ring. He would've made it fifteen steps and courage would've let go
all down the inseam and into his socks.

It rang three times. It went to voicemail. There was no message.
Just a short marker tone: a sour beep the color of red indicator light.
The sort of thing on intercom panels and old English cars. Small and
round. Three rings and a flash of sound the color of history. Foster
felt like standing. Saw himself standing. As though it were the action
to follow a cue. A comment for bodily articulation. A judgment in
self-reliance. But he did not stand. He sat in the chair. And the chirp
of sneakers and the animated rasp of thighs in cloth and the tick-
over of escalator handrail and the high, empty gymnasium sound—
all lifted away from him in murmuration.

3.

"Why would I not be sure? Memory troubles?—eyesight? A question to do with integrity? For what reason? Why wouldn't I be sure?"

"Certain. I just meant—certain," said Charles Foster, kneading his jaw with his thumb. He'd stopped off at his dealer's—a little tramp of Kirkwood house—sat in a threadbare recliner while he'd waited for his prescription to be filled, and been served an appetizer of four stiff lines on a china plate. And now his jaw cramped painfully.

"Whether I'm certain or just goddamned sure, look pretty well the same from here. From right here. I'm certain I would like to know on what basis you ask? Right? Like who are you? Right?"

Foster had stepped out of the dealer's with high voltage ringing in his ears—vibrated down the dog-shit lawn to the car; folded a paper rose with gritted teeth; stashed the laminated brick in the seat springs, and drifted east. And now squinted across the bar at a rare 1950s edition of ethnic Mediterranean stereotypes.

"I'm a friend," said Foster.

"Right, because her friends all come up here to ask after her. Her mailing address, right? Milkman leaves cold bottles at the door, right? No: 'patron,' man, 'patron' is the word you want—you were a friend you'd know what the hell, right? You'd know."

He stood opposite Foster at the bar. For all he knew, a doorman just slipped back to crib a drink. His brow was smooth and untroubled. It bore the dimple of a once-sharp impact and a lone crease bisecting shallow crown from heavy Cro-Magnon slope. A cape of neck fastened at his shoulders, and the nose was pressed flat at the bridge. Foster's own nostrils were numb and dry and tender all at once, and he pressed them with a sniff to compose whatever thought would come.

"Lilith? Lilith," he said.

"Only horses with fast names race, right? Look man, I told you, nobody's seen her; the girls haven't; I haven't; and she's not on the schedule for any shifts. Maybe I should be asking you."

"Would she go by something else? Would someone else know?"

The man straightened. "There's nothing else. And there's no one else to know it. One friend to another: have a drink—go have a sit with one of the girls; or maybe you've just got other shit to do."

Foster stepped back in a centering reflex and looked down at the man—a flesh boulder in fabric wrap: his gaze flitted over the club— its horizon of paisley carpets; its decorative accents in black enamel paint and corrugated metal sheet; its thin brass pillars—fire poles of material need down which seraphim slide but never ascend. He was no longer looking for the girl, but landmarks, anchors of recognition, and finding none he turned from the man at the bar and left.

He crossed the knurl of gravel lot; mounted the high chair of the Suburban, and sat in hungry dejected silence. He was raging with deep and convulsive loneliness. A reservoir taking collection for days; rising with each precipitating subversion; an ungovernable lust for witness, for the anechoic presence of company—he'd left the club and felt the moment of overtop, felt the inundating motion. And this time when he lifted the phone; this time when he dialed; this time when it rang, there was an answer: the cool and childlike voice of Kim Soong.

4.

Charles Foster broke eggs in a skillet. He searched refrigerator drawers, but in vain. A tomato with frost of mold; onions tumbling in rubbery desiccation; bag of peppers mottled with disease. So he took his eggs with ketchup. Runny whites over scritch of fork. He sat with the computer folded to the side and paper rose for breakfast cordial. He ate to the sound jowls and cutlery and cleared the plate to yellow entrails. And he opened the paper rose, carefully unfolded and admired its tuft of pollen. It was Sunday. The blinds were lifted. The curtains pulled. And light was in the room, smoky and new. It didn't make Foster hopeful, but it gave him the mood of hope. He fashioned a straw; rolled the bill carefully against the table, and leaned in to celebrate the promise of the rose. He had called Kim Soong—made a lunch date for today. He'd sit elbowed up to the plate glass on South Grand and look over the table at her; her simple smudge of airbrushed features, and he would smile, he would feel easy and relieved; he would be pressed into service as a physical being, and he would be saved: absolved from his terrors and his doubts and his loathing—by the company of woman. Not a special or beautiful woman, perhaps, but woman nonetheless. He'd reached out to grasp at a common ordering principle—and by this common ordering principle he would be saved. A catch-rope to stop his slide; to resurrect him from his opened cavity. He felt pride at the insight: the ingenuity—the commission of action. He would save himself by the tools at hand, and had bent them creatively to purpose. He would endure; he would meet Soong; he would reset; he would work; he would hear from The Familiar; he would craft the script. He would persist. Prosper. It's all in the head—he said aloud. It was decided. These were matters of the mind: thinking and making and being. They were cause on cause on effect. It's a change of mind—he said. Just concentrate. Reset. And for the reset, a change in mind. He rolled the straw on the table. He put a hand on the laptop. The force required to crush him was the same force required to bind him together. He remembered the thought. Replayed it with its epiphanic pearlescence. He caressed the computer: the toolkit of his escape: his vindication. And he considered the straw: a bit of new currency: tight and perfect tube of bill. Not even once spent and already adulterated to a purpose. He considered the rose, touched its delicate petals, turned it to observe its alternative angles. He thought of his fingers' touch against those petals; he thought of his mind enlivening that touch; he wondered where between the petals and the fingers and the touch and the mind which animated it, might he be? The thought was rare and quick and exhausting—like the misfire of a cantankerous vapor lamp. It was intrusively unfamiliar; dazzling; and it left a voided cavity in its retreat. Foster wanted to be outside then. Something in the thought made him want to be outside. He wanted to drink coffee and go to the gym; he wanted to be in the light. And he would be. He decided he would be. He tenderly refolded the paper rose—untouched, unvisited—closed its petals and pushed it away. He moved it across the table with the index of both hands. He pushed it beyond the computer and past the yellow plate, leaned forward with extended arms, until it was nearly on the opposite side of the dining room table—a closed lotus floating in a high-stain lagoon. Just so far the distance was appreciable. Just so it was out of reach.

5.

When he arrived he threw the doors wide. Wide, so that they whistled on their dampers. He'd left the epiphany at the table and dressed for the gym; stopped in Clayton for coffee. He'd sat in the window and taken on the lazy patter of conversation, the Sunday blazers and broaches, the exclamations of steam wand. It felt civilizing, to sit among the amused and astonished, to be a professor with a corner table and coffee, to imbibe crooked paintings and periodicals, thumb-worn and castaway. And when, finally, he'd arrived at the gym he'd thrown the doors wide in exaltation. A deacon in adulated rush to sermon. He threw the doors and strode in to be received—muggy with the spice of forgotten wash—it was a threshold, real and discernable, and where it touched him now, it was honest and aspirational—today it was the stink of the approach.

Foster felt cheerful and gracious, despite the welling of the nag at the back of his sinus—the dull and needful itch. He worked light weights in the mirror and walked vigorously on the treadmill; he reflected confidently on his work to do—on the coming school week—on his lunch with Kim Soong—on the view onto Forsyth through tinted windows—on the exquisite hatchling: on little Pauline. He resolved to see her; that he would find a way to D.C.—soon; that he would love her better. When all this was resolved he would see her, bring her blankets and soft things, and new and better love.

He took this thought down the narrow passage to the locker room—changed to trunks and towel: changed for the pool. Institutional white, and tiled, with an exposed trellis of joists and ceiling beams: the room was large and enclosed; sealed from the natural day, and rippling in strange polychrome artifacts of light. Lane markers and buoys and depth registers and the full, chlorinated brine of a manufactured sea, neither moving nor still. Foster had padded down the hall and past the elaborate counter and its elastic and joyful attendants and through the moistened door and into the pool room, warm to breathe and cold to touch, and oddly and happily, empty. It was a gift, he thought lightly; a token offering to his new good humor and his virtue. A sign that, however unsteadily, he'd managed to stumble both his feet upon the beam: a high, and right, throughway to the end. He eased off his sandals, slipped them neatly beneath a chair. He lay his towel, removed his shirt and entered the alkaline waters gently from the edge.

He knelt into the shallows and let the water hold him to the chin. It was soft and firm and tingled with discomfort everywhere it did not touch: above the waterline; his cavities; his muscle fiber. He was shimmering and porous. His edges fluttered and swelled; simultaneously expanded and contracted. He thought of Catherine bending the folding knife. He saw her handing it to him. Saw it in his palm: his incredulous palm. He saw her working at the cap of a baby food jar with it—a surgical point in high carbon steel. Wrestling at the lid, as if it were a screwdriver or butter knife—all the while imperiled. In perfect ignorance and material danger. You said it was a good knife—she'd said. He and the knife had misled her. He could feel himself receding; his envelope withdrawing: arms and legs, to torso, to chest, to lungs, to heart—and simultaneously expanding into the pool; impregnating its matter; crystallizing; vascularizing. He was populating its volumes; he was making bodily contact with hollow buoys; with slurping drains and traps; with greasy walls and gritted floor.

But he was startled to find that he was wrong. He had not forged new chemical bonds; he had not worried nerve roots and crystallizing chains into the pool. He could not feel its volumes, and the pool was not empty. Foster was yet to throw his first overhand crawl—had yet to turn the first lap in his forty-minute program—when a man emerged from the far end of the pool. He rose sudden and unaccountably from the depth: to Foster, not violent, but swift and eerily. From the furthest marine-shaded deep, he rose, and slung a dive weight onto the pool deck and pushed back close hair. He cleared his nostrils and read time from a dive watch. He set the bezel with a faint but perceptible ratchet, and he climbed out. He was not lean, but muscular. Foster thought: hardened. He said nothing to Foster, but left. And as he left, Foster noticed a substantial bruise against his right inner shoulder. It looked purple and yellow and green: some brief, localized punishment. When the man had gone Foster began his routine, began his laps and forward crawl; kicked off from the poolside, and tried to resume his optimistic reflections. Unspent cash in bands at home. Himself, sitting down at the computer. Sailing to class in the morning and returning home enlivened and ready to work; to write inspired and effective code. Kim Soong, in a few hours time. And he reflected again on the bruise; the man's bruise. His musculature wasn't gym fluffed, it wasn't swollen and watery, but seemed labor-wizened: calcified; permanent. Foster thought of his own welts; the angry marks on his side and abdomen from his collapse against the gun; the box of shells. Marks of mania and folly. The man's bruise stood out to him in relief, and the more he thought of his own fleshy wounds, the more this was so. He lay back into the cloistered shadow of his mind. Swam laps: forward crawl; breast-stroke; backstroke—in their turn; climbed his fluid advance. And when his mind surfaced from these silences, he thought of the paper rose. He thought he'd resolve not to visit it the rest of the day—one full calendar day away from the florist. Just this one, and then tomorrow he would remeasure. And the bruise. It kept rising to mind like the recurring form in a kaleidoscope. The mind returned to it; to it, to his own welts, and by them back again. He'd fallen on the gun: they were gun welts: marks of an instrument. He kept working this ground, passing over it again and again, and despite forty minutes swimming, couldn't make the ends join. It was much less a thought than an emotion, and as Foster finished his swim; climbed from the pool to his towel, his clinging shirt, and slick bathing shoes—this emotion rang discordantly. It hove like some formless pall above his daylight cheer and deliberated optimisms.

He left the pool, turned the sweating handle, traipsed again past the front desk, pushed open the metal flange of door, and thread down along the narrow crook of passage to the locker room. And then he stopped mid-stride. A shotgun; a rifle: it was a shooting bruise. How simple could he be: a shooting bruise. Of course, a shooting bruise. Charles Foster thought this just as the man from the pool appeared in the passage. He was dressed, in heavy sober clothes, with a towel over his arm, and leaving. He entered from the opposite end. He moved quickly and closely past him, brushed him in fact, and it was not until he'd exited, firmly out through the swinging metal door, that Foster noted the pain in the back of his thigh.

XII.

The television was wood-print decal and aerials to catch echoes of the universe and course-grain static—a diarist reliquary in three-color radio. On it, Lleyton Hewitt clapped the ball overhand and shuffled crabwise. Airline engine howl poured into the stadium and eventually passed in fine Doppler thread. Far court Roger Federer launched left and right with volleys. LeFrance thought he moved like an old Pong curser: back and forth on a track, an Atari paddle in white pixels and headband. The court might have been any color, but the screen shown only in blue-green, gray, and white—somewhere a reality in high-vis felt and grunting ball boys, rendered for LeFrance in Eastern Bloc pointillism. And like his bracelet Timex, it too was inheritance. The watch: a cigar-box heirloom from his grandfather; the television, a gift in refuse from his mother. It sat on a moving box with a casual lean and the girl watched it from the mattress. She lay on her chest and her elbows, feet up at the knee, and she watched it. She watched it under the terms of affectionate communion. And from the doorframe Edmund LeFrance watched it too.

LeFrance had stood in his t-shirt, his pajama pants, his flip-flops—whose clapping followed him everywhere about the house like the nick of animal claws—and had stood at the window over the sink. The girl, his lover, had rung repeatedly to stay, to visit. She missed him. Couldn't she come?—why couldn't she come?—and he wanted her to. He wanted her company and had longed to have it for days, despite telling her whatever might be necessary to keep her away. He wanted her compassion and body-volume of heat and her black frame glasses and her heavy eyes when she smiled and her strange fluid bearing when she did not and he wanted her emotional binding. These were the dressings which healthy men sought, and these were the dressings whose administration kept him so. It was a vitamin, a mineral, an electrolyte to fire the senses—a hormone supplement to render coherence and use of the various and contrary parcels of man. LeFrance had seen the new men—wispy and louche, anatomical and ungendered—and the women who wanted them. But what he knew was that for men like him, bearing an authentic woman along his way was the final condition of man's prime—whether pelts and cudgels or courts and daggers, she is a hearth of her own; woman is the azimuth of man. And so he had told her to leave, had stayed her for days, and relented late last night—just and only late last night—when his want and his worry bore that temporary clearance of strike-plate and latch. LeFrance had stood in the kitchen and rolled a cigarette and lit it on the stove and ashed into the sink and stare through the window into the long grass of the back yard and he'd thought about the man at the bar, and how to ask her to leave.

He'd eaten greens from the bag and taken a Corona from the fridge loosely by the neck, and accompanied by the clap of his flip-flops, he'd returned to smoke in the doorway and watch the Indian Wells tournament and ask her to leave and wonder if he'd work out how to do it beforehand. She'd slipped in late last night and had been happy, and he'd been happy too. But it troubled his intuition—this lapse—and had all the afterglow of mistake. It was too soon: phobia or no, reasonable or no—too soon.

Hewitt knitted his face in the hem of his jersey, and LeFrance said, "I was glad to have you here."

"You were," she said. She rolled on her side and stretched a languid arm for the beer. She was handed it, drank from it, and returned it. "And you're not now?"

"I was. I was glad to see you. Glad that you came, and I look forward to seeing you again. Soon."

She reached for the bottle again and was handed it. She studied LeFrance, checked him above her glasses and through them again, pulled comparative focus on him—and when he reached to retrieve the bottle, lifted a searching hand for it—she said, "Get your own."

"I'm not trying to be clever about it. I have some things I need to do," he said. He smoked and searched for a place to ash. Failing to find one, he ashed in his palm—made a fist as though to perform magic on a coin, and then opened it to observe the residual grey smudge of his conjuration.

"You said you've been to the casino all week," she said.

"I did."

She motioned to the pair of chips at the bedside. "This your booty? Maybe you've done plenty. A week on life-support over a stool—burned through whatever to keep that...pair of chips...and you want to toss me to fix the image; mark the occasion? Make it better?"

"There's more than that."

"How much you down?"

"They don't let me tell," he said, and brushed out the cigarette in the smudge of his hand, and then clutched it in a fist as before. "It's a few days. That should sort it."

"It was a few days before. This is the final: can we just watch the final?"

She looked away to the match, and looked back, and he shook his head.

"It was a few days before, and it was a few days too soon."

"The final," she repeated.

"You're not watching the final, I am. And I have to go, and so do you."

"But we could."

"We can't."

"But we should."

"Yes. We should. But we won't."

"Is there a problem?"

"You took my beer."

"Do you have a problem?"

"That it'll be a few more days before I can see you."

"You're terrible."

"You should see the view in here—it's goddamn panoramic."

"You're a liar," she said, and she took a deep slug off the bottle.

"I am. The worst. But you gotta go."

"Now?"

"Or sooner," he said, and he watched her climb out of the bed and stand before him to finish the bottle. She put on pants and shirt and shoes and a flimsy coat.

"Times like this . . ." she said and opened the door.

"Cause I'm so good to you."

"You are?"

"As the Maharaja to all his harem. And possibly his wives, too."

"I'm not kissing you," she said going down the front stair. And then stopped, and climbed the stair again to kiss him.

"Maybe what?" LeFrance had asked. He'd sat at the bar, belly to the brass at the Delmar Lounge, and had drunk the man's Oban, and the man had said—"Though I think you may be."

"Maybe what?" he'd said.

"A literate sort," the man had said.

"I don't think so," LeFrance had muttered. His mouth was dry and his throat, inexplicably hoarse, and he'd croaked out as though whispering into vacuum.

"The Rilke says otherwise. Or that was just laying about," the man had said.

LeFrance had lit his cigarette with the man's lighter and been turning it over in his hands, and noticed the snare, the barb, the mar in the finish that felt like a kind of tragedy for so fine a thing; and at the remark on Rilke he'd felt himself touching the chapbook and envelope with his forearm: adjusting them, bracing them.

The man uncurled his palm to LeFrance, into which he'd replaced the lighter; and trimmed his ash, LeFrance had thought, with a remote and automatic care—a motion like a draftsman lathing his pencil lead—and had repositioned the lighter with a squaring precision beside the remaining cigarette.

"It's beautiful," he'd said.

"It was."

"You dropped it."

"I never did. It was a gift—and dropped the once," said the man. "Ignorance is hazard to perfection, time is hazard to order; and to beauty: use."

LeFrance had smoked and watched the man drink and stare at him, disarmed and discomforted; as though his vision were troubled—not as though it was blurred, but as though the object of focus were: as though he couldn't make it sharp; as though he couldn't understand what it was. "And you are...whom?" he asked, at last.

"Arbeit," said the man. "Only and ever, Arbeit. But I tire quickly to talk of myself. You are...a native. How do you find it? Speaking...as a native."

"How do I find it, here? St. Louis? Like everyone else: without a seat when the music stops." LeFrance had smoothed his bald crown in a self-placating gesture that failed to serve. "And how does it find you?" he'd asked.

"Like a spirit distilled from its own hangover," said the man, and they both shared a brief and uneasy laughter.

LeFrance smothered his cigarette in the ashtray, and the man had looked at him for what seemed a long and unnatural time. The look was not stern, but hard, he'd thought, not antagonistic, but predatory—something loading forward onto haunches.

"Should we have another?" said the man. He'd drawn up the last cigarette from his arrangement and offered it to LeFrance. "Make it an even six. Breach protocol...just the once."

LeFrance had grown clammy and disoriented. The moisture, from his esophagus to his lips, seemed all at once to have vanished. It wasn't fear—or he thought it wasn't fear—but some coiling uncertainty. This character—this man, he couldn't read or understand him. LeFrance couldn't reconcile whether he was eccentric, dangerously authentic, or if he was just terminally strange. His speech was uncommon and his bearing was uncommon and his statements were uncommon, and his intention seemed simultaneously saw-toothed and inscrutable, as though somewhere an imperceptible low-pressure of menace had rolled in about him. He thought his ears might pop. It was a feeling with a touch of the apartment in it: something overwhelming.

"I'm fine, thank you," LeFrance had said. It was an answer to a question which now felt muted and far away: long ago. Imaginary. "Excuse me for a moment."

"Of course," said the man.

LeFrance drank and scooped the chapbook and envelope into his coat pockets and stood.

"Of course," said the man.

LeFrance had turned down the hall for the restrooms and out of view. He'd forced open the men's room with the flat of his hand, and it struck off the stop and fell hard closed. He'd backed slightly up the hall and through the service door into the kitchen. The staff had looked up from their stove burners and dish tubs and their pickup shelves, from their smoking into the exit-draft of the fire door opened to an alley-court of dumpsters and dolly trucks. "Scotch and pasta— end of the bar. Didn't see the bartender," said LeFrance to the server at pickup, and stuffed a new hundred in his breast pocket. "Good food. Bad company," he'd said, and slipped out through the fire door and between the sweating staff and their tobacco, and into the night.

LeFrance had this and the doings at the apartment fully in mind when he'd first cast her out: asked her to leave days ago—and then again in the morning and then again with a renewed and fortified persistence in the kitchen, eating greens with his fingers and fishing a bottle from the fridge; and now he stood on the stoop in flip-flops and pajama pants with his fist of extinguished cigarette, which he brushed from his palm like discharged moth parts, and he watched her leave. He watched her strike up the little maroon boot of Volvo wagon, and drive away.

LeFrance washed his hands in the kitchen, and when they still felt gritted he washed them again. He lifted a bottle of beer from the fridge for his own, and dressed. He thought of where to go, what to do in his camouflage of activity; his pretence of idleness—an indolence of one, made virtuous and constructive by company. He dressed in clothes and shoulder harness and Redhawk; top coat and pouch of shag and chapbook and padded envelope; a pair of speed loaders he checked with his hands as they might be car keys and wallet. And then he shuffled in the doorframe and drank the beer and watched the final and waited for the end of service or a commercial interruption or some other natural terminus for redirection. And after a moment, there was a knock at the door.

Through the peephole there was a girl—a mousy Asian with a black mantle of shoulder-length hair. LeFrance sighed at the door handle and looked again. She was still and slightly off to one side. When he opened the door to the end of the chain, the girl drew up her hair and spoke: "I'm supposed to wait in the car."

XIII.

I t drooped from the point of the ornament to the bridge of the hood and with a slack-line ease. A hammock string, he thought, loose fiddle bow. It was a gossamer dragline, a bit of spider filament picked up by the prow of his ship—clipped off by the Daimler star and fluttering in the perfect stillness of light and sky. He urged it to piss off to wind, but none rose and he turned to observe Soong instead.

He'd waited on Hartford across from Mekong and watched Soong's gaze tip occasionally over the low bar of curtain and through the window. Divorced from her features, her eyes seemed uniquely glazed and expressionless, had that ocular vacancy of fat house pet: illucid and prosthetic. At another time it might have served its own gratifying irritation, but now—at five after the hour—it seemed a punctuation in puerility fanning at his temper. Who wants goddamn Vietnamese in the first place?—thought Hoyt Gamlin—nothing but Chinese food in half-size portions and flavored with napalm and ginger. He'd been waiting an hour in the car staring cross the street at the brow of Kim Soong, when the thought had risen like an irritable smoke ring. "Alright, that's fucking torn it," he muttered, and shut off the car and stormed across the street and into the restaurant.

When she'd seen him coming she shook her head violently through the window and bounced in the booth so that her whole face to the chin might clear the curtain rod. "What? What! What are you doing?" She was nervous and exasperated, her wrists shone a firm, pleading bent, and she looked everywhere about as though the audience might notice Gamlin's break in character; the director might shout him out of the scene.

"He'll see you!"

"The hell you say." Gamlin had swung through the door and rolled down the aisle, and stood now simmering beside her table.

"He will! He'll see you."

"That's your one line. He's not coming—let's go—we're going."

"No, no, he could—he might," she said. "Leave. You should leave."

"Don't be a twit. He's onto you, or he's not—but he's not coming—and we're going, now. I've enough of this fucking about," he said. Gamlin reached down and grasped her by the wrist and she collapsed like tent poles, and lifted her out and set her on loosely-hinged feet. "There's nothing for it. Come, little Soong."

Soong had taken the call yesterday. It was Charles Foster, strange and manic, she'd said, and entirely out of thin air. He'd called her for a lunch—offered up the place and time—confirmed it by text: here, Mekong, an hour ago. It was the place they'd met for dinner on the fourteenth, and Soong had narrowed it to the table. She'd set in the same windowpane, and he'd been two cars back on Hartford to see. She'd approached Foster at Gamlin's urging—wound him up a touch—and watched for the chime. Foster had come, she said he'd been animated, friendly, weaved heavily between topics and grew more emphatic and fidgety, intoxicated and incohesive with each return from the loo. It was inconclusive, and what Gamlin learned from it was he was tiring of waiting in cars, and that Foster profess to pleasures of a Vietnamese cuisine he couldn't be bothered to touch.

But today Foster was absent—though Soong still was pleading to wait—and on a day when Gamlin would very much have had it otherwise. Soong was wrestling away to catch loose bills from her bag: a matter of miso and tea. And a waiter and cook shuffled into the aisle—two-hundred pounds of chicken gristle, together—and Gamlin said: "Lover's quarrel, chaps." And when he began toward them with Soong in tow, and they remained, Gamlin thrust out his arm as a battering ram—"None today, thanks," he said, and they scuffled back and out of the way: "Now you lads be good, and go get your own," he said, and they crossed to the car and Soong fell in with a shove.

"Wasting our time . . ." Gamlin muttered, as he lit the V12 and pulled out.

"What is wrong with—?"

"Wasting our fucking time! Kim Soong. *This* . . . is wasting our time."

Gamlin had never settled on a plan—a concerted vision for what might happen had Foster come; certainly he might've sat across the street in the car and watched until he'd stumbled onto the curb with his swerve of forelock and his big-n-tall suit clothes, as he'd done before. But Gamlin was working an impulse that he wanted more, that he'd wearied of toeing about in pointe shoes—watching and waiting, for tells and confessions; for mistakes—collecting. He wanted something entirely more decisive, resolving—interactive. Gamlin wanted answers, he wanted results and clarity, and this cocking about seemed a practice in high-speed sitting; seemed fruitless and ineffective—a turn of juiced-up hand-wringing for action, in hopes the various parties would step forward and announce themselves; reveal their intentions, as a matter of courtesy or sympathy or perhaps, boredom. Gamlin wasn't clear on the method—maybe he would grab him, have a talk, intercede—but he was increasingly sure the solution was something direct: un-sedentary. Something meaningful; and before another 'painter' turned up in a panel van, or 5 series; pulled another e-brake turn cross traffic—or some other novel acrobatic shit—and left him curbed wheels and a creased fender to keep; before the remaining players cashed-in or vanished, or bumped their heads. Or whatever the hell was happening, Gamlin had an acute sense of a stopwatch marking it off in the background; metering out the portions. His sense of it was compressive and anonymous, and unwanted.

He tramped left through the light onto Grand and still she was shaking her head—it was on a spring, and in a minute he was going to make it still; clench it to submission beneath his fingers.

"You're still just pissed about the car," she said.

"I am," said Gamlin, "but that's nothing to do with it."

She was peering back over the trunk lid down Hartford as they turned—peering back in certainty and optimism—and, Gamlin thought, a wistful resistance.

"Go back! I think I saw him."

"You didn't."

"I did—I think—down the block. His black truck…"

"Suburban."

"His black Suburban! I saw it down the block."

Gamlin slowed to a crawl and leaned toward the shoulder of the lane.

"You didn't."

"No, I did, I did. I think I did."

"Well, we're not going back now, are we."

"Why not?"

"Don't be a fool."

"I think I saw him!"

"It's ten after the hour, Soong. He'd be an hour ten minutes late—no call, no text—just now sauntering up . . . It's a bit much— Keep watching: watch the intersection! If that is him, he's either full-on hopeless, or he's pulled one around on us."

"Watching us?"

"Watching us. You see him?"

"No. Go slow."

"See him? Is it him?"

"Go slow! Wait. Wait! There! Yes! There—his Suburban. I can see the nose. Just pulled to the light."

"You sure?"

"Look for yourself."

"I can't see."

"Would he really stake us out? Foster? Maybe he's just late and didn't see me: thought I'd left—which I did."

"Let's find out."

"Wait! Slow down—"

"Let's find out," said Gamlin. "If that's him—he's playing shadow—I'm raising the stakes; and if not, I've a notion where to cross paths."

2.

Kim Soong sat on the front step with an arm wedged between her chin and her knee, and she threw Gamlin a heavy-lidded, disparaging look. With the other she smoked. She mouthed at him as she exhaled, mouthed out silent exaggerated vowels and consonant shapes: This . . . Is . . . Stupid: You . . . Are . . . Stupid. Gamlin shone her a smile in deflecting confidence, but over twenty minutes his doubt now resembled her own general pulse of loathing. They'd left South City, left Mekong, and Soong had lost sight of the Suburban in the sprint to 40. They'd spun the noisy pea-gravel lanes and set up before Foster's place on Greenway—the old brick and stucco Tudor with the yard wanting trim like a four-day-stubble. "Why are we stopping? Go—keep going," she'd said.

Gamlin had looked at her silently.

"What? No. What? Why are we stopping?"

"Go see if he's there."

"You're a crazy person—what are you doing?"

"And if he's not there . . . we'll just wait a bit."

"Gamlin."

"Say: you waited, you didn't see him; say: you didn't have a ride—say: you called me to pick you up—that you'd really hoped to see him, and that you want to introduce me—I'm fucking fascinating."

"Oh, you are. And why didn't I call him?"

"Why didn't he call you? You want to see him; you were worried there might have been a mix-up—and you want to introduce your friend," he'd said.

"It's like you're lurching from one attempt at calamity to the next."

"When he answers—if he answers, say what I've told you and then summon me over," he'd said, removed the Browning Hi Power from his coat and inspected the breech. "Who dares, wins—little Soong. Be a dear and hand me the spare magazine from the glove box, would you."

She'd gone to the door and knocked, and waited, and rung the bell, and waited. Check for his car—he'd said through the window, and she'd shaken her head uncomprehendingly. He'd pointed at her and made a half-circle gesture with his finger, and she'd lit a cigarette and left her tote on the step to go around back. She'd returned with another shake of her head and a redundant shrug, and set herself beside the bag—collapsed beside it in ropey despondence. And again they waited. Soong had lit another cigarette after the first and ashed from an outstretched arm; tapped them off with exaggerated theatricality—stage taps—and watched them sail into the grass or onto the step or onto her pant legs and sneakers—watched them in hopeless indifference, while Gamlin sat in the car thumbing-over the first round in the high capacity magazine, depressing it against the spring and turning it, while his gaze lighted on the dash and the wheel and the shifter the vents house numbers the road the curb the tree the yard—restless and birdlike: in thoughtless concentration.

"Call him," said Gamlin.

Soong stared.

"Call him," he said, and lifted an illustrative hand to his ear. "Call him, now."

She rooted through her bag for the phone and called him. She dialed Foster, and it rang, and Gamlin watched her listen. They watched each other, and again she shook her head, and closed the phone and crossed to the car and sat heavily in the passenger seat. "This going to plan?" she said.

Gamlin watched his lap where he rolled the cartridge and they sat to this sound of the cartridge being depressed and released, the faint click and grind, and the bloom of full-day quiet—of the whisper-rattle of things in small capitulating motions, of the outdoors reciting in illuminated verses—mumbling to itself.

"You have a piece, little Soong?" he said, and roused the engine against the self-genuflecting day. He pulled off and they moved swiftly down the gritted lanes.

"I do," she said.

"You have it on your person, little Soong?"

"I do," she said, and folded herself into the bolster as though she might be turning over in bed.

Gamlin hustled the Mercedes out onto Delmar and round the corner to Big Bend, and down along its troughs and swells. "I've a thought," he said.

"Why not? The last was a success."

"Look for Zephyr on the left," he said, and they saw Zephyr and turned across traffic and parked-up. "Third on the right. Dart gun, I suppose."

"That's right, Gamlin: bull moose tranquilizer."

He gestured to the white dually in the driveway.

"August Reams?" she said.

He shook his head—"Here we are making house calls; I figured we had another call to make—our good man, Edmund LeFrance."

"Team August?"

"Last and precious remnant, it seems."

"We still daring?" she asked.

"I'm in a visiting mood. I feature it," he said. "You'll go; you'll knock; say what you like when he answers; and you'll put your ass back in the car and leave it." He handed her the car key. "I'll be a few minutes."

"I'm waiting."

"In the car: you see moose, you give 'em the dart."

On the stoop Gamlin stood from view and waived Soong to the side; waived her again. And she knocked. When the door opened it snagged on a leash of chain, and Soong said, "I'm supposed to wait in the car."

"What?" was the utterance from the door. It was a single syllable wet-honed of enervation and discontent, and Gamlin marked it with a running leap at the door—feet up.

The door burst open, smashed off the wall, and the man skid backward shoulders against the floor and Gamlin climbed up from the threshold with the Browning and reset the door in the frame. "Knees up Mother Brown! Let's chat," said Gamlin. "Have a seat."

Gamlin motioned to the small dining table and chairs. "Come. Sit. If you prefer we can put you back on the floor after a bit. Come, Edmund LeFrance, come tell me about your August Reams; about his Mexican holiday; about the flat on Nebraska—that seemed to go well."

Edmund LeFrance collected himself from the floor and sat at the table. Gamlin turned out a chair and joined him. "We in private?—anyone in the cupboard?"

LeFrance was silent, tipped his head, and stretched his fingers on the table.

"Any denials to peddle?—wrong man, wrong house, just visiting— all that? No? Ever hear of Pavel Kashkin? Your mate August capped him in Mexico City; left him in a bathtub to dry. You help with that? Huh? Why'd he do that?"

LeFrance was silent.

"Who'd he do that for, huh?"

LeFrance was silent.

"His idea to slip the city and put him down? Little recreation?

"Howard Charles Foster—hear of him? Was it his ask? Kashkin find out he was cheating on his taxes? Huh? His wife?

"Something else? Somebody else?

"Here I am, top of my courtesy, Mr. LeFrance. But, your lack of cooperation, I find, highly unprofessional.

"That's right.

"Discourteous—mm-hmm.

"Anyone else make it from the flat? August—anybody?

"Didn't look it.

"August impart anything to you—before his untimely passing— words of wisdom?—little granule of information? Did he take something from Kashkin in Mexico, hmm—something he might've mentioned to you, something he might've given to you—passed along for safe keeping, right?—a note, a document, schematic . . . a drive; little computer drive, like—the clap?—anything?"

Edmund LeFrance looked at his hands then, and past Gamlin through the narrow angle of doorway into the bedroom, and at the corner of the television which shone there. Gamlin saw this look, this flicker of tell, and the sighting over his shoulder and he heard the television and turned to see it, turned to see a bisection of screen through the doorway, and the oblique angle of rally playing out, the two dancers with rackets performing a ballet of service and volley—"Queer game," said Gamlin—and Edmund LeFrance snatched right-handed into his coat for the Redhawk and cleared the holster and Gamlin turned to the sigh of clothes and sense of motion and loosed the Browning unsighted into LeFrance's chest and the Redhawk discharged beside LeFrance's shoe and the room sang with the diatonic overpressure of the two cartridges.

"Fucking hobbyist."

The toll of the Magnum played dim nausea in his ears; choked Gamlin's hearing with its convulsion, and he worked his jaw to dispel it. And then he shot LeFrance again.

"You people are really starting to piss me off."

"Now, why would you do that, ya sodding heathen? Look," said Gamlin, pointing emphatically with the Browning, "you nearly spoilt your goddamn shoe!"

Gamlin rose and fetched his casings from the baseboard. He considered the weeping puncture in LeFrance's sternum and the one beside and he considered the Redhawk still looped in the fingers of his hand. "Shall I leave Thunderclap with you?" he said. LeFrance set tipped ponderously over the chair back. "As you wish," said Gamlin, and moved to check his pockets: his speed loaders, pouch of Drum, wallet and keys, his chapbook, and the padded envelope with the slender thumb drive; which Gamlin held out between them.

"You were about to mention this?

"I see.

"Cut you off in mid-sentence, did I?

"Well, my apologies.

"Perhaps, I'll just keep it till you're feeling better," he said.

Behind Gamlin sports commentators were muttering between themselves and tennis shoes chirped with odd, irregular punctuation; and the players danced and leaped and swatted and called out in occasions of deep guttural exclamation—as though it might be a children's game, with vocalizations imparted by rule. Gamlin turned and rest his mind and senses upon this momentarily, upon the television's quavering noise and light; until, from outside there came a sound of struck flare—its snap and bristle and rush—and he went to the window, and saw the Mercedes was filled with smoke, saw that it vented through the driver's window, that a fountain of sparks showered the interior—ricochet off the glass, and that against the opposite curb was a black Suburban.

XIV.

He'd sat on the rug on the floor and leant upon the Eames and play Satie Gnossiennes on the stereo, advanced the volume till he set between hammer and string, and stripped and cleaned the Barrett and drank coffee from the simple white cups that pleased him. The Atlantic lay to his side and he'd lifted and folded and turned it through in late-morning leisure: Saddam Hussein was on trial; Vladimir Putin was inscrutable; and Chistopher Hitchens, heart-burnt for some erstwhile issuance of praise, had leapt on a dyspeptic scattershot of contrarian screed—and together, they appeared on the company of pages in collective agitation.

Marek Hussar had read and listened and pulled at the stubble of his beard, and refit the rifle. He'd sat in deliberation, and when he'd settled into the product of his thought he'd replaced the rifle and drawn the car from the garage into the driveway and closed the overhead door. He'd lain down heavy plastic sheet where the car had been and prepared a bucket of warm soapy water. He turned through the flight cases for the articles of his intention. He produced a Tyvec coverall and wore it, prepared a final Americano in the kitchen and then filled the double sinks—one soaped, one flat—and adjusted the stereo volume again so that the garage too, was live with it. There were nitrile gloves and outer gloves beside, a filter mask and cinched hood, a high capacity autoinjector pen which he'd disassembled to parts; there were three more he'd carefully placed to hand—atropine sulfate, pralidoxime chloride, diazepam—and there was a chest with six latches and three unbroken seals and two locks, and Hussar set it cautiously upon the plastic over the floor, and he sat down before it and reviewed his preparations.

He unlocked the chest and broke the seals and there was a vacuum canister like a large thermos, and a small manual pump. Hussar broke vacuum on this canister and removed a threaded lid, and from this removed another smaller version of the same. He broke vacuum on this second canister and removed another threaded lid, and two thick glass vessels separated by pad insert and stacked one upon the next. He inspected these both carefully and replaced one, and from the other he removed a further lid and revealed a rubber diaphragm which he pierced with a syringe. It was odorless and colorless Ethyl N-2-diisopropylaminoethyl methylphosphonothiolate, and he filled the syringe with it. He transferred this to the disassembled autoinjector pen—rebuilt it, refit the chamber reservoir and needle, the drive assembly, the load spring and trigger; he replaced the canisters and pulled vacuum on them once again, fit them in the padded chest, and doused the completed pen and forearms first in the bucket and then the water of both sinks, before stowing the chest and the antidote kit and removing the suit and gloves into the plastic—and disposing of it. And then he'd bathed.

Marek Hussar had stood in the master en suite the night of the fifteenth. He'd taken the Parkway back from his maneuvers in the Central West End, and he'd pulled off onto DeBaliviere and waited for the Mercedes to come back along—sniffling instinctually after him, lifting a leg for every oil stain and coolant dribble of the way—and quietly and from great distance he'd followed it back to the parking garage at the Ritz, Clayton; he'd gone in after it and noted its plates and VIN and particulars. And then, that evening, he'd gone up into the en suite, with the lights put out, and he'd looked out at the house backs of Greenway with field glasses and double old fashioned for whisky, and the bottle. He'd watched for hours, for opportunity, for signs, and when he'd finished with vigils—this, and all others beside—he'd gone to bed, had put the car nose-out in the garage, and looped bells over the handles of the entries, turned the lock of the bedroom door and taken the Barrett and its sudor of powder-flash and gun oil, and full charge of magazines, to bed.

In the morning he'd blown the moldy decay of civilization from his nose—black, earthy and contemptuous, and he could not stop tasting it: a scent of florid bacterial end times, of soil distillates and corporal depredation—solvent of the very agents of undoing. Greed gnawing its own micturated tail: this was the smell. He'd cleared it from his nostrils with glycerin soap and cleaned the Barrett and had espresso crema and aromatic volatiles, and music. He'd prepared the autoinjector pen with extraordinary care, and had gone with a modest cache of supplies, to the gym.

He'd stowed his things in the locker room—down the passage, along the damp concrete, chipped and slippery epoxy, sloped and drained, and amenable to the hose as a stable—and for Hussar—at all times a space persisting in want of it. He'd staked out the treadmills and cable-rows, the dumbbells in their five and fifteen pound presentations, the pool, and the men's locker. That day, at first, and for what seemed a term of afternoons to follow, Hussar had made a place of routine for himself in sight of these. And, one by one, this radius of midday had begun to pile on, until, Sunday, March 20th— when Howard Charles Foster had come to swim.

Foster had swung through the doors in some imagined triumph, Hussar had thought—a pied piper, soon to be followed by all the rats of Hamelin. He hadn't spared a moment for Foster's emotional complexion—the rudder setting of his mental state—but whatever he might have conjured, this was manifestly apart from it. Foster had floated through the doors and past the counter at reception, and off to the lockers to prepare; and Hussar was impressed by this show of mood—this mania of witless delusion, or this fantastic turn of resilience, whichever it may be. Foster had a look of deep and recent haunting in the shadow of his features, but as one in chipper and animate recovery: a convalescent for whom sugar-wafer and words have expiated and exorcised. Foster appeared at the treadmills and at the other stations of his way before he'd entered the pool. Hussar had gone and lain in wait there. He'd anchored himself to the floor with dive weight ballast and the motion of his watch face and the slow stroke of his heart. And then he'd immerged. He entered the tank from above, pierced the mirrored veil of ceiling with a toe, a foot, a shower of effervescing air that lifted away on impossible winds. And now there, he was a body lowered to the earth, eased in low gravity onto the pale floor of the world; a pair of legs, hard-white and knobby, like beanstalks rising off to break the sky. He stepped in and down the grade and clapped at the water and eased back in baptismal recline. And Hussar sat in crocodilian suspense, and watched him—the languorous chicken hide and bandy, articulating wishbones, the cold meat to be tonsured down to ivory. Hussar had watched this approach, and then, at an interval of his choosing—at the trigger of his intuition—he'd risen, come up, pushed off the bottom and ruptured the placid lid of the pool. He came up in a motion and toss the weight on the deck and cleared his nostrils and set the bezel of his watch to mark Foster's forty minute routine—and with a glimpse of him startled and static, he climbed from the water and left it for the lockers.

There, he dried and dressed and collected a slender steel rod from his things. Foster preferred a locker, and he identified it by number, and had intended to wrest the padlock from the stamp-steel catchings with a twist—but it wasn't necessary: in his bliss or stupor, Foster hadn't bothered to fix a lock at all, and from it he swiftly removed effects: Foster's wallet, identification cards, key ring, and phone. He readied his own materials, prepared the autoinjector pen, and when the hand swept at last to the bezel mark at forty minutes, he stood, and with careful measured steps began his progress toward the door. A bag on his shoulder and a towel over his arm, he counted these steps and watched his stride closely. He'd worked a place to start, a time to stand and turn to leave, a length and speed of common step approximating Foster's shambling gait returning from the pool. He'd calculated the distance by time, by step and cadence and carriage; and so not merely to be loitering, if the intervals were right they should arrive to enter the narrow, dim, and crooked passage, from opposite ends, at once.

But Foster was there. Hussar made the mouth of the passage; entered the eternally darkened hall, his body mechanics now liberated by sight. Somehow, already Foster was there, premature; he'd rushed with unease or left a moment early—cut short his routine by fractions, some foreboding, by some startling emergence of a man from the depth of an empty pool. He stood stopped mid-passage, shackled to the floor by some emerging quaver of thought. Hussar imagined he could see it—the thought bubble forming and its punctuated ellipsis, and he meant to lance it—approached now sinuated with false ease, elastic with a javelin thrower's first steps. He advanced and swept close; brushed him with an arm and shoulder, punctured him with a quick, smart jab of the pen to the back of the thigh, and pushed out through the steel door.

One three-quarters hour in the maculated uterine dark of the locker room had made the gym and its hem of day white and biting. Hussar forged out into the lot and spotted Foster's Suburban by the key fob's call, and he took it. He climbed up and situated his shoulder bag and cautiously wadded the towel over the pen and peeled the one glove from his pen-hand, and put these in a trash liner and hove them into the back. He fit a fresh pair of gloves and passed briefly through Foster's wallet and scrolled through his phone, and stoked the truck by its wheezy furnace, into life.

The phone was a rectangle fresh with petroleum esters and the aroma of new electronics—of solders and silicone microchips and lithium ions taking current and passing charge for the first time: a BlackBerry with shiny un-oiled keys and the protective display decal intact and straight from packaging. It shown a call, yesterday, and thirty minutes later a text; a message sent in psychological super-script; a conformational Tourette's—as though the earlier call had been entirely free of detail, or they'd all come last minute in reve-lation. Hussar did not know, nor did he particularly care, but had practical interest to understand where Foster had thought to be in the hours after he'd wrung off the last of his swim. And that answer, or so it seemed, was in the company of a young Chinese at a restau-rant, the corner of South Grand and Hartford. Kim Soong occupied no place in his awareness, but there she was, put down in Foster's contacts—recipient of the call and text—and after some time in the tight queue of parking down the curb of Hartford, he recognized a black Mercedes, an S-class that let out a little black-haired waif; and this, he thought, offered suggestions. She'd been set down at the half-block and traipsed back to the restaurant on foot, and the Mercedes doubled back toward Grand for parking with better view. Whatever his interest in the girl, however, it was the prospective heavy in the

Mercedes that most occupied his attention. And for that attention there was a further hour without amendment.

This was the figure, Hussar presumed, who'd rolled past the Dutchtown apartment moments before call time—which meant he'd been onto the wheres and whos of Howard Charles Foster, or of August Reams and Co. Despite precautions, this was the figure who'd tailed him to the rental return, and not unimpressively, clung on for dear life through the doings on the Parkway—the so far insistent, but not infallible figure who'd shacked up at the Ritz. And about an hour and a minute after he'd arrived, it was the figure—the meaty, sparse-blond, figure—who'd leapt from the Mercedes and stormed across the street into the restaurant and drug out the girl a moment later as though she was his own wayward child. And he toss her in the car and pulled off, and Hussar, far down the block, hurried out after them.

Traffic on Grand palpitated unmuffled and with frenetic working-class urgency, like bees before the fall of dusk. Hussar made the next light out and followed, back into University City, where, he thought—rather unexpectedly—they'd gone to pay visit to Foster. They'd parked up in front—and Hussar very much behind, sat beneath the brow of a hill, where, just under his visor he could see the girl camped and smoking on Foster's front step, and the bare roofline of the sedan. Hussar was interested and amused that they'd come, to stake out the house in its living presence. It spoke to what was known, whom they followed and how closely, and onto which beat in measure they fell. But, for what it told, it cast light also on what was not known: whose players were these and what outcome were they advancing?

They'd been there some time before the call, her in a pout on the step and the man in the car and out of view. There was some exchange: she listened, didn't hear or didn't believe, looked in confirmation; dug a phone from her bag, and then the phone rattled in the cup holder—Foster's phone. Hussar picked it up. He didn't answer, but observed its screen glowing through the protective decal, and he caressed it with a gentle touch of his hand. He pet the phone with a sort of tickled delight—suppressed but genuine—an appreciation for the charm of a gemstone in irony, polished and perfectly cut. And he smiled, a big warm intoxicated belly laugh of a smile. It was a small, hot pleasure, and life he thought, offers so few. He imagined what she'd planned to say, what message she'd intended to craft: 'Oh, where are you, Foster? Weren't we supposed to meet, Foster? Oh, it's all fine, Charles, but couldn't I just see you now?'

Why call now, Hussar wondered, why not before—an hour ago? They thought they'd had it in hand, was why. They'd thought they were playing the down-stroke, right in front of the beat, on the very toes of the measure. And, just now, it was crossing someone's mind they weren't—they'd lost the pocket and the bar too, and thought they'd catch-up at the refrain. But they were adrift, and Hussar thought, could no longer tell by how much. This call was pulling threads.

The phone ceased its mortal hum. The girl shook her head and got up for the car. And then they sat, Hussar figured, with no square move left to play. Whatever else it might be, it would be an entertainment. Something like watching a blind man stumble in unfamiliar daylight, or a dissectologist earnestly chasing down puzzles for which all the pieces are not disposed. And then they pulled off, with that rudder-slip of urgency and frustration and wheel-spin, and Hussar followed.

2.

The Mercedes turned off Big Bend at Zephyr and stopped a door down from Edmund LeFrance—August Reams' man with the great white truck and card habit—and when they did, Marek Hussar felt that lustrous apprehension of good fortune, that cheerful pique of something gifted, unsought and handy. He cut down the next left and eased four blocks down to Bellevue before doubling back the return distance along Zephyr. He collected Foster's things, took deep relaxing breaths and drove slowly balancing the wheel against his knee while situating his bag and fitting the suppressor to the USP Tactical. And when eventually he edged up quietly opposite the Mercedes, the girl was looking the other way. Hussar rolled down the window and waved, and the girl noticed the wave and then noticed the Suburban, and with a hasty and eager familiarity stooped from the passenger seat to see the driver under the roofline and brought a smile with her to show, and Hussar put two rounds through the side glass and then a thermite grenade as well. After a few seconds the grenade spit and hissed and filled the car with sparks and smoke, and Hussar leaned back behind the B-pillar of the truck and watched.

In a moment a figure rustled in the curtain at LeFrance's house— peaked at first and then pulled a few inch gap to see in disbelief. It was but an instant, but in it Hussar could see that it was the sparse blond—the driver, the heavy—and he could see his eyes go wide to see the car, and he could see them sweep through the smoke, lift across the street to the truck, and Hussar could not tell what they saw when they reached him—if they had understood what they saw— because he sent two rounds through the window where he stood, and he had fallen away.

Hussar swapped the clip for a fresh magazine, pinned another thermite grenade and toss it in the back of the truck near the tank, and rushed the door of the house. He took the stairs by twos and swung through the door and to the side, toward the window. There, the blond lay on his back in a litter of glass crumbs, with taps astride the sternum and the Browning on the floor, and fingers probing to dislodge the suffocating mass, and issuing faintly of pneumatic purge, like a stabbed inner tube's resolving breath. Hussar put a round in his head the look of a carnal bindi, and checked pulse on LeFrance tipped back in a chair. "I see you two've been introduced," he said, when he'd dropped the wrist. He returned to the blond and went through his pockets. He found his identification and spare magazine, and the padded envelope and the small thumb drive, which he kept. Hussar drug the blond by the hands, along the floor into the kitchen and rest him near the stove. When he returned for LeFrance there were sirens which arose and drown the hollow knock of ball and mellifluous prattle of the tennis broadcast; a drone of coarse tires and the organ-grinding diesel notes of heavy machinery, and Hussar glanced from the window to see a fire engine rounding the corner, and drawing to rest in the small fraction of the block unobstructed by the two burning cars.

"That's uncanny," said Hussar, and shared a look with LeFrance. "Do they live next door?" He watched briefly as the fire crew dismounted and deployed hoses and protective gear from locker boxes and compartments and Hussar shook his head and looked again to LeFrance. He looked at the Redhawk and moved to borrow it from LeFrance's grasp and returned to the window where he squeezed off the five remaining rounds into the fire truck where they lighted upon mirror chrome and aluminum panels and heavy windshield glass. As they rang out, the concussion of the first had not dissolved before the last had played, and when the entire crew leaped to ground, Hussar felt satisfied he'd purchased a better disposal—it would be two to three minutes for the police to arrive in numbers, a further ten before they'd have the building fully cordoned, and longer still before they'd let the department break cover to lay hose on the first thing.

Hussar drug LeFrance into the kitchen and put him on the floor beside the blond. He went through LeFrance's coat and withdrew the small worn chapbook and held it between them in appreciation: "The Rilke…says otherwise," he said, slipped the book into his coat and put their armaments and identification in the oven. He put Foster's effects there as well and checked for the standpipe behind the stove; lit the burners and broiler, inventoried his things, released the handle on the last thermite grenade, dropped it down the gap beside the gas line, and he left by the rear entrance.

XV.

Charles Foster watched from the hall as the door closed over the silhouette of the man as he left. The door swung out and paddled back and forth to rest and threw short beats of light into the dim cavity of the hall—pulses of something which kicked back the smoky membrane until the passage was engorged once more in full shade. A can-light overhead that spoke occasionally in white-glinted ticks said nothing today, and sensing it, Foster wondered formlessly, whether the passage in its natural, intended state was illuminated by a working fixture casting shadow, or darkened by a broken fixture casting light. He reached down and touched the back of his thigh and looked at the spot of blood on his fingers and wiped it against his shorts—"For Christ' sake." At first he took a step back toward the door, as though he might follow the man out and have words about carelessness—might share indignant protest into shrugging rebuttal; and then waved off the idea with his hand and turned back down the hall toward the lockers.

His mind shone again on the man—the multi-colored bruise on his shoulder; the shooting bruise; the unaccountable emergence from the pool, like some punched-up water spirit; the stupid collision in the hall—there was some burgeoning association inflating his imagination that had been aborted with a prick—dislodged with a hip-check. He could no longer envision its point of contact, nor even the leads to reach it. It receded before him: the spark, the arc it traveled, the points of termination, the approaching armature, even the electrifying impulse was spending its tungsten-glow. He'd lost the kinetic euphoria of the morning, the level calm of the pool, the bite-force of his presence of mind, and now, he didn't feel well either.

He shuffled past the kink in the hall, round the blind corner of its end, and into the jaundiced splendor of the locker. A man, round and tan as a barrel, changed shorts where he washed hands at the sinks. A pensioner from distant antiquity loitered in tube socks and translucent drapery of hide on a bench beside his things. Down the causeway of lockers, someone crossed to enter the showers with carriage as though eagerly receiving guests. To his side, a man stood in the bank of urinals and looked upon his work in long, confounded fixity; and Foster moved toward the back and toward his locker and toward the bench before it, where he now had a vision to sit. But Foster felt a blanching nausea, and made for the toilets instead.

The first he tried was dappled in bright high-vitamin yellow—so thoroughly marked it seemed a work in contest. The next was fetid with lurid residuals. And the next, he took, because he feared he wouldn't make another. He fiddled with the lock, but it would not latch, and he fell to rest upon the bow of seat. He was clammy and depleted, and sat on the toilet for an age of minutes—one minute; five?—a determination of time which seemed further and further distended with each interceding breath; each pass at calculation. He stare at the glyphs and etchings of the stall, the countless individuated cuneiform ciphers, ad-hoc to a man—to his predecessors—and to their moment in restless and disparaging turn. Cave painting, he thought with a cough that had begun as the impulse to smile—a grim, blinking, curdle of smile—but threatened now to empty him to his toes. Discomfort in his thigh swelled from throbbing knocks to a perfect and singular coal whose heat and dimension accumulated like surf, one lick upon the next. It was his leg—this was a thought. It was the puncture—this was a thought. The man delivered the puncture—this was a thought. But they were, each of them vacant, voiceless thoughts. The thinker did not hold them, did not direct them, lay no claim to possessing them—but rather, saw them: they were pictograms, illustrated panels, ink blots held out before him on flash cards. Foster watched these thoughts, watched the panels swap, watched them strobe and flutter with projected backlight. His thigh twitched and clenched. His leg trembled. He was chill and nauseous and faint, and now the perch on the toilet seat towered above the floor, was high and unsteady and sway with the motion of his shuddering leg. He had a sharp instinct to get down, to retreat toward his faltering pulse and assume the position—to be on his knees and to hang his arms from the toilet and lay his cheek on the cool seat whose first cleansing touch had come in the pool-water damp of his trunks.

It was coming. He climbed to his knees—his buckling knees—and rest his head and slung his arms and begged it to come and to give him at least that small respite that settles between the purges—that still, quiet place where the tsunami bulge draws down the tide from the beaches, and for a moment they are placid and rare. But even here, the altitude was a vertigo-inducing peril, and he coughed into the basin and collapsed down onto the floor. He wanted urgently now to get beneath his heart, to slip down under its yoke. His arms and legs quaked, his abdomen—his chest shook in reedy gasps, wheezing, hacking. His body—his face—rest where they'd made the floor with a slap—against the cold, etched, ammonia-wet concrete. His eyes blinked and his limbs writhed in trembling spasms, or locked in waves of full-body contraction, absolute in their tooth-grinding, toe-pointing totality. His legs splay out somewhere under the verge of the stall and he blinked at the stains of the toilet neck, and the down of coiled hairs, and Foster did not think of Catherine, or frail Pauline, nor his mother, or the man from the Executive Office—The Familiar; not August or Sachs or his plane, or the blade-spoilt knife, or the small company of the paper rose. He pointed his feet and clamped his arms to his side in breathless contraction and looked at the cover of tissue crumbs spread before the toilet and watched his breath disturb the coiled hairs, and he convulsed vomit and felt that his trunks were everywhere moist and warm. He disgorged a bloody sputum then, and felt the contractions abate, and he rest his gaze upon the streaks down the toilet—lip to collar—and the array of crumbs, and the cloudy surge which crept slowly toward, and embraced them.

XVI.

Patricia Harvey parked her carmine red Mercedes Geländewagen in the driveway, and strung balloons from the yard sign. She opened the garage to the bright mid-April day, and placed crisp new orchids on a table in the foyer and baked two sheets of cookies in the oven and set out mimosas in flutes and by ten o'clock she was proudly watching the cars pulling in at the curb of Creveling and handing out listing sheets from the counter and cookies and mimosa flutes, and walking couples through the kitchen features and two-stall garage and the master suite and three beds too, and the impressive barrel-vaulted living room, cherry-paneled, lead-glassed, and amply-spaced for large and various furnishings.

"We're neighbors—" said the man.

"We're agents, too," said the woman.

A family of boisterous children was in back on the pool deck; upstairs a gay couple lingered in the master suite—Patricia knew by their perfect sweaters and black-rim Capote glasses, and they wore no socks with their loafers. A woman downstairs turned through the finished family room and fed appetizing descriptions by phone into her husband's ear—and it was then the couple in running clothes had come in panting and glazed and greeted Patricia by her fine, tan-leathered hands and extravagant jewelry, and shared guilty looks over baked goods and champagne—they were Jan and Thomas Marginot, and they were agents, too, and it was a pleasure.

Thomas was fixing his hair with his hand and wiping it on his hip and drinking the mimosa for water. "Wasn't this on the market a year ago—maybe last winter?" he asked.

"December, January?" asked Jan.

"It was," said Patricia.

"Is it the same seller?" asked Thomas.

"No, it sold to a client of mine at that time—a real estate investor— speculator I think—foreign, very eccentric," she said, and laughed her favorite cocktail laugh: "A Swiss."

"Market's strong—I wouldn't sell," said Jan.

"He isn't holding?" said Thomas.

"I believe he's moving his portfolio to other markets. I've the impression he does it at whim," said Patricia.

"I may have somebody for it," said Jan.

"It's true," said Thomas, "we have a client very much in the market."

"Well, cheers to that," said Patricia, and snuck a mimosa to toast. "Have them buy the house, and you can sell them the land as well."

"The land?" asked Jan.

"Acreage, I mean."

"How much?"

"Where?"

"Out 44," said Patricia, "south of Cuba—south of Cuba and Bourbon."

"How much?" Thomas repeated.

"Three parcels. About three-hundred acres together."

"Are they adjoining?" asked Jan.

"No, they're all very much separate."

"Are they built-out—do they have structures?" asked Thomas.

"One is an equestrian estate with house and stables. Another has a hunting lodge and blinds; and there's an old farm, but the barn burned in a lightning strike—everything wood is ash and everything metal, all the machinery, melted to pools—it was hot." Patricia laughed. "Rolling hills—it's quite beautiful, really—but the barn is a crater with metal puddles," she said, and laughed again.

Thomas traded his glass for another. "What about the house? Is he flexible?"

"It's just what he paid for it—they all are."

"What?" said Thomas.

"You said he's a speculator—how can that be?" said Jan.

"I know! Very peculiar," said Patricia.

"But if we had a close offer, you'd take it to him," said Thomas.

"No," said Patricia. "I can't."

"You can't or you won't?" said Jan.

"No. I can't. I can't reach him—I've tried."

"How can you take him offers?" asked Jan.

"I can't. I have instructions."

"Instructions?" said Thomas, and drank to illustrate his doubt.

"Yes, just instructions. For the sale, and wire transfer."

"But, what if it doesn't move?" said Thomas.

"Your commission?" said Jan.

"He's already paid my commission—isn't it amazing?" Patricia laughed and toasted her good fortune.

"Already paid?" said Jan.

"He paid in advance—on all the properties?" asked Thomas.

"Yes, yes! Can you believe it? Oh, what did he say?—he called it... an 'honorarium.'"